Burnout

The Rise of a Villain

Books by Jordan S. Keller

Ashes Over Avalon Trilogy
Wildfire
Burnout

Coming Soon!
Ashes Over Avalon Trilogy
Combustion

Burnout

The Rise of a Villain

Jordan S. Keller

SPEAKING VOLUMES, LLC
NAPLES, FLORIDA

Burnout

Copyright © 2023 by Jordan Keller

ISBN 978-1-64540-955-7

To my Writing Group family
You're the superheroes in my life.

Chapter One

Abigail was weightless.

Her body levitated over the skylight above the downtown branch of San Arbor's First Financial Bank by a psychic touch she was barely used to. Her stomach threatened to roll over, again, but she forced her lunch to remain below her throat. Twisting the dial on the mini binoculars, she zoomed closer on the hostage situation below. Bank visitors and employees were tied together at their wrists and forced to kneel under a teller counter. Of the few faces Abigail could see, they looked terrified. One of the hostages lay on the floor, blood oozing from a hole in his side, while another hostage pressed a balled-up jacket against the wound. The white floor tiles under them turned scarlet. Behind the counter, two masked criminals filled duffel bags with tightly wrapped bills. A third swept the barrel of an automatic rifle across the hostages making them shudder.

All three criminals continued the heist either unaware or unthreatened by the police and heroes outside. Red and blue lights flashed against the first-floor windows and painted the interior the same colors. The marble statues inside the historic building paled under the lights. Their melancholy expressions made more dire in the face of the robbery.

Abigail tapped the communicator inside her ear, linking her to the other four Round Table Knights. "I count thirteen hostages, at least one injured," she relayed. "Three goons, and it looks like the vault is still secure."

"Best way in?" King Arthur, leader and co-founder of the Round Table Knights, asked.

"Side door." Abigail swept her binoculars across the scene again. "But bad guy number one has pretty good visuals on all doors. They're armed. We need to distract him."

"Or control him," King Arthur decided. "I need a megaphone."

Moments later, King Arthur's amplified voice boomed through the communication link and over the roof of the bank. Abigail knew the criminals inside would hear him too. The hostages turned their heads toward his voice, relief replacing their fear. The voice of a hero had that effect. King Arthur's abilities were known throughout the city and those foolish enough to go toe-to-toe with him. His power of sway allowed King Arthur to command any target that heard him. Glowing a royal purple, his eyes would signal the power's activation. King Arthur was the only Round Table Knight not to wear a mask. It was a dangerous choice, but King Arthur valued the trust of his people over the threat of evil.

It was one of the things Abigail admired most about him.

"Put down your weapons and kneel away from the door," King Arthur finished his commands.

The criminals did not obey. They didn't even acknowledge the hero's order. They continued on with the robbery. The man on the ground continued to bleed.

"It's not working?" Excalibur asked in disbelief over the comms. "Did they not hear you?"

"They did." King Arthur's charming demeanor dissolved as frustration took over.

Abigail examined two of the criminals closely. Their ears were stuffed with a yellow substance. They signed messages across the counter at each other, the conversation short and choppy while they handled cash between hand movements.

"They're using sign language to talk," she said over the communication link.

"Are they deaf?" Excalibur asked.

"No. They're clever," King Arthur corrected. "Here's the new plan. Merlin, I need an opening. The brighter the better. 'Xcal, you're going in first, sorry to use you as bait."

"Not like it's the first time."

"Avalon, Lancelot, once Excalibur's inside, I want you to drop. Excalibur and Avalon will keep the gunmen busy. Lancelot and I will do the rescue. Merlin, be ready out here. Trap anyone who gets out. Understand?"

Abigail looked over her shoulder at the newest member of the Round Table Knights while the others agreed over the earpiece. Lancelot was only a sidekick for the sake of contracts and normality. Abigail knew he'd be a fine hero on his own and be promoted once he completed his year training with the Hero Relief Center. That didn't stop her from worrying about him. She didn't know if she looked that small and young when she joined the Knights three years ago. Lancelot resembled someone on a college brochure, even with his costume and mask, rather than a superhero.

She switched her communicator off and asked him directly, "You good?"

Lancelot nodded from the solid patch of the roof he stood on. "I'm great. We're ready up here, King."

"Let's be heroes today." King Arthur's voice rang through everyone's ear.

The psychic hold around Abigail pulled her away from the skylight. She was happy to have solid ground back under her. The relief was short lived though, and the building shook when one of Merlin's chemical reactions struck the front wall. The rotating red and blue lights faded in the flood of white light stretching higher than the roof. The light and blast were the products from whatever chemical reaction Merlin caused by mixing elements she pulled from the environment around her. The scent of sulfur and charcoal filled the air as if a dozen fireworks had just gone off. As dainty as Merlin tried to make herself appear, her ability to fuse and rip molecules around her matched her terrifying personality. With every mission, Abigail was reminded of how grateful she was that Merlin was on their side.

Abigail listened past the explosive aftermath for gunshots bouncing off metal and knew Excalibur was inside the bank. His armor was forged to withstand a bullet assault, but she didn't want her boss in the crossfire any longer than necessary. One unlucky shot through his mouth guard would end the hero's life. Abigail summoned her cherry-red fire to encircle her wrists. Her skin was immune to its level of heat, and the flames waited for her command. As a teenager, Abigail could only pretend to be a hero and the most action her flames saw was helping her father light the grill when it was hamburger night.

After donning her Avalon ultra-ego, she no longer needed to pretend.

"If I burst through the window, will you catch me?" she asked Lancelot.

"Scared of a forty-foot drop?"

Abigail unsheathed her sword as her answer. The flames covered the blade out of habit.

"I'll always catch you." Lancelot said, and Abigail felt the psychic hold wrap around her. "I'll be right behind you."

From the very first spark of fire she could summon, Abigail knew she wanted to be a hero. She wanted to save people. Today, thirteen people needed saving, and she would not let them down. Taking a running jump from the roof, she dived for the skylight as if she were diving into a swimming pool. Just before impact, she unleashed a massive breath of blue fire that shattered the glass. Her scorched black tongue protected her mouth from the intense heat, and she fell into the bank.

Her descent was much slower than it should've been. Through the haze of Merlin's blast, Abigail saw sparks of bullets scraping Excalibur's armor and she doggy-paddled through the air toward an unsuspecting gunman. She landed like she jumped from two steps instead of a rooftop. As the psychic hold vanished, she rushed to the criminal guarding the hostages. He raised his gun, but Abigail sliced the barrel in two with her blazing sword. The bullet jammed in the chamber with an audible *thunk*. Abigail heel kicked the man in his stomach and knocked him into the marble counter. The gun flew from his hands and clattered on the floor.

"Lance, it's clear!" she yelled over the noise into her communicator.

Several more shots rang out around her, and Abigail dropped to the floor. She saw the third criminal firing wildly around him as he retreated inside an office. The blinds on the door banged against the window when he slammed it shut.

Abigail took a quick inventory around her; King Arthur and Lancelot untied the hostages, and Excalibur broke the second man's gun over his knee like a broom handle. This third man was hers. She rammed into the locked door shoulder first. The thin wood splintered away and granted her entry. She scanned the office but found it empty. Abigail was about to jump atop the desk where she suspected he hid under, but, from his position beside the door, the man smashed a potted plant over the top of her head. Her vision spotted, her knees buckled, and the ground rushed up to her. The man yanked her up by the collar of her costume before she completely fell. The cold bite of a gun barrel burrowing into her side removed the remaining pain in her skull.

He laughed in her ear. A relief-riddled chuckle two steps away from madness. The hammer clicked back in slow motion. Unlike the Knight who trained her, Abigail was not immune to bullets. The one preparing to rip into her would kill. She took a deep breath, filling herself with oxygen, and released a blast of fire around her. Flames leapt off every bare patch of her skin. The laughing ended abruptly as the fire licked up both their bodies. Only one was fireproof.

The gun wasn't either.

The weapon exploded like a tiny bomb under the heat and knocked Abigail through the drywall and into the lobby. Her flames vanished as the air exited her lungs. She expected to feel glass carve through her costume and shred her skin as the front windows drew nearer. She covered her face with her arms and braced for impact.

When the pain didn't come, when the glass didn't bite, when she didn't feel the sidewalk outside, she moved her arms. Her breath fogged against the unbroken window. She touched a shaking finger against it. The glass was still intact. She drifted down and settled back on her feet.

"I told you I'd always catch you," Lancelot said behind her.

His psychic touch left her, feeling like cold tentacles trailing off her skin. "I owe you one."

"Help me with this."

Abigail joined him, taking one of the two citizens from under his arms and helping them to the door where a paramedic waited. It was a good day to be a hero. Abigail helped the rest of the now free hostages get to the paramedics, cutting off their binds and offering comforting smiles. The bleeding man was lifted out on a stretcher with the help of Excalibur, and two of the criminals were cuffed and carted from the building to waiting police cars. Surrounded by uniformed personnel, the remaining criminal was hidden behind their blue shirts. Across the room, Abigail chewed the inside of her cheek as she waited for their diagnosis.

"You guys okay?" King Arthur asked, stepping in front of Abigail and blocking her view.

"Feeling great, boss," Lancelot answered at her side.

Abigail didn't share her sidekick's sentiment. Unease and uncertainty gripped her. A section of the office's door frame broke free and crashed to the ground. The entire outside wall was blackened, and she imagined anything remaining inside was charred.

King Arthur locked his normal brown eyes with Abigail's. "I'll finish up in here, you both wait outside."

"I'll need to give my statement."

Abigail peered over the top of King Arthur's crown and saw the paramedics enclose the third criminal inside a black bag. The bag was loaded onto a gurney with far less care than the hostage had been. The message was made clear in case the body bag wasn't loud enough: there was no hope in saving this one.

King Arthur grabbed her shoulder. "You can give that at HQ. But right now, I need you to smile and show everyone that things are alright. You did good today, don't forget that."

"Yes, sir."

Abigail followed Lancelot through the hole Merlin had created, and they were ambushed with cheers from the crowd surrounding the barricades around the bank. Lancelot waved to the crowd and shouted 'hello's back to them. Abigail knew this was part of the job, too. Saving the people of the city she loved was the greatest honor; her face on the side of buses and the line of Avalon merchandise were unavoidable side effects. She smiled and waved to the spectators. The cheering pushed the body bag away for a moment. It was just a criminal, she told herself. She saved the people she needed to.

Through the noise, a whistle caught Abigail's attention. A high-pitch signal that dipped an octave before ending. The voice following it bewitched her completely. She knew the low rumble like she knew her street address. It sounded like home. She was powerless to the smile that appeared when she heard him, the praise meant nothing compared to the sound of his voice.

"Nice work, heroes!"

Abigail couldn't deny how good Thomas looked in his turnout coat. The firefighter's uniform hung protectively around him, and the hardhat flattened his raven hair close to his ears. His face was perfect, all the burn scars removed to reveal the man he was truly meant to be. The man Abigail knew he always was.

"Sorry to leave the cleanup work to you guys," Abigail addressed the five member squad, but her eyes were locked on Thomas. Just seeing him across the street lifted her spirits.

"As long as you didn't set too many fires, we'll be fine." Thomas grinned under the shadow of his hat.

Abigail started to reply, but an invisible tug against her hair reminded her where she was. Reminded her of who she currently was. She needed to finish her own job, and, sadly, it wasn't teasing the firefighter.

"I'll see you at— at the next call," she tripped over her words. *I'll see you at home* still lingered against her tongue. "Be careful in there."

"You guys got all the bad guys out, yeah?" Thomas raised an eyebrow.

Abigail nodded.

"Then there's nothing to worry about."

She resisted rolling her eyes. Even if she had missed someone, they wouldn't be a match for the supercharged firefighter. Abigail knew Thomas' fire abilities were stronger than her own, but that fact didn't stop her from worrying about him as he walked into the bank. It was the same breathless sensation she felt every time his squad was called to a fire. One day, the smoking buildings may not return him.

Another invisible hair tug forced Abigail to look away from Thomas and to Lancelot, who pursed his lips together.

"Are you done flirting with the firemen?" Lancelot asked with a laugh. "I think the main one knows you have a crush on him by now."

"It's not a crush." Abigail playfully shoved him. Was it even a crush if you were dating the person outside of costume? "It's just being friendly."

"Could've fooled me." Lancelot interlaced his fingers and rested his face against them to imitate an infatuated woman from some romance movie. "Oh fireman, please be careful saving the day. Will you accept my token of love—"

Abigail shoved him again, although a little less playfully. "Knock it off, Lance. Media is coming our way."

"Aren't I the funny one, though?" he muttered the comment.

In the three years after the passing of San Arbor Ordinance 7-59, fondly referred to as the Call To Action ordinance, heroes were allowed to stop active crime without being called on the scene by first responders. It allowed the heroes to patrol the city, act in real-time, and was a huge success in lowering crime rates and protecting the lives of the first responders.

It was preferable for the armored knight Excalibur to approach an armed gunman than a detective wearing just a Kevlar vest.

The only negative effect of the Call To Action ordnance was the creation of an even bigger celebrity storm around the heroes. When the Round Table Knights wore their masks, it kept their true identities a secret but invited the world to zoom in on their alter-egos.

"Avalon, Lancelot." A reporter held a microphone between them. "Walk us through what happened inside."

"We stuck to the plan," Abigail explained with her cheerful media voice. She always felt like she was selling something on an informercial. In most cases, she sold safety and security. The promise that so long as the Knights were here then San Arbor would be protected. "King Arthur had everything figured out and we followed his plan of action."

The reporter turned to Lancelot. "This is only your second month working with the Knights, were you scared?"

Lancelot laughed. It was charming and ended with a smile that could easily melt as well as mend hearts. "Of course not. I trust Avalon completely. I knew she wasn't going to let me down." Lancelot slung his arm around Abigail's shoulders and pulled the two of them closer together. "I'm pretty sure the only scaredy-cats in there were the criminals. Please tell me you got a shot of Merlin and her magic spell?"

The reporter looked to her cameraman who nodded back at her. "We've got it."

"And the Round Table Knights have you, San Arbor." Abigail ended their interview with a wink and untangled herself from Lancelot.

The camera clicked off and the reporter flipped to a blank page in her notepad. "Lancelot, could I ask you for an autograph?" She handed the notepad and pen toward the sidekick. "I wasn't able to ask you last time, and I know it's not professional, but—"

Lancelot accepted the notepad and pen. "Don't worry about it," he glanced at the press badge around her neck, "Monica. I can't believe I missed you last time. Channel 9 is my favorite station. Especially your reports."

Monica cradled the notepad when he returned it. "You were really busy last time. It's when you lifted—"

"—The motorcycle!" Lancelot exclaimed with her. "You really got my good side with that story."

"You don't have a bad side." The young reporter blushed.

"Come on." Abigail grabbed his elbow and steered him away from the reporter. "Thank you!"

Phone cameras from the sidewalk clicked around them as they returned to the rest of the Knights. Greedy hands stretched past the barricade trying to get their own signatures and faceless voices requested selfies and hugs. Four ambulances were parked in a semicircle patching up the rescued hostages that wouldn't need transporting to a hospital. Merlin gave her report to the Chief of Police, Vincent DaVodi, who looked happier to talk to her than the rest of them, and listed the chemicals she used for hazmat purposes. Every piece fitting together in the chaotic calm that marked a job well done. Abigail joined Excalibur who claimed the watchman position over the two criminals as they were loaded into a squad car.

"You okay, sir?" she asked.

Excalibur stopped rubbing his shoulder. He probably didn't feel the pressure of his hand through his armor. The angry brass eye of a bullet stared at Abigail through the silver armor. The rest of his pauldron was peppered with indentations.

"Absolutely." Excalibur's voice sounded robotic as it filtered through the mouthguard of his helmet. "Just need some repairs."

"I can take over if you need me to." Compared to her boss, Abigail was untouched. Even her blonde curls were perfect.

"And give you any more of the glory?" Excalibur asked, and Abigail knew a grin was forming under his helmet. "Don't worry about me."

Abigail patted his forearm. "I still think you're really cool."

"Even if you could pass for a cheese grater right now," Lancelot interjected.

Abigail glared at Lancelot, but Excalibur chuckled. "I'm glad the bullets got me and not you. Could you even take a punch in that little thing?"

Lancelot looked down at his costume. Dressed like he just stepped off a bus headed to the Renaissance Festival, he wore blue and white pants tucked into brown boots, a flowy white shirt, and a baby blue cloak clasping around his shoulders with a silver chain. He used to wear a hat with a blue feather, but it kept flying off in battle. He tapped his head. "I've got all the protection I need right here."

"I hope you don't mean your smarts," said Abigail.

"At least I'm pretty, right?"

"Sure." Abigail shooed his psychic touch away as he tried to tug at her curls again.

Chapter Two

The distraction Thomas created at the scene wasn't strong enough to fully stop the cobwebs inside Abigail's mind from snagging fragments of the fight. After returning to the Hero Relief Center, she locked herself inside her office and waited. She waited to give her statement to the police, she waited to apologize to President Samuels and her team for embarrassing the company, she waited to get the phone call saying the criminal was actually a good citizen who got hired for a job too big for him just to afford the operation that his kid needed to survive. Abigail tried to shut her eyes, but every time she did, she only saw the criminal's face; pale in the dim light, small nosed, shaking bottom lip. She only saw the explosion that killed him. The explosion that she caused.

Abigail had been a reckless sidekick. She would not become a reckless hero.

She couldn't afford it. The media would devour a story on a killer hero. Her days as a hero would be over. Not even a costume change could save her. The life she spent a decade fighting for would be lost. She'd never be able to do hero work again. The longer she waited in her office the harder it became to breathe. She pulled her mask off, maybe for the last time, and ran through her sword drills in the open space of her office.

Strong body. Strong mind. Strong body. Strong mind. Strong body. Strong mind.

She'd come too far to give up now.

The door slid open an exhausting two hours later. Abigail searched King Arthur's expression as he entered the room. She searched for something to comfort her, but his charming face gave nothing away.

The door closed behind him, and King Arthur sat in one of the plush chairs opposite the desk. Abigail set her sword on the desk and sat on the edge of the other chair. Torn between fully committing to the seat, fully believing she was safe, and having an easy exit in case King Arthur hid bad news under his crown. She worked with the man for over three years, and yet he still made her feel like a child.

"Tell me." Abigail broke their silence.

"Tell you what?"

"What's going to happen."

"I imagine the First Financial Bank will shut down while they do repairs," King Arthur answered but didn't. "The money is being sorted out in evidence right now, and the people are being sorted out in the hospitals."

"That's not what I mean."

"You want to know about the criminals?" Abigail nodded, her mouth dry, and King Arthur continued. "Two were being booked when I left the station. Samuels' will get a full report once it's done."

"The third?"

"Unfortunately, he was dead at the scene." King Arthur shrugged, unfazed by Abigail whose eyes still begged for answers. "Apparently, his gun misfired and shot him."

"King, that's not what happened."

"Sometimes the bad guy gets killed by his own gun. That's what the police believe and that's what the media will report."

"Did you—"

"Protect my team?" he interrupted her with a smile he reserved for interviews and product endorsements. This King Arthur was saving face, and Abigail hated he now used it on her. "I will always do what is necessary for us."

Abigail wasn't sure how to respond. She didn't know what she should say, she didn't know what he wanted to hear. Her mistake was covered up by his ability. She should be grateful, but instead she felt suffocated. A dark secret festered between them. He covered up a *murder*.

"What do I do now?"

"Something normal," King Arthur encouraged. "I meant when I said you did good today. Go home, relax, and come back tomorrow ready to do more good."

"Thank you, King."

Abigail didn't think she deserved the praise. A *good* hero wouldn't have panicked like she did. They would have handled the situation without killing anyone. The thought was bile in her stomach, acid in her throat; it was guilt. She committed the ultimate crime, and because she wore a mask and the man held a gun, it wasn't considered wrong. It was justified. King Arthur rearranging the city's perception of the truth was justified.

King Arthur picked at a loose string at his armrest. "But the next time you get careless there will be repercussions. Do you understand?"

Abigail blinked. "Yes, sir."

"Very good." King Arthur stood and exited Abigail's office without a farewell or further instruction.

A chill settled over the office once he shut the door. A chill too cold for Abigail to burn off.

Ever since Thomas officially moved into Abigail's seventh story apartment, the hallway outside their door smelled of smoke. Not the campfire smoke that clung to her sheets after his past late-night visits, but the thick fumes of house fires. A trail of ash stained the carpet between the elevator and the door from whatever had traveled home on his boots. Thankfully he kicked them off just before entering, leaving the mess out of the apartment, and the dirty shoes greeted Abigail as she unlocked the door.

Thomas, sidekick turned villain turned firefighter, sat in the living room with his socked feet on the coffee table. The television remote was in hand as he aimlessly flicked through the channels. Nothing seemed to keep his attention longer than four seconds.

Nothing except for Abigail.

"Hey babe." He muted the television, the screen locked to a cooking show, and met her in the kitchen. "How was work?"

"Before or after the robbery?"

Thomas' arms wrapped around her waist and he kissed the back of her neck. "Before."

"Marketing meeting. I'm getting a new action figure." Abigail leaned into his warm hold.

Thomas was the most normal thing she knew. He chased away her troubles without even trying. She rotated in his arms to kiss him quickly on the lips.

He smiled. Either from the kiss or about the action figure, Abigail didn't know. "Do I get one?"

"Don't your buddies think your little shrine to me is weird?" Abigail teased.

She'd been to his firehouse several times as Abigail Turner, girlfriend, and almost every horizontal surface contained an Avalon figure, doll, lunchbox, or pen set. Even his current socks sported her flaming sword logo.

"It's cool to have the flame hero around," he admitted. "Maybe you could swing by as Avalon one day. The guys would get a kick out of that."

"Coming to see my biggest fan?" She raised an eyebrow.

"I won't tell anyone I'm your favorite." His crooked smile held a permanent residence on his face. Just as it did in Abigail's heart.

Abigail, unhappily, removed herself from his arms and peered inside the fridge. Even with a roommate, her shopping habits remained poor. They ate enough take out for the restaurants to know them by name, phone and favorite combo number. The fridge was bare except for the half carton of eggs and a jug of orange juice. She shut the door on the poor choices for dinner.

"How was your day?"

"Before or after the robbery?" he echoed.

"After."

"Small kitchen fire," Thomas said casually. "Dish towel on the stove, you know how it goes."

"I'm glad it was small," Abigail admitted. "You running into those blazers scare me."

She turned to see an amused look on his face.

"Babe, I'm fireproof. Did you forget?"

She never did. "Doesn't hurt to be careful."

"Like you were?" It was his turn to tease. The deadly scars that once covered his body had vanished, but his playful nature remained. "I saw your handiwork inside the bank. You know burning the dollar is just an expression, right?"

She punched his shoulder, but he didn't acknowledge it. She changed the subject far away from the robbery and what only she and King Arthur knew. "What do you want for dinner?"

"Popcorn," Thomas answered automatically. "Let's see a movie tonight."

A low-key movie night definitely counted as normal.

"Let me change."

Even outside of her costume, Abigail kept a watchful eye over the movie theater lobby. She noted the quickest exit route, possible entry points for attacks, and eyed the soda dispenser thinking how it could be used as a weapon. Excalibur called it *Hero Vision* on a mission once. He had promised he found a way to turn it off. He hadn't shared the secret with his sidekick at the time, nor did he grant her the knowledge after she graduated to hero. The lobby was filled with teenagers depositing quarters in old arcade games and a group of children ripping into a box of candy; tiny and colorful pieces bounced off the carpeted floor. It was not filled with criminals or villains, she told herself. Tonight was a normal night.

Thomas squeezed Abigail's hand, and it snapped her attention back to him and the woman across the counter. The only super thing she wanted tonight was the super-sized popcorn. For the current promotion, the container was covered in tiny cartoon rodents. One wielding a sewing needle like a sword faced Abigail with a button shield. Thomas handed her the popcorn bucket while he finished the transaction. The greasy bottom coated her fingers with butter.

"Think we missed the previews?" Thomas poked two straws into the soda and took a sip.

"Maybe the bad ones," Abigail answered. Their movie started four minutes ago according to the time stamped on their pre-ripped tickets. Traffic had been worse than usual.

"Film House," Thomas mimicked the theater's opening credit that advertised its fresh popcorn, cold drinks, and upgraded sound system. "Your home for the movies you want."

"Where popcorn flows, and your drink never empties," Abigail finished with him in a whisper while they found their seats in the dark theater.

Their seats were two in the second to last row, left side. Abigail was pretty sure the cushions had molded to their butts from all the time they spent in them. She didn't know when *movies* became their thing, but ever since Thomas returned to San Arbor, they had been buying tickets like they owned stock in the film industry. Thomas set the drink between them and grabbed a massive handful of popcorn. He reached for another handful before Abigail settled in her seat.

The final preview faded away, and the opening scene of the movie flickered to a beach with soft waves lapping against the sand with meditative intent. Abigail sank into her seat with a handful of popcorn. Thomas snaked his arm around her shoulders. This was the beginning of a perfect, normal, night. The sound of a gunshot didn't fit into Abigail's plans, nor did it match the on-screen visuals. Members of the audience gasped at the sudden sound, and others waited for the screen to match. An old man and a young dog jogged across the screen, and a second shot rang out. The film characters didn't notice the commotion, but the theater patrons noticed the scream somewhere outside. Murmurs covered the first line of dialog.

Thomas sighed and then whispered into Abigail's ear, "Hero time."

He sounded more annoyed than concerned about the noise outside. He slipped something into Abigail's hand. She knew the soft material instantly. It was her red domino mask.

"When did—" she stopped herself. "You don't mind?"

Thomas took the popcorn bucket from her lap. "As long as you bring me back a slushie when you're done."

She kissed him twice, missing his lips on the first time and getting scratched by the stubble around his chin on the second. One peck for love, and one peck for an apology. "Be right back."

Avalon, the Dragon Slayer, wore a pleated skirt resembling something from a Viking television drama. Abigail, date night, wore a leather jacket zipped over a cute dress that her mother gave her last year. Instead of a sword, she was only armed with her fists. It was a lucky day for the criminal. She tied her mask over her eyes and ran into the lobby.

She grew tired of seeing guns pointed in peoples' faces. She grew tired of street thugs demanding wallets and jewelry. She was getting tired of "busy work" crime. Today, at the First Financial Bank, was exciting. Tonight, at the snack counter, was boring.

"Hey buster," Abigail shouted over the wheezing popcorn maker. The glass case was shattered by one of the shots, and the second vanished somewhere inside the drop ceiling. As she approached, baby blue smoke oozed from her mouth. "Didn't you read the sign? No outside food, drinks, or weapons."

The gunman looked over his shoulder at her. A ski mask hid his face, smashing his two chins against each other beneath the fabric. He moved the gun from the snack girl, who dropped behind the counter, and aimed it at Abigail. At the click of the safety, she unleashed the breath she'd been building. Brilliant indigo flames filled the air in front of her and absorbed the bullet. She ran through the fire, her jacket singeing, and bull-rushed the criminal.

He didn't fall like Abigail expected. He was as solid as a rock and used the butt of the gun to smack the side of Abigail's face. Her cheek stung, but she wouldn't be in a top-rated hero company if a blow so small could stop her. Cherry-red flames blossomed across her knuckles, and she attacked the man like he was an HRC training dummy until his hoodie burned away. She targeted his face next and a single punch burned away his ski mask. Abigail yanked the remains of the mask off before the fire could do more than blister.

The man tried to swing his gun into Abigail's face a second time in a desperate attempt to end her assault. She grabbed his wrist and twisted until his fingers loosened and the gun dropped. Abigail caught it, placed it on the counter, and pinned the man's arm behind his back. She grinned, realizing she'd make it back to the movie before missing anything too important.

"Can you get me a blue slushie?" Abigail asked the girl still behind the counter.

"Avalon, watch out!"

It was not the answer she expected to hear.

With his free hand, the man snatched the gun from the counter and spun around to aim at Abigail again. She dropped down, the bullet missing her head and embedding into an arcade game behind her, and kicked the man's knee. The man tumbled into the snack display, breaking the glass. Abigail slid the gun farther away from him and grabbed the man's wrists. The fire she used to burn him was not as hot as the glare she seared him with. The *snap* at his wrist was quieter than his knee, but both blows resulted in broken bones. The man stayed in the snack display and whimpered as Abigail got off of him.

"Blue slushie," she ordered from the snack girl when she found her shaking eyes below the counter. Abigail opened her phone and dialed the Hero Relief Center. She gave her statement quickly, tying the man's hands together with a pair of zip ties she pulled from her pocket. "Move and I'll break the other knee," she growled at him.

Abigail exchanged the gun for the slushie and slipped back into the dark theater. Half of the audience had left, using the back exit of the building, but Thomas still sat where she left him. Half of their popcorn was gone. He eagerly accepted the slushie.

"Miss anything important?" Abigail stuffed her mask into her pocket.

"The dude lost his wife to cancer, and now he and the dog are going back in time to save her."

"Really?" Abigail looked to the screen where an old man walked with a young dog. They got to the edge of the beach and started on the other side after the screen flashed a grainy yellow. "Was that the time travel?"

Thomas laughed. "I was just playing. I think the film's broke or the guy left. It's been on this loop since you left."

"Oh." Abigail felt like this was her fault. Her cheeks shaded to the color of her mask.

"Want to sneak into a different movie?" Thomas wiggled his eyebrows while he sipped from one of the two straws in the slushie. The image was boyish, and cute. It was Thomas. It was solace.

"Yeah." Abigail reclaimed the popcorn bucket, the fight already miles away in her mind. "I want to see the fighting mouse one."

Chapter Three

Abigail stopped mid stride when she saw an image of her face across the street. She neared the newspaper and magazine stand, frustration and embarrassment darkening her features with each step. She was on the cover of at least three of the tabloids claiming shelf space on the outdoor display. The images were from the movie theater robbery last night. The headlines demanded the details of the situation. But not about the attempted robbery. Everyone was dying to know who Avalon had gone to the movies with, what film she had seen, what snacks she had bought.

"How do you even know she went with someone?" A tired looking schoolboy asked his friend who flipped through one of the magazines beside Abigail. "And why does it even matter?"

Abigail shared his opinion. It didn't matter.

His friend slapped his arm with the copy before she continued reading. "It's obvious Dean. Why would anyone see a movie by themselves when you can rent almost everything online?"

"Because they wanted to see it the week it came out?"

"Sure." The friend didn't seem convinced. "But why risk your privacy going to a crowded theater when you could just stay home?"

Dean pointed at the cover. "Avalon clearly wasn't there as Avalon or else she'd be in her costume."

The friend smiled. "Exactly. Avalon was there on a date! Just look here. You and Sam used to do this when you were dating."

Abigail watched the school kids examine the zoomed in photo of the twin straws inside the slushie. She wanted to bang her head against a light post. She wondered who even snapped the photos last night. She'd like to think the citizens of San Arbor would value their life more than the quick buzz generated by posting photos of superheroes on their social media accounts, but apparently, she was wrong. While the school kids continued their theories, Abigail flipped the magazines around to hide her face. This would blow over in a couple of days, she hoped.

"Hey!" the cashier barked in Abigail's direction, and she and the two kids froze. "What do you think you're doing? Stop messing with the books."

Abigail leapt back from the rack, her hands up in peace. She didn't have a proper excuse. The cashier shooed her away with a rolled-up newspaper without leaving his chair. Abigail departed, ducking her head below her shoulders, and returned to her route to the Hero Relief Center.

Perhaps if she were in costume, she would have more authority to remove the tabloids.

Walking into the HRC, Abigail thought she'd be safe from the headlines and speculations, but the same magazine cover stared her down from the front desk. She could never wear the blue paisley dress again in case anyone made the connection that Abigail Turner looked a lot like Avalon, The Dragon Slayer. She stomped her sneakers harder against the tile floor as she neared the desk. Shannon, the receptionist, loved the muddy rumors about the heroes she worked with.

When Abigail approached, Shannon looked over the top of the magazine and read aloud, "It's unclear who Avalon was with last night, but breaking down the eligible bachelors in the hero community—"

Abigail yanked the magazine from Shannon's grasp, and the older woman laughed at Abigail's annoyance. Rolling the magazine as tightly as the thick pages would allow, Abigail stuffed it under her arm. "This is stupid."

"For you maybe," Shannon agreed with another cackle. "I think it's pretty entertaining. If you get asked to go on to *Tonight in San Arbor*, will you take me?"

Abigail was pretty sure the late-night gossip show fueled most of the rumors about the city. Their *sources* targeted everyone that stood in some sort of limelight; heroes, politicians, athletes, anyone with something to lose. Abigail was also pretty sure she would eat a bowl of nails before she'd willingly go on the show.

"You can just go in my place," she promised Shannon.

Shannon comically tossed a strand of her hair over her shoulder. "I'll make sure you look good."

"Thanks." Laughing, Abigail retreated to the employee elevator with slightly higher spirits. "See you later, Shannon."

The secret lairs of superheroes were no longer secret. The hero companies operated out of downtown skyscrapers and corner offices just like the other big businesses. Half of the Hero Relief Center was blocked off with a series of security scanners requiring employee badges and thumb prints to proceed. The other half was a flashy showroom dedicated to the heroes containing a museum and gift shop. Abigail tapped her foot inside the elevator as it traveled to the twelfth floor where the other Round Table Knights would be waiting with the company's president Quinn Samuels.

It was Samuels' idea to start the HRC, but it was King Arthur's idea to have the Knights of Camelot theme. Modeled after the old legends, the table in their meeting room was constructed from a single round slab of white marble. All the lighting in the room was produced from artificial wall candles. The room was over the top but served its purpose. It also served as a beautiful backdrop for press announcements and social media updates.

Being a hero in the modern age was complicated.

Abigail dropped the rolled magazine in the trash bin outside the door and sat in her unassigned seat next to Excalibur. The table was large enough to seat twenty-four people, but only the five knights and President Samuels filled them. It was King Arthur's dream to see all the seats filled with heroes one day. But, for now, San Arbor's top heroes knocked knees and elbows in the intimate space they created on one side of the stone table.

President Samuels began their routine morning meeting by turning on one of the three monitors behind him. Abigail dropped her head into her hands, muffling a sigh. Another front-page cover of Avalon stared across the table from her. If she wasn't so embarrassed, she could have been impressed by the number of photos captured from her fight in such a short time. It seemed each tabloid had their own front-page photo.

"This is a good reminder to always be prepared." Samuels was not good at hiding his snicker. "Even when you're off duty, make sure you've got some sort of mask in case something like this happens. Good job, Avalon."

Abigail gave him a thumbs up and a dirty look in response.

Samuels composed himself and switched the monitor to another screen and handed out their patrolling assignments. King Arthur and Excalibur had the downtown area, Merlin was stationed in the open shopping district where her chemical reactions had less chance to damage something, and Abigail and Lancelot were given school duty.

"A first grade class needs a lesson on teeth cleaning," Samuels explained.

"Then send a dentist," complained Abigail.

Lancelot knew better than to argue with his boss while he still only had the temporary sidekick badge, but Abigail saw him eye Samuels with the same distaste she did. Their powers were worth more than showing a group of kids how to floss. A hero saves *people,* not gums.

"You know it's in your contract," Samuels answered, shutting off the monitor. "You both need the community service hours."

"Does this really need two of us?" Abigail still argued. "Lance can handle this on his own. Send me to Jolt Station, Uptown, anywhere."

King Arthur's royal voice spoke over Samuels. "Are you ignorant or just forgetful?"

The insult stung worse coming from King Arthur. It wasn't a playful jab or flippant words thrown just to hurt. They were carefully chosen and spoken with an evenness reserved for truths. The room turned cold.

"I told you there would be repercussions if you were careless again."

Abigail started to fold her arms across her chest but stopped. She didn't need a shield against King Arthur. "I stopped the bad guy."

"You broke bones," King Arthur corrected. "On some low-level grunt that was going to steal less money than the property damage you caused the company."

Abigail admired King Arthur's hatred for the media and how it and the city tried to keep the heroes on a short leash. Now, she hated his loyalty to Samuels. The Call To Action Ordnance was still new in the eyes of the law, and any slip up could jeopardize it. King Arthur was on a shorter leash to Samuels than he ever was to the media's cameras. It was a fact only Abigail seemed to notice.

"The only reason I'm letting you out today is because San Arbor is more focused on your date than the criminal you mangled."

Abigail matched King Arthur's glare until she thought she saw a flash of purple over his eyes. She looked back to President Samuels before she could confirm the color change. "Where's the school?"

The first grade class at Westcrest Hills Elementary School was beyond ecstatic when the heroes entered their room. The waist high army of kids leaped from their seats and shouted incoherent sentences at them. The more determined kids ducked between their teacher's legs and gripped onto Avalon's and Lancelot's costumes. Abigail shoved their hands off her skirt fearing an accidental wardrobe malfunction. Beside her, Lancelot scooped two of the children into his arms and bellowed into the room with his own howls of laughter. The children surrounded him like he was their oversized child king.

"Who's ready to brush their teeth?" he called out to them.

The children reacted like he asked them if they wanted ice cream instead. Kids began hovering in the air before lowering gently into seats. Lancelot used his abilities to spin and twist a few kids before they found their destination. The giggling intensified.

"We'll handle it from here," Abigail told the teacher as Lancelot telekinetically lifted more of the class into the air.

The teacher's eyes were glued onto her floating students. Abigail wasn't sure if the wobbling smile on her face was in fear of the two heroes taking over her class for an hour, or excitement of having an hour away from the goblins.

"I'll just be outside if you need anything," the teacher promised.

Abigail made her own promise: "You won't have to worry about us."

At a glance back into the chaotic room, Abigail hoped she could keep it.

The teacher vanished out the door covered in construction paper rainbows and flowers. The children watched hungrily and wide-eyed from their seats. Abigail put on her media smile and joined Lancelot at the front of the room. He used his powers to juggle their props, a toy mouth, toothbrush, and floss above his head. He looked like a court jester instead of the fabled knight he stole his name from.

"Hey kids," Lancelot lowered the items onto the demonstration table, "Avalon and I fight bad guys every day to keep you safe, but did you know you can be heroes too?"

The children's *oohs* filled the silence. Abigail cocked her head, waiting for Lancelot's catch. As a first grader, she could only dream about being a hero. There was no way she was actually saving anyone at that age.

"You can be the hero to your teeth!" Lancelot was too excited, and the kids fed off his energy. "By brushing every day, you can fight the bad germs that want to damage your gums and teeth. Today, Avalon and I are going to teach you how to defeat the three worst villains that live inside your mouth."

Several of the kids screamed in terror. Their high-pitched wails left Abigail's ears ringing.

"They're level one baddies," Abigail chimed in, grabbing the toy mouth off the table. "Nothing you can't handle."

"The first villain?" Lancelot said in a low voice. "Cavities. Can anyone tell me how a cavity is formed?"

"Sugar!" answered a chorus of students.

"Right!"

Abigail didn't know if that was totally correct, but she let it slide. The quicker they were done the quicker they could get back to real hero work.

"The sugar will invite scary cavities to live inside your mouth." Lancelot sounded like he was telling a ghost story around a campfire. "Once inside, the cavity can cause enough damage to destroy the tooth. We don't want that, right Avalon?"

"Right!" Abigail agreed. She chomped the toy mouth together. "Without teeth, you couldn't shout 'I'm here to rescue you!'"

"Or smile at your best friend." Lancelot smiled goofily at Abigail. She chomped the teeth closer to him. The children laughed. "How do you defeat a cavity?"

"Brushing!"

"Right again." Lancelot picked up the toothbrush. "Your teacher must be very impressed. Alright, Avalon, open up! Time to brush."

Abigail pulled open the toy mouth, and Lancelot brushed over the teeth while singing a terrible song she assumed he made up. Each verse was the same, and the kids caught on quickly.

"Brush-brush-brush, back and forth, back and forth. Brush-brush-brush, side to side, side to side. Brush-brush-brush, back and forth, back and forth. Brush-brush-brush, side to side, side to side."

Abigail thought she slipped into a nightmare. The children chanted the words in a ritual to please their child king. She was glad this wasn't filmed for an instructional DVD. Most of their presentation, she didn't know what Lancelot was about to do next. Her mind ran a marathon trying to keep up with him as he taught the kids to fight gingivitis, and bad breath. At the end, the children lined up to high five the heroes, and receive their goody bags of dental care products and sticker sheets from the Hero Relief Center.

Most of the stickers were removed and stuck to places before the teacher returned. Several places that didn't need stickers like the floor, lamp shape and windows were suddenly covered in colorful heroes. The teacher clapped her hands together, and the students found their seats.

"Tell the heroes thank you," she instructed.

"Thank you!" the goblins shouted before erupting into more chaotic energy.

"Remember to brush, brush, brush!" Lancelot bid farewell to his small army while Abigail led them into the hallway. "Wow, that was fun."

Abigail shook her head. "You looked pretty at home in there."

"Teaching the youth?" he grinned.

"Thank you for coming," the teacher squeaked, standing on the other side of the door keeping the children back. "I'm sure the kids will talk about this all week."

"It was our pleasure," Abigail said.

"We love helping out the next generation of heroes," added Lancelot.

"You two make such a good team," the teacher commented before shutting the door. "I hope your next date doesn't get interrupted."

"What?" Abigail asked, but the door already separated them.

Lancelot howled with laughter.

"Stop." Abigail swatted at him.

"She thinks I was your movie date?" He composed himself. "Man, that's funny."

Abigail shoved him with her shoulder as she felt his psychic touch on her hair. "Let's get back to HQ, maybe we can get restationed."

"If you're not grounded anymore."

Abigail glared at him, but her look didn't pack any real fight. "I'll leave you here."

Lancelot stepped beside her, matching her stride as she walked down the hallway. He scrolled through his phone. "Traffic looks clear," he muttered reading the news feed. "The others aren't involved with anything media worthy. Probably going to be a slow— Woah, woah, woah! Fire at Jolt Station."

Abigail stopped and grabbed his phone. "What?"

31

The burst of media snippets all read the same thing. A fire raged inside Jolt Station, San Arbor's train depot. Cell phone pictures captured dark smoke escaping the arching main doors of the building. Firetrucks were parked outside. Nameless first responders populated the foreground. Abigail zoomed into the backs of turnout coats and engine numbers searching for Thomas. Her stomach flattened when she saw Ladder Company 3 stitched into one jacket. He was inside the building. He was being consumed by the fire.

"We have to go."

Lancelot grabbed his phone. "This fire started over an hour ago. They'll have it under control by the time we get there."

"I have to help him."

"Him?" Lancelot asked.

"The firefighters," Abigail corrected over her shoulder, now jogging down the hallway. "All of them."

She knew it was pointless. She knew worrying about the fireproof Thomas Sanders entering a burning building was like worrying about a fish jumping into water. Thomas was born in the flames. There wasn't anything else he was meant to do. There was a better chance of winning the lottery than Thomas getting hurt on the job. But it never kept her from worrying. Thomas was back in her life, and she wasn't going to let anything take him away again. She ran to the car once outside the school and willed Lancelot to hurry along.

"Come on!" she muttered as Lancelot chatted with the crossing guard before walking to the parking lot.

To Abigail, the Earth rotated several times before Lancelot opened the car door. Instead of his body entering the seat, he held his phone across the space. A video was paused on the screen.

"Get in," she ordered.

"Watch this first."

Not wanting to waste time arguing, Abigail snatched the phone and threw the car back into park. She rapidly tapped the screen commanding the video to interchange between play and pause. When it finally played, Abigail tightened her hand around the device. A helmetless Thomas walked through the smoldering entrance of the train depot. Smoke rolled off him, and his turnout coat was covered in dark burns. In his arms, he miraculously carried three small bodies. The crowd around the videographer cheered as Thomas delivered the children to a paramedic. He wiped his forehead with the back of his glove, smearing black soot across his face, and returned to the building. The camera moved from him to a reporter holding a Channel 9 microphone.

"That makes seven rescued," the reporter announced in disbelief. The crowd on the other side of the camera cheered again. "And he keeps going back inside to get more. Right now, we know the fire has been contained to Bank C of Jolt Station, and fire crews are working to put it out. It is unclear how the fire— oh my!" The camera panned back to the depot. Thomas walked out with two more people. His turnout coat draped over their heads. "Two more rescued! This is truly—"

Lancelot pulled the phone from Abigail's hand. "That was posted twenty minutes ago, I think your fireman is okay without you." The seatbelt clicked together and punctuated his statement.

Abigail switched the car out of park and drove. At the intersection, she forced herself to turn left, toward the Hero Relief Center and not speed toward Jolt Station. He would call her. Just like every fire before. Thomas would call.

Chapter Four

It wasn't a call, but Abigail heard his low rumbling voice as if Thomas had whispered the text message in her ear.

Alive and smoking. I'll be home late. Have to smile for my adoring fans.

Abigail clutched the phone to her chest while she ascended the elevator back to her office. It wasn't quite the proof of life she wanted, but relief still filled her. She typed a response as the elevator let her off ten stories later. She whistled Lancelot's annoying song as she entered her office. The chant had painfully wiggled its way into her head and, knowing her luck, would stay there for the rest of the day.

Despite the Call To Action ordinance, strict rules still regulated the hero's day-to-day and until it was her time to patrol, Abigail was stuck on desk duty. She logged onto the HRC system and inputted her time at the elementary school as social engagement hours. Members of the Round Table Knights were required to log in 35 social engagement hours a month. Whether it was to keep their ratings up, ensure good public relations, or to actually help San Arbor, Abigail preferred to spend her required time helping sort packages at the food bank, or aiding the physical therapy ward at the children's hospital.

Reminding kids to brush their teeth didn't seem as beneficial as the others.

A knock sounded from her door, and Abigail looked up. President Samuels smiled at her from the doorway next to King Arthur.

"Hey." Abigail glanced between the two of them. "What can I do for you?"

President Samuels crossed the room and sat in one of the two chairs on the other side of Abigail's desk. His suit was pressed as it always was. His burgundy tie matched his burgundy handkerchief. The matching cufflinks snagged pieces of light and tossed it back around the room. King Arthur casually took the other seat next to him and leaned into the cushioned back looking like he'd be there for a while.

"I ran into Lancelot in the hallway," President Samuels said. "He tells me your field trip was a success."

"Lancelot must have worked with children before us, he's a natural at it," agreed Abigail. "I'm sure the kids will be talking about it for a while."

"Not as bad as you thought?" King Arthur asked.

Abigail heard the warning undertone and shook her head. "Not bad at all. Enjoyable even."

He nodded and Abigail turned back to President Samuels. Despite his title, the president was a lot easier to address than King Arthur. "Any new information on that Jolt Station fire? The reports didn't have a lot of specifics in them."

"SAFD had it contained," answered Samuels. "It would have been nice to work together with them but sending in our heroes would have been an insult when they had it under control."

"More of a reason for us to have been there."

President Samuels ignored King Arthur. "It's my understanding that the transportation department is going to do a full investigation and check of the other train engines to ensure this doesn't happen again."

"That sounds good." Abigail filled the silence that followed. King Arthur still looked bothered by their lack of appearance. She couldn't say she didn't share it. "Is there anything you need from me, sir?"

President Samuels frowned. "I hate to ask this, but can you work late tonight?"

"Sure, what's happening?" It was difficult to say no to the president. It would not be difficult to work patrol. No matter the time.

"You've been requested to go on *Tonight in San Arbor*." The president's frown was replaced with a sheepish smile. "I already told them you'd be available for the segment."

Abigail clenched her fists under the desk, and neither her boss nor her leader witnessed the micro tantrum. "What do they want to talk about?"

"It's a fluff piece, nothing serious," President Samuel's explained. "Just a little coverage on your date."

Abigail's sigh was louder than she expected. A wisp of blue smoke exited her mouth along with it. "Is that really necessary? There's nothing to cover about it. It wasn't even a date."

"It's something fun for the city, and after the hostage situation San Arbor could use a distraction."

"This might not be as bad as you think, either." King Arthur leaned forward in his chair. Abigail caught a glimpse of her reflection inside his golden crown. This was part of her punishment; she just knew it.

"What time do they need me?"

"The show's recording at 7 tonight," answered President Samuels. "Take a member of staff with you. Mitch will drive you to the studio at 6."

Adding grumpy Mitch into the equation made the night far worse. Abigail knew he'd blame her for keeping him out late and sitting through the show's taping. "I'd like to take Shannon. She'd really enjoy seeing the show."

At least someone should have a good time during all of this.

"Very well, I'll let her know."

"Sir?" Abigail stopped President Samuels and King Arthur before they completely rose from their seats. "If we're able to discuss the Knights, anything I should mention?"

"Try to keep it on the date, okay?"

"The city doesn't need to be reminded about the beating you issued during it either," added King Arthur with a dangerous glare.

"Understood."

"I can't believe this is seriously happening," groaned Abigail, watching her reflection receive a second dusting of makeup from a stagehand backstage. Other staff members of *Tonight in San Arbor* bustled around her in a chaotic symphony of television production. Almost all of them had a headset covering an ear.

Shannon snickered in the seat beside Abigail and said, "I warned you this would happen."

"I can't believe you were right."

"Can you lift up your mask?" the stagehand asked.

She looked younger than Abigail, but it was hard to tell with the makeup caked around her eyes possibly hiding wrinkles or acne. Abigail raised an eyebrow and the stagehand suddenly decided she was done with the eyes and checked that Abigail's lavalier microphone was properly strapped to the underside of her cape.

"It's not too late to sign me up for the interview," Shannon said. "Slap a publicist credit to my name tag, and I'll tell Graham all of the juicy details."

"There are no juicy details," Abigail reminded but it didn't stop Shannon's laughter. "I grabbed two straws by mistake. I had just stopped a robbery; the straw count was the least of my concern."

Shannon pursed her lips. "I wouldn't say that on air. San Arbor's environmentalist would have a field day if they believed Avalon didn't support the sea turtles."

Abigail sighed. "You should have that publicist credit."

"You're good at this Avalon, don't worry too much."

"Avalon!" a different stagehand called from outside the green room. "You're up in sixty."

"Then why did falling through the roof the other day feel more enjoyable?"

Shannon stood with Abigail, more eager to follow the staff to the side of the stage than her and shrugged. "Shouldn't you do one thing a day that makes you afraid?"

Abigail wondered what magazine Shannon picked that out of. "I'm a hero. We don't scare easily."

The applause from the other side of the red velvet curtain muffled Shannon's comment, but she didn't look like she believed Abigail.

A booming voice cut over the applause, and Abigail listened for her cue as *Tonight in San Arbor's* Graham Green introduced Avalon and her segment.

"We've all seen the pictures and we've all heard the speculations, but now it's time for San Arbor to get some answers!" Graham riled the crowd again. "Ladies, and gentlemen, and viewers at home, please welcome Round Table Knight: Avalon, the Dragon Slayer!"

Abigail pushed through the curtain and waved toward the crowd and cameras. She was used to the bright lights, the dull roar that pulsed in her ears, and the trip-hazard floor covered in cables and wires. She stepped onto the platform stage, shook hands with Graham who kissed her cheek, did a quick spin to show off her costume and sat in the chair next to him.

"Wowza! Sometimes I wonder if being attractive is a requirement for a superhero."

"It's just all this makeup," Abagail assured, her cheek itchy from Graham's kiss which was more mustache than lip.

"Then when do my powers kick in?" The crowd laughed along with Graham, prompted by the red *LAUGH* sign that turned on above the set. "How are you doing tonight, Avalon?"

"Doing well, Graham." Abigail forced another smile with her tense muscles. She felt like she was waiting for a punch; this small talk was just a distraction from the talk show's real attack. "I'm flattered to be on your show tonight."

"It's always a pleasure to have one of the Round Table Knights here with us. After Saves the Day shut down, you heroes are surprisingly busy."

"San Arbor is a big city. We like keeping a good eye on everything. Being able to work with the San Arbor Police Department has been one of the best things to happen."

"For you?"

"For everyone. Us, SAPD, San Arbor. The city has never been safer." Abigail beamed with pride.

"Yes, I'm sure that it is." Graham glanced to someone off stage before saying, "Avalon, do you like games? At *Tonight in San Arbor*, we're big fans of them."

"As long as it isn't Monopoly." Abigail glanced around looking for a hint of the challenge about to occur. Last week, Graham had a player from the San Arbor Majestics wade through a pool of pudding to recreate his game-winning homerun. Abigail didn't smell smoke, so she doubted Graham built some sort of flaming gauntlet to test her.

"I'm not much for Monopoly, either. Lost a wife once because of it. Anyway, here it is!"

A stagehand set a silver tray on Graham's desk. There were two slushies, one blue and one red, and three straws stacked between them.

"Are you ready for a race?" Graham handed Abigail the blue one. "I heard you're an expert of the double-straw technique."

Abigail resisted rolling her eyes as the television host wiggled his eyebrows. "I grabbed two by mistake. There's no need to be wasteful."

To prove her point, Abigail selected only one straw and inserted it into the drink.

"Count us down!" Graham shouted at the crowd who quickly started their chant at five.

The game was ridiculous. It was a waste of Abigail's time. The whole evening was. All she wanted to do was be home and see Thomas. Make sure he was okay. *Alive and smoking* wasn't good enough until she made sure of it. If anyone should have been celebrated tonight it should have been him. He would have enjoyed this far more than she. Abigail slurped down the slushie hoping the quicker it was gone the quicker she could leave.

Graham pulled away with more than half his slushy remaining and grabbed his head. He pushed both palms against his forehead, his face twisting in discomfort.

"Brain freeze, you win," he declared after sucking down a breath.

"I guess I do have a bit of an unfair advantage." Abigail did take joy in besting the host. She pursed her lips and exhaled a puff of blue smoke.

Graham composed himself. "I guess with anti-brain freeze technology you wouldn't need anyone's help finishing one of those."

"Nope."

"So, no secret boyfriend?"

Abigail sighed, "No."

"A secret girlfriend?"

"Again, no. I grabbed two straws by mistake."

"But if there was a beau for Avalon, what would they be like? What is it that you look for in a partner?"

Thomas flashed in Abigail's mind. Her smile was automatic, and she couldn't help but say, "Someone funny."

"So, definitely not Volcanic."

The audience roared with laughter.

Abigail scrunched her nose at the idea. She guessed it was a little funny, but not in the way the crowd probably laughed about. "Volcanic? He's old enough be my father!"

"Ah. So, someone younger?" Graham continued to fish for clues, to fish for ratings and reactions from his audience.

"Someone my age."

"Similarities are important! What else would be similar? A profession maybe?"

"I do love a man in uniform," Abigail said sardonically, but it wasn't technically a lie.

"A hero's uniform?" Graham rose to his feet. "San Arbor, you heard it right here! Avalon is looking for a hero!"

"No!" Abigail blushed and laughed around her outburst. "I'm not *looking* for a hero."

Graham's eyes twinkled, "Because you've already found one."

Abigail held up two fingers like a spartan shield to deflect Graham's assumptions. "Two straws by mistake."

"And that's her story, and she's sticking to it!" Graham looked into a camera. "Head over to our socials and cast your vote on who you think Avalon's most eligible bachelor is. We'll be back right after this."

The spotlights peeled off Abigail, and Shannon was suddenly on stage receiving the same kiss on the cheek greeting from Graham. Abigail sighed. She was finally free. Abigail yanked the microphone's battery pack off her back and wound the wires around it. She looked around for the closest stagehand to return it but caught Graham instead.

"Avalon, before you go?"

"What's up?" she asked.

"Make sure you and your friend stop by the gift shop on your way out. I told the studio to give you both a free shirt."

"Mr. Green, that's so nice," Shannon said.

"And, unnecessary," Abigail added.

Graham took the bundle of microphone wires from Abigail. "Not to me. Consider it an advance payment."

"Advance for what?"

"When you do snag yourself a bachelor you have the breaking story with us."

"I don't think my love life requires all of this fanfare," Abigail tried to sound polite.

"It will when you hook up with another super. I can't wait to see how the viewers vote during the airing tonight. I bet the top contender is Lancelot. What a scandal that would be!"

Shannon's cackling laughter followed Abigail as she stomped off the stage and out of the studio.

Chapter Five

The apartment was empty when Abigail finally got home. She hadn't thought her televised appearance would last longer than Thomas', but no smelly and soot-stained boots greeted her outside the door. She turned on the television and flipped the channel to the local news. *Tonight in San Arbor* wouldn't air until later, hopefully when she and Thomas were both asleep and could avoid it, but she hoped to catch Thomas' interview or some coverage on the fire. When the channel refused to offer any more information than the currently revealed letters on a game show's board, Abigail forced herself to do something productive. But every deep laugh from the on-air sitcom caused her to jolt to the screen with a soapy dish, half-folded shirt, or broom and dustpan in hand. She was disappointed each time when it wasn't Thomas waiting for her on the television. She checked her phone again. It's emptiness also disappointed her. She finished the chores, straightened their shared closet, and returned every shoe back to the rack instead of their haphazard positions on the floor. A frozen pizza was tossed in the oven. The dry dishes put away. Pens in the junk drawer tested for ink.

And then she heard it.

The undeniable sound of Thomas. The thunder in a storm. His voice, made scratchier from the day's events, filtered out of the old television's speakers like a siren's call. Abigail's butt planted on the couch before she could react. On the screen, a line of soot covered Thomas' nose and forehead. The darkness around his eyes made them appear a brighter green than they naturally were.

"I just did my job," he answered the reporter's question with a shrug. "A hero saves people, right?"

The reporter next to him lost his composure, his mouth dropping to a gasp. "You pulled eleven people from Jolt Station. What kept you going back inside? Weren't you scared?"

"If fires scared me, I wouldn't have become a firefighter."

The apartment door opened and the door snagging against the welcome mat silenced the reporter's next question. Thomas looked like his recorded twin on the television. Soot still stained his face, his clothes smelled like smoke, his hair greased back with sweat. His boots were kicked off in the hallway and calf-high Avalon socks protected his feet. He never looked more handsome.

Alive and smoking.

Abigail ran to him, joining the ash, sweat, stink and everything else that clung to him.

"Miss me?"

"Hush." She squeezed him harder then released him. "You're incredible."

Thomas smirked, even his teeth were coated in soot. His pink gums were tinged black. "This city councilman seems to think so too. He kept yapping at me. Even wanted to tag along back to the station with us."

"What'd he say?" Abigail followed him into the bedroom, claiming a seat on their bed.

"Nothing important." Thomas tore his shirt over his head and tossed it into the laundry basket. "Wanted to give me a key to the city and a new car. Told me I was better than any of those superheroes."

Abigail stuck out her tongue. "What'd he really say?"

"Did the political thing and thanked me," he answered seriously.

"I'm really proud of you."

"I am too." Thomas' reflection smiled from the dresser mirror as he dumped the contents of his pockets; wallet, badge, and loose change all tumbled into a leather tray. "This hero stuff is pretty cool."

"You could be a hero with us, you know."

"Think I could pull off tights?"

"You could wear a dress."

Thomas laughed with her, and then said, "I'll stick to the mask-less kind of hero work. It's working out a little better for me."

Abigail dropped her gaze from his reflection to her hands. His playfulness hid a darkness just below the surface. It was the same shadow she saw flash in his eyes when he didn't think she was looking. Side-kick. Villain. Civilian. First responder. Thomas had seen all sides of their hero world.

And the hero world hadn't liked any of his roles.

"What started the fire?" she asked into the quiet room.

"Train engine overheated," he answered. "Probably an older one. The councilman was talking about getting everything upgraded in the middle of praising me."

"I bet." Abigail slid off the bed and kissed him on the cheek. "I'm so glad you're safe."

Thomas retreated to the bathroom, then stuck his head back into the room. "I'm so glad you're dating a fireman. Whatever's in the oven is burning."

Abigail looked into the kitchen and saw smoke rising from the stove. "Shit!"

Thomas' laughter followed Abigail as she raced to the other side of the small apartment. She reached her bare hand into the oven and re-moved the burning disk of cheese, dropping it on top of the stove. She'd seen house fires in better shape than the darkening strips of mozzarella. After a taste test of the burnt crust, Abigail decided this pizza was an insult to the pair of heroes and opted for takeout. With the promise of a properly cooked pizza in 30 minutes or less, she began airing out the apartment by fanning the smoke out an open window with a dish towel.

Most of the burnt smell was gone by the end of Thomas' shower, and the rose scented soap overpowered any lingering pepperoni ghosts as he emerged into the kitchen.

"A new one is on its way," Abigail said in apology as Thomas examined the pizza on the stove.

The charred remains clattered on its side when Thomas dropped the burnt pizza. He turned his investigation to a junk drawer. "I think it's edible."

"Then it's all yours." Abigail joined him. "What are you looking for?"

"Pizza cutter— oh!" Thomas yanked out a portable CD player instead. Faded orange headphones wrapped around the player several times. Both item's brand names had rubbed off a long time ago. "What do we have here?"

"Wow. I haven't seen that since high school." Abigail peered over Thomas' shoulder while he pried the player open revealing a blank CD inside. "I can't believe I moved it here with me."

"Did someone make you a mixtape?" Thomas removed the CD and checked the bottom side for scratches before returning it into the player.

"I did." Abigail pointed at the date written in pink marker on the CD. "I made them a couple times a year with my favorite songs."

Thomas stuck an earbud in his ear and let its mate dangle between them. "What was the great Avalon listening to way back then?"

"We don't need to remember." Abigail chuckled and tried to wrestle the player away from Thomas.

"Oh." Thomas already hit play, lifting the player above his head and out of Abigail's reach. "You *liked* this song? So girly."

"Give me that." She snatched the dangling earbud and listened. "Come on, this is a good song."

Thomas smirked. "Sure, for teeny boppers. What else is on here?"

They leaned against the kitchen counter while Thomas shuffled through the CD. Abigail tried to defend her Senior year taste in music, but a couple of songs even made her cringe. She didn't think today's music was much better compared to her *classics*, but she was glad a few of the bands fell off her radar. The final song began much slower than the others on the CD. Instead of computer-generated beats, this one was composed of piano keys and soft acoustic guitars.

Abigail blushed. She'd forgotten the love ballad. The same sappy song had played at the homecoming dance that year. She was about to end the listening session, but Thomas tucked the CD player behind him in the waistband of his pants and captured her hands. His smirk softened and she melted. In the confined space between the stove and the sink, Thomas guided her in a Waltz neither of them knew. They shifted over the tile, bumped into the fridge's handle, and missed the notification of the arrival of their new pizza. As the song ended, Thomas dipped Abigail so close to the ground her hair brushed against the tile. Their headphones pulled out of their ears, and neither was able to catch the CD player as it dropped onto the floor. Thomas' grip only held Abigail, and she knew she'd never meet the same fate as her old CD player.

Chapter Six

Abigail watched in horror as a coffee mug floated toward her. The few yards between her and the office door became an infinite expanse under the beverage. Her skin squirmed when the dark liquid *slooshed* against the mug's rim. The computer, the papers, her red scabbard, everything on her desk had a big red target for the coffee to spill on. She didn't dare move from her seat, fearing the extra movement would push the mug off its invisible tether. When the mug did set itself magically on her desk, the thirty-second ordeal feeling like an hour, Abigail glared at the man standing in the doorway.

"Why? she moaned. "You could've brought it over here like a normal person."

"But I'm not normal." Lancelot grinned before sipping his own coffee with both hands wrapped tightly around his mug. "Besides, you could've gotten it yourself."

"But you asked me if I wanted one." Abigail checked the papers on her desk, they were all dry. She shuffled a pile of folders together as Lancelot sat across from her, and she moved the documents protectively away from him. Cream colored coffee dribbled from his mug onto her desk.

"Excalibur said it's a sidekick duty."

"Excalibur was also joking."

"Just say 'thank you.'"

"Thanks." Abigail flashed him an award-winning smile.

"You're welcome." Lancelot returned a smile just as bright. They both chuckled at the exchange. Their media expressions becoming their own inside joke the public would never understand. "What are you working on in here, anyway?"

"Reports," Abigail answered with a hiss. "I always let them get backed up and get stuck with a mountain."

"Shouldn't you have someone who does this for you?" Lancelot flipped one of the folders open.

"You."

"I'm a sidekick, not an assistant," he said with a wink.

"I don't see you doing anything sidekick worthy." Abigail closed the cover of the file he attempted to read, embarrassed for him to see how behind she let herself become. The incident date was almost three weeks ago.

"I brought you a coffee," he reminded before switching subjects. "What'd you get into last night?"

The memory of Thomas' hands around her waist and their clumsy dance beside the kitchen counter seeped into her mind. It warmed her more than any coffee would. "Nothing crazy. Caught up on laundry. How about you?"

"I checked out this new restaurant near my house. It's a fusion place with Asian and Mexican flavors. It's a lot better than it sounds."

"What'd you have?" Abigail was happy for the distraction from her paperwork. "Egg roll tacos?"

"An egg roll burrito. You should come with me next time. I promise this place will knock your socks right off."

"An egg roll burrito and missing socks?" Abigail teased. "You're not selling this place too well."

"Then just trust me."

Abigail eyed him. He shifted under her gaze, halfway raising his mug to his mouth, then stopping to lower it again.

"We can go outside of costume," he suggested with the smallest amount of pink dusting his nose. "If you're worried about people seeing

Avalon and Lancelot together? I saw that I'm the winner of Graham's poll."

"You watched *Tonight in San Arbor*?" Abigail hoped he hadn't.

"Of course. I always watch when one of us are on. My mom has my first appearance recorded. She's planning on playing it after Thanksgiving Dinner this year for the whole family."

Tonight in San Arbor and Graham's poll evaporated from Abigail's mind. "Your mom knows what you do?"

"She was the first person I told," he smiled fondly. "So, this new restaurant?"

The loudspeaker overhead interrupted her polite decline.

"We've got a fire on Ninth and Broadway," President Samuels announced over the intercom. "The Twin Leaf Bar in the Grand Hotel. Avalon, Lancelot, run point until backup arrives."

The desk shook as Abigail stood, both coffees dumping onto the files as she grabbed her sword. "Let's go!"

Lancelot was a step behind her as they exited the office. The most usable application, in Abigail's mind, of Lancelot's telekinesis was the ability to fly. They rode the elevator to the rooftop and ran to the edge of the building. His psychic hold wrapped around her torso, and Abigail hovered in the air with him. She was fine so long as she didn't look down. Their first flight together resulted in her looking down, getting sick, and owing an enormous apology to the woman who was standing below her. Lancelot grabbed Abigail's hand to keep her upright and moved their bodies mentally through the air as if they stood on a conveyor belt rather than thirteen stories above the ground.

The smoke wasn't visible until Seventh Street which Abigail knew was a good sign. The smoke she did see was a dirty mixture of gray and white, also a good sign. When the smoke turned black was when there was trouble. There was time to stop it before it turned bad. The street outside the Grand Hotel was blocked off, nosey cellphone users, hungry reporters, and concerned citizens stood along the perimeter. The red and white lights of the ambulance and firetruck flashed against the building.

Abigail was relieved when her boots landed on the ground, and she could get to work. She started walking before the psychic hold was completely off her body and approached the fire chief overseeing the crews inside. The older woman's hand wrapped tightly around the radio strapped to her shoulder. The chief commanded someone inside the building before addressing the hero. Abigail recognized the chief as Bridgett Warren. She was Thomas' chief. The 3 stitched into her uniformed tied the two of them together the same way Avalon's and Lancelot's mask did for them. Abigail forced herself to listen to the woman instead of looking for Thomas.

"I've got three inside doing rescue," Bridgett explained. "A kitchen gas leak caused the blaze."

"How can we best help your team?" Abigail asked. *How can I help Thomas?*

"You're the fireproof one?"

Abigail nodded.

"Get this line going." Bridgett pointed to the hose at her feet. "It's too hot for my guys to get close. Can you help with rescue?"

Lancelot nodded. "I can access the higher floors. Can your men get any remaining people to the windows? I'll bring them to the ground."

Bridgett spoke into her radio, "Purvis, Maddox, get those people near a window. You've got hero support coming in. Everyone else, clear out of the bar. Water is coming for the kitchen."

Abigail didn't wait for any more direction. She couldn't wait on the sidewalk any longer. She grabbed the hose, yanked it twice to start the release on the truck, and ran into the hazy hotel lobby. She followed the smoke, smelling of grease and char, through the lobby to where it billowed menacingly around the entrance of the Twin Leaf Bar. Sinister red and orange flames flashed between plumes of the dark smoke. It was equal parts a warning and an invitation to Abigail.

Running into fires never got easier. Even though she was fireproof to the common house fires and car explosions, Abigail's body fought against her mind. Charging headfirst into flames was against human nature. But standing still was against hero nature. Abigail tugged the hose, creating several feet of slack and ran into the dark smoke.

Three steps in, and she couldn't see the doorway behind her.

The light sensors on her mask became obscured by smoke, and the thousands of sensors inside turned on. Hidden objects in the smoke were highlighted on the sensor's screens before her eyes, and two pin-point flashlights on either side of the mask tried to illuminate the room. The light bounced off the smoke clouds and did a better job at blinding the hero than aiding her. Abigail focused on the readout screen inside her mask instead and twisted the hose nozzle. Water shot through the hose at the hungry fire currently consuming tables, chairs, and wooden support pillars. A great hissing filled the room along with hot steam.

She traveled deeper into the blaze, heading toward the kitchen in the back, targeting the flames she passed with either the water or her own flames. The temperature rose around her. Her sweaty palms made holding the wild hose difficult as it thrashed under the water pressure. More steam filled her vision. The flashlights bounced off the vapors, and the mapping systems confused the ghostly smoke-made forms as real objects. She was forced to advance blindly. Only the heat was able to guide her.

The fires she doused seemed to double instead of die. Each spark she produced took more oxygen from her straining lungs. More patches of red appeared through the smoke rather than vanishing. The thermal gage on the mask readout warned against the dangerous temperature. Abigail moved from burning table to burning chair, the flames beacons in the dark. The Twin Leaf Bar was famous for its compact size and speakeasy feel. Walking blindly through it, the space seemed endless. Rounding an art deco column, flames coiling along the raised spiral, Abigail finally found the stream of fire pouring from the kitchen's door like an angry river. She aimed the hose at the bottom of the blaze and twisted the nozzle for maximum power.

The blaze hissed, wounded but not defeated, and sparks spewed at Abigail. Behind her, the column crashed to the ground with a mighty *bang*. Burning bits of rubble shot in every direction. Unleashed embers erupted into the air resembling a mushroom cloud. Pieces of wood clawed into Abigail. Her back became a target for the shrapnel. Her costume absorbed some of the force. Her fireproofing ignored most of the heat, but her bare skin was just human. She bit her tongue as sharpened pieces of wood cut into the backs of her legs. She clamped her jaw, focusing her attention on the raging beast in front of her and not the pain. She could take care of herself after the job was done. Black smoke twisted out of the kitchen, invading Abigail's space and forcing its way under her mask. The heat was unfathomable as it tore into her eyes. Abigail was losing her breath.

She tightened her grip around the hose and dropped to a knee. Partly to stable the hose, partly to stable herself. Curious flaming tendrils stroked against the newly opened cuts on her back, finding one of the few ways past Abigail's fireproofing. She cringed at the intrusion. Something dug painfully into her knee from the floor. Abigail pushed it all aside. She focused on her fingertips, how they wrinkled under the pressure against the hose, and not the shallow breaths she was only managing to take. Abigail didn't know if her vision faded due to the smoke and steam, or from the lack of oxygen. She pressed more weight onto her aching knee to stay upright. She yowled as the pressure pushed the foreign object deeper into her patella. Black smoke raged against her throat and stole more of the space oxygen.

"You okay, hero?"

The voice sounded like a faraway echo, but the touch that followed was real. A hot mask appeared over Abigail's mouth and nose, and she greedily breathed in the concentrated air. Her vision cleared and her savior's blurry face focused in front of her.

Wild black hair held back the wilder flames around them.

Thomas.

Abigail's eyes watered, but the heat stole her tears.

"I told you to invest in a rebreather or something," he scolded. "You're okay?"

"Yeah," Abigail returned the mask to his face. "Are you?"

Thomas nodded. "A little scorched, but I've had worse."

His twisted smirk was a comfort only Abigail could understand. It made the fire feel miles and miles away. The heat was an afterthought.

Thomas returned the mask to her. "I'll make a path. The gas is off outside, all that's left is the fire. We have enough water?"

Abigail checked the gauge, passing the mask back to him. "Enough for this."

"I love you."

"I love you."

Thomas stood, raising his palms to the fire. The buoyant cinders floated to him first, then the wispy smoke. The red fire twisted up and laced through his blackened fingers before absorbing into his hands. He was an elegant monster commanding his fiendish friends home. The doorway to the kitchen was clear, and Abigail rushed in with the water hose on full blast. She focused on the lowest level of the fire, while Thomas absorbed the higher flames.

After the final patch of fire was doused, Abigail twisted the nozzle closed. The charred remains of the kitchen dripped around her. She didn't care that the pristine kitchen was now in shambles. She didn't care about the water soaking inside her boot. She didn't care about the cleaning her costume desperately needed. She didn't care about the stinging and burning on her back and legs. All she cared about was the man who left everything behind to join her in San Arbor. Thomas shook his hands out at his sides and approached her. Instead of the kiss she thought was coming, he shoved his oxygen mask against her face until she took several deep breaths. When he pulled the mask back, his fingers were scorched black from tip to the second knuckle. Fear snaked in her chest faster than any five-alarm fire. Abigail grabbed his free hand. It was still hot and stained her own fingers with ash as she tried to rub them clean.

"I may have absorbed too much." Thomas playfully wiggled his fingers in her hold. "They'll turn back to normal in a few hours, promise."

Abigail released his hand and shoved the mask to him. "You're incredible."

Thomas smiled at the praise. "Best in the world?"

She knocked her shoulder against his. Not refuting his statement but being careful not to let his ego get too big. The way he looked at her, all crooked smile and bright eyes, she could tell he saw right through her plan. "Let's get out of here."

Thomas spoke into the radio attached to the shoulder of his turnout coat. "Kitchen is secure, you can return the hose. Headed out the main door."

"Damnit Sanders," Bridgett Warren's voice crackled back. "I told everyone to evacuate that area."

"Someone needed my help." Thomas smirked at Abigail.

She rolled her eyes and followed him out of the kitchen. The hose tugged forward as the truck's winch wound it back in place. Abigail limped behind it and Thomas. Each step caused her knee to buckle. She gritted her teeth but kept going.

"You're bleeding," Thomas said when they stepped into the lobby where the light illuminated her injuries.

A thin veil of smoke encased them. Abigail looked down. Her knee was raw and bloodied. A fork-sized splinter from the column poked from the wound. She pinched the splinter and yanked it out, wincing as she did. Blood oozed to take its place and dripped down her leg, spilling over her golden greave.

"It's fine."

Thomas raised an eyebrow. Abigail stood her ground as he gave her a once over, but her damaged knee buckled as she attempted to keep her weight on it. Before Abigail could protest, Thomas scooped her into his arms and walked to the front door. The hose in her hand felt like an oversized rattle to her oversized baby. She frowned at him which only made him laugh.

"I can walk just fine."

"Just let me have this, babe," he said. "The guys will get a kick out of it."

Abigail shook her head but allowed him to carry her over the threshold of the hotel and onto the sidewalk. The flashing cameras were brighter than the flames. The cheering crowd was louder than the roaring fire. The audience around the barricades easily tripled since the heroes' arrival. They only saw one thing: a firefighter carrying a hero out of a burning building. Abigail's bloodied knee looking horrific. The burns on her legs looking like a vulnerability.

Chapter Seven

"I'm fine," Abigail assured the paramedic currently listening to her lungs. The metal stethoscope was a cool relief against her back. The paramedic's watch scraping over a cut was not. She took another deep breath at the medic's command.

"Let me do my job." The paramedic rounded the gurney to address Abigail's next injury: her bloody and swelling knee. From the opened bag also seated on the gurney, the paramedic retrieved a tube of cream and gauze.

While the paramedic assessed her injuries, Abigail assessed the situation around her. The ambulance she sat near was the last one at the scene. The others were moving their cargo to the nearest hospital. She knew Lancelot would have done everything to get the citizens out, but until she saw the numbers she couldn't stop wondering if they arrived too late.

How long had the fire been burning before the Hero Relief Center sent them?

Why had they wasted time for her to change into her costume?

The paramedic examined a singed cut on her leg, causing Abigail to wince. Her leg almost smacked against the paramedic's face in the process, and she grabbed the hero's boot to keep her still. Whatever goo was in the tub was applied, and an arctic tingle chased away the stinging. The paramedic moved to the next cut, and Abigail found something better to focus on.

Thomas stood with his company down the sidewalk. She'd get the details from him later about the start of the call. For her report and her curiosity. Thomas and his crew were storing equipment back in the truck, their heads bent together in conversation. Abigail knew the redhead, Purvis, and the blond, Maddox, from a company picnic Thomas brought her to after his first month at the San Arbor department. They were nice men and accepted Thomas into the station like the upperclassmen on a football team.

Teasing included.

Abigail overheard parts of their conversation as the trio drifted closer to the ambulance once the final bit of equipment was properly stored. She picked at the soot under her nails, being mindful of the paramedic who continued to disinfect her open wounds. Her attention perked when she heard her name.

"Come on man, you saved Avalon," Purvis said to Thomas.

Maddox added, "She's only your favorite thing out there."

"I wouldn't say that," Thomas defended with a chuckle.

"This is your chance!"

"Probably your only chance."

"To do what?" Thomas asked.

"You know," Purvis said suggestively. "I know all your posters aren't just for looking at. Aren't you going to like, ask for her phone number or something?"

Maddox shoved Purvis on Thomas' behalf. "Tom's dating Abby, right?" At a nod from Thomas, he continued, "And doesn't Avalon have a secret boyfriend or something?"

Abigail was equal parts impressed and sickened by his tabloid knowledge.

"You're going to regret it if you don't at least say something to her."

Thomas shrugged. "Think she'll let me take a selfie?"

"If you don't ask, I will." Purvis threatened with a snicker.

From under her lashes, Abigail watched Thomas cross the sidewalk. His turnout coat left a speckled trail of ash and dust behind him.

The material seemed to be molded to his skin. No matter how often he washed up, the soot clung to him like a magnet. Abigail smiled when he got closer. It was an automatic response.

"You okay?"

"This isn't necessary," Abigail answered. The paramedic made another loop of gauze around her knee, clearly ignoring her bravery. "Looks like you made it out fine."

Thomas sat next to her on the gurney. "Just a little smoky."

Abigail laughed, then said, "Thank you for your help, sir. But you should really follow your superior's orders and fall back when told."

"And report to *your* house's bus for treatment," the paramedic interrupted them. She stored her gauze and goo back inside her bag and addressed Avalon. "I suggest you get a tetanus shot, otherwise you're clear with me."

Thomas knocked his shoulder against Abigail's when the paramedic vanished inside the back of her ambulance. It was an affectionate touch shared just between them. Something as intimate as a kiss, but subtle enough for their documented lives. He continued their conversation as if the paramedic never existed, as if the world around them didn't matter. "I didn't want to lose the opportunity to work with a hero like yourself."

"The HRC is always accepting applications for new heroes."

"Don't I need a superpower to do that?" Thomas winked. "Being an everyman hero is fine enough for me. I've been told there's a lot of paperwork involved with you guys."

"Who told you that?"

Thomas shrugged. "Listen, I don't want to be too forward, but my buddies dared me to come over here and get a picture with you. Would that be alright?"

Abigail looked across the street to Purvis and Maddox. Their attention dropped to an interesting crack in the sidewalk when she did.

"I wouldn't want you to lose a dare."

"You're a real hero." Thomas slipped his phone out of an inner pocket of his coat.

Abigail scooted as close to him as she could. He pinched her hand with his in the hidden space between his coat and her costume and raised the phone. Their dirty faces appeared in the screen, Abigail's hidden behind her red mask and Thomas' obscured by ash. Just before clicking the camera, he kissed her on the cheek which resulted in a "hurrah" from Purvis and Maddox. Thomas slipped off the gurney.

"Hope to see you again, hero."

"Don't run into any more fires." Abigail was grateful her mask hid the heat rising in her cheeks ignited by his kiss and fanned by the crooked smile hanging off his lips.

"No promises."

"Mr. Sanders!"

The booming voice burst the quiet moment Abigail forgot wasn't private between her and Thomas. Using the force of an agitated hippo, San Arbor Mayor Owen Benton maneuvered his way over to them. A woman, who was probably his secretary, clicked behind him in two-inch heels. Lancelot floated her purse between them. The woman was all smiles, a side effect of Lancelot; the mayor was in a huff, a side effect of heroes.

"Mr. Sanders," the mayor greeted. His breath labored as he tried to breathe through his nose pretending the short walk hadn't winded him. "That's you, correct?"

"It is now." The mayor only stared at him, so Thomas added, "Call me Thomas."

"Splendid. I heard you're the one who saved this hero?" He said *hero* like someone would say *urchin*.

"She didn't need saving." Thomas was quick to defend Abigail, although he did so much nicer than Abigail would have.

Owen Benton didn't hear him. "I want you to know that I think it's absolutely incredible that one of my city's first responders put a stop to this tragedy. Let's have a quick interview."

Thomas rubbed the back of his neck. "I try to keep my media appearances to a minimum of once a lifetime. Channel 9 already got me this week, so..."

"Nonsense." Benton ignored him. "This is for *my* website, none of the news stations will have it. Cindy? Are we ready?"

The woman who was definitely his secretary pulled herself away from Lancelot. From her floating purse, she retrieved a digital camera mounted to a monopod. She powered it on and gave Owen Benton a thumbs up.

"Perfect." Mayor Benton pulled Thomas away from the gurney so they stood in front of Abigail and the ambulance lights. He waited for a second thumbs up from Cindy and beamed into the camera.

"Mayor Owen Benton here just outside the Grand Hotel minutes after today's fire was extinguished by one of San Arbor's finest. Fireman Thomas Sanders risked his own life to save our city's people and a treasured landmark that is the hotel. And, best of all, our first responder even saved the life of a superhero. I got to say, you're redefining what 'super' means, isn't that right, Thomas?"

"I was just doing my job," Thomas said flatly. "Avalon and I both stopped that fire."

"But she was helpless until you arrived!"

"That's not true."

Mayor Benton laughed, his large belly compressing against his suit. "You're too modest, Thomas. You were the hero today! Take it in. Oh—" Benton squinted his eyes and looked past the camera at Cindy who mouthed a reminder. "That's right! You also saved over ten people earlier this week at Jolt Station. Absolutely incredible."

"It's been a good week for fires."

"You need to be celebrated, Thomas!"

Pink dusted his face under the remaining soot. "What?"

"Cindy, mark it down. Friday night, San Arbor will be holding a celebration for Mr. Sanders and his fellow firefighters. What's your favorite food?"

"I'm not picky," Thomas answered.

Mayor Benton shook his hand vigorously. "Cindy will give you all the details. Good work in making San Arbor safe. You did a real hero's work, Thomas."

Cindy turned off her camera and took notes on the mayor's plans for the celebration. The more he spoke about it the louder he became. Through the spit and bile of the mayor, Abigail accepted a small wave given by Thomas before he returned to his captain and crew. Purvis waited with a high five.

"Can you believe that guy?" Lancelot whispered, stepping in front of Abigail, and replacing her view of Thomas and his turnout coat with Lancelot's puffy sleeves. "We did the work in there."

Abigail stood, her feet piercing with needles from the lack of blood flow to them. "Benton's always opposed us. He's been fighting to remove the ordinance since he got into office."

"So, this is the reason we have to be on our best behavior?" Lancelot sounded like King Arthur. Abigail shared in their frustration.

"It's going to take time before everyone likes the change."

"How many years does this guy have in office?"

Abigail laughed and it caused Lancelot to drop his snarling demeanor. "It's okay for the others to get credit."

"Yeah, but they already got Jolt Station this week. We should get the hotel."

"It's not a competition, Lance." Abigail reminded him. "We all serve the same city."

"Are you ready to go?" He extended his hand to her, clearly finished with their conversation.

Abigail took a final glance toward the firetruck and Thomas as he loaded himself inside.

"Would you count this as your first date?"

"Shut up," she teased, but grabbed Lancelot's hand who greedily tightened his hold around her.

Psychic energy enveloped around them, the icy tendrils locking around Abigail like an extra rib cage, and Lancelot lifted off the ground tugging Abigail with him. The return flight to the Hero Relief Center wasn't as hectic as their departing one. Without the sirens leading him, Lancelot flew slower and closer to the ground. He dipped around buildings and lingered through San Arbor's downtown park. The twisting green leaves and colorful blooms was a pleasant sight compared to the earlier fire. The cool air soothed the injuries on Abigail's legs, and she was grateful for Lancelot's detour. The softness in his face returned as he floated them inside the HRC's lobby. The sore Mayor Benton caused him must have soothed in the flight as well.

It seemed both of their irritations applied to Mitch in their absence, though. He looked more annoyed than usual standing atop the white tiled floor. Abigail hoped he wasn't there for her. His hand, cloaked in a plastic glove, waved her over and her hope evaporated.

"Hey Mitch." Abigail's smile wasn't returned. Neither was her greeting.

"Of course, you'd be the one needing this shot," Mitch grumbled. "Can't leave it to the rookie to mess up."

A syringe gleamed deadly in his hand. Abigail wasn't sure how she missed seeing the medical tool which looked more like a weapon in Mitch's possession. Abigail didn't have to guess how his bedside manor would be.

"Did the paramedics call?" Abigail asked, assuming Mitch held a tetanus shot.

"I did," Lancelot answered her. "I didn't think you'd go to the hospital to get one on shift."

He was right. The Twin Leaf Bar wasn't some back-alley junk yard. The thought of getting tetanus from anything in there was comical. Going to the hospital would be a waste of time. She turned to the side allowing Mitch to choose which part of her arm he'd like to stab her in. The swash of an alcohol pad came first, and Abigail made a face at the cold temperature.

"You can hold my hand if you're scared." Lancelot offered his hand, wiggling his fingers at her.

"A little shot doesn't scare me." Abigail said, but still flinched at the sudden jab in her arm.

"Don't make me give you a second one." Mitch warned, tearing his glove off with a snap of rubber.

"That I can promise." Abigail rotated her arm in large circles. She imagined it was like getting a flu shot. More movement now, less stiffness later.

"Didn't bring any stickers for your patient?" King Arthur asked, coming up behind them.

"No, sir." Even with his respectful reply, Mitch's attitude didn't adjust around the leader of the Knights and his second in command. He didn't excuse himself from the group of superheroes. Mitch was gone as quickly as King Arthur and Merlin arrived. Most likely catching the elevator that brought them down.

"Impressive saves today, Lancelot." King Arthur addressed his newest member of the Round Table Knights. "We just heard from the hospital that all six you levitated down will be going home to their families."

"It was an easy job." Lancelot knew nothing of humility.

"Not easy enough, it appears." King Arthur's gaze fell across Abigail, clearly noticing the bandages more than her damaged costume.

"All superficial," she tried to assure.

"I'm glad to hear it. I have an assignment for you and Merlin."

"Right now?" Lancelot interrupted. "Avalon's injured. I can go with Merlin. What's the job?"

"Avalon said she's fine, isn't that right?"

It was a question with only one correct answer, another test from the hero king.

"What's the assignment?" asked Abigail.

King Arthur smiled but it didn't warm Abigail like it would a TV crowd. "A building demolition in the south. I want you two there in case the demo crew needs help."

"And, in case a camera crew is rolling?" Merlin asked.

"Make sure they get your good side." King Arthur answered. "I don't want anyone thinking a superficial wound will keep my heroes off their feet."

Abigail swallowed hard and forced the heel of her injured leg down. She'd been unconsciously favoring it. A mistake in front of King Arthur who surely saw it as a weakness of herself and their hero brand.

Chapter Eight

Abigail was surprised to find an actual building demolition crew waiting for her and Merlin at the end of the long car ride. The double tinted windows of the HRC car made it impossible to grasp her whereabouts, and after King Arthur's comment, Abigail was left with a sinking feeling in her gut that was strong enough to pull a cruise ship down. Terribly filmed movie scenes of mob hits creeped along Abigail's thoughts during most of the silent ride. Also standing around the dated and abandoned parking garage were bored looking camera men kicking rocks in the parking lot while their field reporters prepared their notepads. If this was a hit, at least there'd be documentation of it.

"*Is* this a media stunt?" Abigail asked as the car pulled into a parking spot away from the crowd. "Or do you think they'll really need backup?"

Merlin flattened out a crease in her red dress formed by the seat belt. "A lot could go wrong today. A chemical dust cloud, an inferno, a missing foreman. It's best to be proactive."

"You did call the media being here." Abigail cupped her hands against the window to see through the darkness at the waiting news crews. "Must be a need for content."

"I knew Arthur would send us somewhere with a camera." Merlin sighed after her statement, peering out the window on her side.

"Why's that?" The Round Table Knights' ratings had been steady throughout the month. There wasn't a need to add focus to them right now.

"He wasn't too pleased with your performance earlier." Merlin exited the car.

Abigail scrambled after her. They had maybe two minutes before the crowd noticed them and any conversation became public record. "I did my job."

"I know you did, the building still stands, but being carried out by a first responder," Merlin stopped herself with a chuckle. "I haven't seen Arthur lose his cool like that in a while."

I don't want anyone thinking a superficial wound will keep my heroes off their feet.

Abigail stopped her eyes from rolling. "For someone who wants us on good terms with the first responders, King can sure give off mixed signals."

"Arthur knows what's best for us. All of us." Merlin ended their dialog. "I'm going to inform the demo crew we're here, go mingle with the cameras, answer their questions about the Twin Leaf fire."

Abigail wasn't ready to close the book. "Merlin, don't you think we can be doing more than playing to the media?"

"Yes," Merlin answered simply. "But, until they don't ultimately control us, I'll continue to blow them kisses while protecting San Arbor."

Merlin's heels deftly led her to the yellow hardhat wearing men across the lot. The shadow cast by her witch's hat grew the further she walked away, its curly top attempted to trap Abigail's ankle. Something festered inside Abigail, but she swallowed it down as a two-person news crew scurried over to her. She smiled wider than necessary, but her pulling cheeks forced any doubt from her eyes as she faced the reporter.

It was the same one Lancelot had flirted with after the bank robbery. Her name tag confirmed it. She pushed a microphone toward Abigail and glanced at the camera man whose large camera already blinked red.

"Avalon, I'm surprised to see the Knights here." Monica dived right into the interview with the same force Abigail recognized from herself running into fires. "Is there something happening that we don't know about?"

"Not at all. Merlin and I came by as a precaution." Abigail hated how automatically her voice switched to its higher pitch press release mode. It was part of the job, a part she was well versed in, and if King Arthur doubted her work ethic, she'd ease his fears right now. "Being one step ahead of disaster is the best way to avoid them."

Monica nodded. "While we have a minute with you, Avalon, can you tell me about the Twin Leaf Bar fire today?"

"What would you like to know?"

The reporter smiled, looking like she was just given the map to Atlantis. "Walk me through what happened inside. Give me a real first account."

Abigail did so. She retold the frightening account of becoming one with the flames inside the bar. Using just the dangerous heat as her guide to the blaze. Dodging the falling column that would have surely broken her back if she hadn't rolled out of the way. Using the water hose in one hand and her flames in the other to combat the blaze. Dousing the stream of fire pouring from the open gas valve inside the kitchen. Monica's eyes widened with each turn of events, her pen scrambling across her notepad marking each white lie as fact.

"Both me and the dining room got a little roughed up," Abigail ended with a grin. "But we'll both be back in no time. I think San Arbor is as fireproof as me."

Monica didn't laugh at Abigail's joke. "What about the firefighter who saved you, you skipped that part."

"He found me coming out of the bar," Abigail answered, the lies forming quicker than her mind could process them. Protecting Thomas and his abilities were more important than his ego. "He thought my knee was a lot worse than it was and thought it best to get me to an ambulance as quick as he could. Walking wasn't fast enough, I guess."

"Not as fast as flying, I'm sure."

"It does lack a little in that department."

Monica pointed at the camera and the red light faded off. "Thank you for the interview, Avalon, this is a big exclusive for us. Is Lancelot here? I'd love to hear about his rescue, too."

Monica kept her head down, gazing at her scribbled notes, but Abigail caught the blush she tried to hide. Another victim of the newest Knight. Lancelot's crush count was astronomical in the city. HRC Marketing was already designing a Valentine's Day campaign for him. Abigail decided to be nice.

"Lancelot isn't with us, but I'm sure he'll be jealous I got the Channel 9 exclusive without him."

Monica retrieved a business card from her suit jacket and handed it to Abigail. "If any of the Knights decide they'd like a Channel 9 exclusive, feel free to call me."

"I'll pass the invitation along." Abigail tucked the card away, knowing she wouldn't remember to pass the reporter's hungry request along. She, as were the rest of the Knights, was not a puppet to the media. She was a hero to save people, not the company's ratings. "If you'll excuse me, I better get back to work."

Abigail narrowly dodged another interview from a rival news station and arrived at Merlin's side. Her witch's hat had changed into a ruby red hard hat, and she examined a blueprint of the old parking garage. White X's dictated where explosives were placed inside. Whoever was paying for this demolition must have held a grudge against this structure from the number of X's. There would be nothing left but rubble.

A construction crewman approached Merlin's other side. His hard hat was regulation yellow. He sanded his hands together. Abigail couldn't tell if he was nervous or excited that Merlin held onto his blueprints.

"We're ready for the demo," the man said. "I was hoping one of you would like to do the honors?"

Merlin answered, "I'll leave that to you, Vic. Your men set this up, they should have the fun."

Abigail nodded in agreement.

Vic called over his shoulder, "Alright Sean, get ready to detonate! Sixty seconds."

There was a loud *whoop* from somewhere to the left, and Vic said to Merlin and Abigail, "Today's his first official demo, the kid's pretty excited."

A second crewman joined them with a black box. The sides were painted with bright yellow stripes and a red button on top begged someone to press it. The crewman's fingers fluttered above it. He seemed more interested in his bomb box than the two heroes beside him. Abigail enjoyed that. The kid's hand was on the button the second before his sixty seconds were done. A set of car lights flashed inside the garage, and he pushed the button.

The lights signaled again. A car horn baled urgently.

"You didn't check if this place was empty?" Abigail shouted, her wrists igniting with fire.

"How long is the fuse?" Merlin demanded.

"About two minutes," Vic stuttered out.

Merlin shoved Abigail forward. "Stay away from the X's. Get the civilians out of there. What's the weight strength of—"

Abigail was gone. Knowing the rest of the questions would be for the foreman and his crew. If anyone could stop the dynamite, it would be Merlin. But, in case she failed, Abigail could not. Inhaling deeply, she forced all of her flames to her feet and rocketed to the third floor of the garage where the car still signaled desperately.

Once inside the garage, flashing red lights greeted her on either side of the rows of parking spots. The dynamite sticks looking just as eager to be set off as Sean was to do so. The garage became a cave of angry red monsters. Abigail rushed to the only white light in the area.

"I can only buy you time." Merlin's voice crackled inside Abigail's head piece. "It'll blow in four minutes."

"I'm almost there."

Abigail slid into the car. Flames dripped off her legs and burned to ash below her. Yanking open the driver door, Abigail found a small girl operating the lights and horn. Fear streaked the girl's face as easily as the grime also clinging to her did. The child was small, and her malnourished bones protruded from her thin skin.

"Let's get you out of here." Abigail reached for the girl, but she squirmed away attempting to hide behind the gear shift. "This whole building is about to fall down. We really need to get out of here."

The girl shook her head, refusing to cross the gear shift.

"Update." Merlin demanded.

"I've found one girl in the car, trying to get her out."

"Three minutes."

Abigail reached into the car and grabbed the girl before she could jump into the back seat where a mess of blankets would make the rescue more time consuming. The one thing Abigail didn't have right now: time. The girl thrashed against Abigail but was too small and too weak to prevent the hero from doing her job. Abigail tried to soothe her with a series of shushing sounds, but the girl's struggles persisted. She pulled at Abigail's hair, clawed into her arms, and shrieked inside her ears. Abigail barely managed to pull her from the car's interior. In her wild movements, the girl pulled down the visor and bonked Abigail's head. She swallowed her curse. A stuffed rabbit stared up at her from the floorboard. Its matted arm reached for the child writhing in her arms.

"Here!" Abigail shoved the rabbit into the girl's arms. The girl quieted down after receiving it. "I have the girl, we're heading out."

"Less than two minutes," Merlin replied into the earpiece. "Mother's outside."

"Roger."

Abigail ran toward the edge of the parking structure. The people and their vehicles looked like toys from her height. Only Merlin stood out from the crowd with her bright red outfit. The red lights flashed rapidly at her approach. She turned the girl's head into her costume and leapt. The edge of the concrete floor bit into her boot before Abigail ignited her feet into tiny rockets. The ground was nearing too quickly. Abigail was going to crash into the pavement if she didn't slow down. She tightened her arms around the girl. Her tiny heartbeat rattled against Abigail's body like a small rodent's. Abigail snuffed the flames at her feet but ignited them again as she felt their descent quicken. She repeated the process several times until she stumbled onto the ground. Dark smoke covered her and the girl.

The dynamite ignited.

The ground shook as five levels of concrete collapsed. Pale dust flooded the parking lot. The shock wave stole papers from reporter's notebooks and ripped hardhats off crewmen. A sheet of concrete armed with rebar steel shot toward the landing zone of Abigail and the girl.

They were two tiny lady bugs under one large shoe.

"Avalon!"

Abigail's ash cloud blocked the sight of the threat, but slowly the pocket of darkness illuminated. The crash never arrived despite the shouts inside and outside her earpiece. Abigail located the light source. The little girl's hand glowed lime green. She pointed to something outside the cloud. The more the dark smoke dissipated the less Abigail understood.

The concrete missile hung in the air, suspended by an unseen force. Exposed rebar along the cracked edges glowed the same green color as the girl's fingers. When the girl shifted her fingers, the concrete slab shifted the same way.

"That's you, isn't it?" Abigail whispered.

The girl didn't deny the statement. Her outstretched arm trembled and when she dropped her arm, the slab crashed to the ground. Small debris rolled toward Abigail as tiny snowballs compared to the avalanche that would have crushed them. Abigail stared in awe at the little girl who was picking a piece of a straw wrapper out of her stuffed rabbit's fur.

"Lillian!" a voice cried out.

Turning away from the broken concrete, Abigail came face to face with a woman somehow smaller than the girl in her arms. A crewman followed her across the barrier and cameras flashed behind all of them. The lights created small stars in Abigail's vision. The woman fearlessly grabbed the girl from Abigail's arms and delivered a hundred rapid kisses to her head. Tears tangled with the dirt on the little girl's face. Abigail didn't know which of them was crying more. The mother and the daughter looked inches from hysteria.

"You saved us," Abigail finally said, staring at the little girl. Few things surprised the hero in her line of work, and this definitely earned a place on the list.

"Didn't you see the signs?" Vic demanded while interrupting the happy reunion. "This garage is off limits."

"It wasn't a week ago," the mother growled.

"Were you living there?" Abigail asked, recalling the blankets nested in the back seat of the car.

The mother refused to answer, choosing instead to examine her child. Lillian pointed at the ground and two steel nails turned lime green like her fingers and floated around her. She wiggled her fingers and caused the nails to dance. Her mother kissed her fingers and whispered something to the girl. The nails dropped back to the ground.

"Don't let them leave," Merlin's voice appeared in Abigail's ear. "Bring them over here."

Abigail scanned the area and found Merlin standing by an ambulance. The back doors were opened, and a paramedic waited with a gurney. She gave Merlin a thumbs up before turning to Lillian and her mother.

"Ma'am," Abigail shifted herself between them and Vic who still waited for answers to his demands. "Lillian needs to be checked out by the paramedics. If you'll follow me, I'll take you to them."

The mother's arms tightened around Lillian. She became an unmoving Gorgon of motherly protection.

"I won't hurt either of you," Abigail tried again. "My name is Avalon—"

"I know who you are," the mother cut her off with a spit to the dusty ground.

"Then you know I'm only here to help." Abigail switched to her media worthy tone and smile.

"Mommy? Did you find any cookies? Or carrots for Snuggles?"

The woman holstered her glare on Abigail and tended to her daughter. "I'm sorry baby, I couldn't find anything today."

"But I'm hungry."

"I know, I know."

"They'll have food on the rig," Abigail lied. "Come with me, please."

The woman finally gave in. "Fine."

Abigail led her to the ambulance, keeping her and her daughter shielded from the media as best she could with her body. She would make sure the media didn't profit from this family's situation. Unless they approached with checkbooks, Abigail would make sure the girl and her mother retained their privacy. Abigail grinned at Merlin as they neared, but the witch Knight remained solemn.

The mother set Lillian on the gurney and the paramedic got her vitals. Lillian giggled when the paramedic listened to her lungs.

"Do you have her registration?" Merlin asked.

"No."

"Will I find it when I look her up?"

"No."

"Registration?" Abigail asked but was ignored.

"She needs to be registered. They'll take her to San Arbor Medical for the assessment. I'll inform Chief DaVodi of the news."

The mother acted quickly, lunging toward Merlin, but Abigail was quicker. She put herself between the woman and Merlin, flames twirled around her wrist and dared either to cross. She stared down Merlin.

"Stand down, Avalon." Merlin never turned away from a fight.

"Lillian was only saving herself," Abigail challenged. "She isn't a vigilante. You can't take her from her mother."

Merlin's face softened for a moment. "No one is taking the child. The girl's mother will accompany her to the hospital. After all, the child is a minor."

"I don't want her on some list," the mother declared behind Abigail's flames.

"She will be," Merlin's answer wasn't up for negotiation. "Every powered individual is recorded. Instead of fighting me, I'd suggest you use this time to remember why she wasn't registered before today."

"All clear," said the paramedic, his work up complete. "Ma'am, you can ride in the back with me."

Merlin's icy stare chilled Abigail's fire and the woman's fury. The mother stepped around the heroes and climbed into the ambulance with Lillian, who was preoccupied applying bandages to her rabbit.

"Do a secondary sweep of the area," Merlin instructed, her tone more sour than usual. "I'll be in the car when you finish."

Abigail gritted her teeth but didn't press her increasingly bad luck. After her call to the chief of police, Abigail was sure Merlin was going to fill King Arthur in on her disobedience. The Round Table Knights were a team and standing on the opposite side of Merlin was an insult to that partnership. Abigail set to her task, hoping to return to Merlin's good side before she could talk to their leader.

Chapter Nine

Despite having an on-call hero company, disasters still happen in San Arbor. She was a city like any other, and crime and accidents were attracted to her like an insect searching for a porch light on a summer evening. But two large scale fires in the same week was unprecedented. Public transportation in and out of Jolt Station turned into a maddening experience as displaced passengers from Bank C were forced to use new routes. The trains became crowded, late, and unsanitary as bodies pushed together and trash caught under the seats. The Grand Hotel was shut down until the first floor was cleaned and the Twin Leaf Bar repaired. The estimated closure was three weeks. The loss of profit from the hotel, and the equal loss of tax dollars for the city, ticked along the bottom of the screen during all Channel 9 newscasts.

The only effect Abigail focused on after the fires was the toll they had on Thomas. The following morning his fingertips were still stained in black ink. Not even the half-worn bar of soap in the bathroom could rub them completely clean. The following night in bed, the dark color was an evil contrast against the white bedsheets. Lying beside Abigail, Thomas held his hand above his head and stared at the staining. His fingers disappeared into the darkness around them.

Abigail didn't know what he was thinking as he stared at them, but she knew the nagging pull in the back of her head and prayed it wasn't the same for him. She reminded herself for the tenth time that day that his fingers were stained and not scarred. The markings were not from a self-inflected burn. Tired of watching his fingers vanish into the darkness, Abigail plucked his hand from the air. She pulled it to her mouth and kissed each of his fingertips. They were as soft as they always were. The rose petals to the thorny demeanor of the man that controlled them.

"It's weird that it won't come off."

Abigail nodded. "Does it hurt?"

"Of course not," he answered. "It keeps fading. That's good."

"It's just from you absorbing the flames?" The question was simple, they both knew the answer, but Abigail asked anyway. The double meaning of the question was heavy against her tongue. She had to be sure.

"Yeah, I guess I never noticed it when the scars were there."

Abigail released his hand, but he left it laying between them, reaching out for her. His low voice was solid and sure. Abigail knew she'd follow the sound anywhere it led. If Thomas wasn't concerned about the ash-soaked skin, then she shouldn't be either.

Stained, not scarred.

"Hey, babe?"

Abigail tried to find his eyes in the dark but was unable to until he smiled. The flash of his teeth guided her to his face.

"I've got this party to go to tomorrow. Some kind of hero thing. Want to be my plus one?"

"You're not going to ask your hero girlfriend?"

"She's busy." Thomas' mouth struck out of the shadows and landed a kiss on Abigail. "Besides, it's a non-super event."

"How'd you get an invite, then?" she pestered.

Thomas laughed once and pulled her across the small space between them. Their abnormally warm bodies sparked against each other.

"I've got the whole city fooled." Thomas admitted before ending their conversation with a burning kiss.

By Friday evening, it seemed the entire city forgot about the fires. The attention was spotlighted on the mayor's office and the party his staff put together on the office lawn. The party planner had been a force to be reckoned with. The lawn area looked normal at lunchtime, but now the hot dog cart was replaced with a five-piece string band, several dressed tables were stationed around a small platform and podium, golden balloons marked the corners of the pretend room and the small bar operated by black tie employees was ready to serve the mayor's guests.

Abigail patted down the front of her dress as the car they arrived in peeled away from the street. She felt strangely out of place wearing something as nice as a formal dress outside, but she didn't mind seeing Thomas in a suit jacket and tie. Even if that tie was printed with tiny flaming Avalon swords. She was certain he had every connection to the merchandise world, legal and illegal printing rights, when it came to his countless Avalon-themed items.

They found their table near the front of the stage by its marker. A plastic 3 hung from a toy firetruck's aerial ladder. The other tables were reserved for the other ladder companies and police districts, each marked in a similar fashion. Abigail stopped herself from saying hello to Chief DaVodi as they passed his table. He wouldn't recognize her without her Avalon gear. Mayor Benton waddled from table to table, keeping him distracted from his guest of honor's arrival. Abigail appreciated his delay and hoped the mayor stayed away a little longer.

"Thought you weren't going to make it." Purvis greeted them as they sat down.

"You think I'd miss my own party?" Thomas replied. "Hey, Tawna."

"Hi Tom," Purvis' wife replied from the seat next to him. Her hands were clasped over her growing belly. "Hi Abby."

"How're you feeling?" Abigail excitedly asked. "How's the baby?"

"Kicking." Tawna smiled. "I'm ready for her to be out in the world."

"Have you ever felt it?" Purvis asked. "It's too weird."

Abigail and Thomas both shook their heads no.

"When she starts up again—"

Thomas ended Purvis' statement, "I'll be keeping my hands off your wife."

Tawna laughed. "I don't mind if you want to feel."

Thomas *shooed* the offer away with his still stained fingers. He turned to Maddox and his purple paisley tie. "Where's Harvey?"

"He couldn't get out of work," Maddox answered. "But he sends his love."

Abigail watched as Thomas interacted with his crew. The normal conversations about life and sports, the lack of evil conspiracies and government espionage, was a needed culture shock compared to the HRC after-work hangouts. She didn't realize how difficult it was to turn off the hero brain until she was just simply Abigail Turner.

Fire Chief Bridgett Warren arrived shortly after. Several other guests nodded to her as she approached the table. Abigail had only seen the chief in her uniform, and now she wore a striking white dress adorned with golden embellishments that matched the golden beads in her hair. Her teenage son had a golden handkerchief tucked into the breast pocket of his sport coat to match. He pulled the chair out for his mom, and Chief Warren kissed him on the cheek when he took his seat beside her.

"You boys going to behave?" She eyed Purvis and Thomas.

"I've got my eye on him," Tawna answered for Purvis.

"I'm done causing trouble," Thomas answered.

Maddox whispered to Abigail, "We'll see how long that lasts. We need to test the portable pool next shift and last time didn't go so well."

"I was pushed!" Purvis whispered back as the stage lights came on.

"You tripped." Thomas laughed, and a mischievous glint flashed momentarily in his eyes.

Abigail twisted in her seat to see the stage better. It reminded her of the press stage the HRC constructed for their announcements. Only, this one had a single camera trained at it instead of the bombardment of flashes from media and paparazzi that usually swarmed the hero company's stage. The mayor's secretary adjusted the lens of her handheld recorder on Mayor Benton as he cleared his throat into the microphone. His suit wasn't flattering. The expensive material made his round belly resemble a beach ball, and the light paled the color to Baby Puke Green.

"Remarkable!" Mayor Benton said. "I've never seen this lawn look so good. San Arbor's best people are here, no superpowers required."

A few people clapped at his awkward introduction and waiters began delivering the first round of salad to each table. Abigail thought the mayor would be somewhat subtle with his distaste of heroes tonight, but he kept proving her wrong.

"You are not recognized enough for the real bravery that you show every day. Of course, someone who's bullet immune would run into a gun fight, but it takes a real man, a real hero, to do it when they know they could be hurt." A louder response of clapping filled the silence as Mayor Benton sipped his water before continuing, "While I'm in office we will celebrate the bravest heroes of San Arbor as much, no, much more than the celebrity heroes who only do it for the paycheck."

Abigail started forming her hand into a fist in her lap, but Thomas covered hers before she could finish. He rubbed his blackened thumb in small circles over her skin. The tickling sensation curbed her frustration. The mayor could think what he wanted; Abigail knew the only reason she did hero work.

Her worth was only measured in the lives she protected.

"And, who better to start this celebration than the man responsible for two impressive acts of bravery and heroics this week?"

Purvis "whooped!" loudly before Mayor Benton could announce, "Thomas Sanders! Of Ladder Company 3!"

The lawn erupted in cheers, table three being the loudest and Abigail being the proudest, as Thomas reluctantly joined Mayor Benton on the stage. His lanky form loomed over the mayor, and he leaned down to mutter "thanks" into the microphone. Mayor Benton reached inside the podium and, without prompting, pulled a golden medal over Thomas' head, knocking his carefully combed hair back into a frenzy.

Thomas gripped the medal hanging from his neck. His look of surprise slowly faded while he examined the round medallion.

"Thank you for your service, Thomas!"

Thomas looked up from the medal, his hand still protectively wrapped around it, and said, "I was just doing my job."

"There he goes again." Mayor Benton slapped Thomas' back. "Modest Thomas. Cindy, get our picture, would you?"

Cindy gave a thumbs up once her task was completed, and Thomas was allowed to hop off the stage. He returned to their table, now set with a spread of food that audibly made his stomach growl, and grabbed a roll from the basket before sitting down.

Abigail pecked his cheek. "Congratulations, babe."

"What's this thing say?" Purvis reached for the medal.

Thomas smacked his hand away with the flat side of a butter knife. "Get your own and find out."

"That'll be impossible with you stealing the show all the time." Purvis poked.

"Don't mind them," Maddox, the voice of reason, said to the table. "Purvis is just mad that he has to get off his butt now."

"Tom's just got to stop making us look bad."

"Thomas is making us look good," Bridgett corrected. She raised her glass to the center of their table. "I'm not sure how we got lucky enough to have you transferred to San Arbor, but I sure am glad. You've given Ladder 3 a new start."

Maddox clinked his glass against his chief's. "We were about to be axed until you showed up. Your addition kept our house from absorbing into Company 7."

Abigail noticed the pink flash across Thomas' cheeks before he tapped his glass against his teammates'. "I only transferred to be closer to home. It had nothing to do with helping you losers out."

"Love you too, bud." Purvis added his glass and the four of them laughed.

Mayor Benton continued to call first responders to the stage to receive similar praise and equally shiny medals. Chief DaVodi was called for his expert handling at the San Arbor First Financial Bank robbery, a paramedic's quick job of stitching up a knife wound to save someone's life, a firefighter from Ladder Company 9 who carried a 92-year-old man down four flights of stairs in a fire evacuation, and a police officer who raised over $700 for a new wheelchair for a young girl. They received matching awards, and the girl accidentally rolled over Mayor Benton's foot.

It was a good night.

After the awards, another speech from Mayor Benton, and dinner, the string band picked up their instruments and played to the sound of the guests laughing and drinking. A couple of people pushed a table back and began to dance in the grass. Pointed heels and suit jackets were left at tables as more people joined the dancing. Abigail turned to ask Thomas to join her on the dance lawn but found him staring at his medal. He rubbed his thumb over the carved cityscape she assumed represented San Arbor. He studied it like it was from another planet. His fingers left bits of ash inside the divots.

"What are you thinking about?"

"If I get another one, I'm going to need a bigger neck." He dropped the medal and looked at her. "Thing's heavy."

"Going to start collecting them?"

Thomas shrugged, glancing at his teammates who dissolved into the crowd talking to other guests. "Purvis could use a good challenge. We could make it a game."

Abigail poked his knee. "I think you like being a hero."

"It's a lot of work," he sighed dramatically. "Do you think they'll start making me kiss babies?"

"You'll have someone to practice on in a few months." Abigail laughed.

"Hope you didn't mind skipping work for this."

"They don't feed me like this on patrol." Abigail ran her finger through the remaining raspberry coolie on her dessert plate. "I wouldn't have missed this. I'm really proud of you."

"So am I!" Mayor Benton's voice shattered their private bubble, again, and he sat down in the other seat next to Thomas. "I want to talk to you about your future."

Thomas cocked his head, and Abigail gritted her teeth waiting for the mayor to continue. Just because Avalon had to play nice with him, didn't mean Abigail had to as well. She'd save face only for Thomas' sake.

"Future like promotions?" asked Thomas.

"Think bigger! You could be the next face of the SAFD."

"A mascot."

"An image," Mayor Benton explained. "A role model, and ambassador, someone normal that normal people can look up to and aspire to be. I can see it now," Mayor Benton made a big arcing motion with his hands, "your face on T-shirts, water bottles, the cover of magazines, radio shows, the whole shebang!"

"I don't want to be in the media like that."

"You're right. That's what those superheroes do," the mayor grumbled. "A smaller, more personal approach then. We'll go door to door!"

"Mr. Mayor, I think you're only using me to increase your popularity before next fall."

"I want to use you to upstage those Knights," Mayor Benton said unapologetically.

Abigail took a large drink of water to keep her mouth shut.

Thomas asked, "Why do you hate the heroes? They keep San Arbor protected."

"Until they don't. What's going to happen when they decide protecting us isn't fun anymore? What's going to happen when tax dollars aren't enough to satisfy them? What's going to happen when they decide they're gods and we're ants?"

Abigail gasped and was unable to control herself. "That would never happen."

Mayor Benton peered around Thomas' shoulders, forgetting there was a third member in their conversation. "How can you be so sure? King Arthur could rewrite the way the whole city thinks, and no one could stop him. Merlin is capable of leveling San Arbor block by block if she wanted. Excalibur is so militarily trained I wouldn't be surprised if he had a whole army waiting for his command. I have no idea what all powers that new one is hiding, and Avalon is so reckless that more non-convicted people go to the hospitals than a courtroom."

"Those people were caught in the act." Abigail shoved her hands under the tablecloth so no one would see the red embers sparking off her fingers.

"They still have a right to a trial."

"The Knights would die for this city and her people, you're either blind or stupid if you can't see that."

"Let's all calm down." Thomas grabbed Abigail's hand under the table, and she felt a burst of fire between his fingers. "Isn't this night supposed to be about me, anyway?"

Mayor Benton adjusted his tie. "It's about the real heroes of San Arbor. People we can trust."

"And detain," Abigail added.

"You shouldn't trust everyone, Mr. Mayor." Thomas' voice rumbled with a coming storm. "I've seen very normal people do very evil things."

Mayor Benton chuckled, but it was cold. "Consider my offer Thomas. You could become a god yourself if you let me help you."

Thomas turned away from the mayor. His green eyes dark in the dim light. "Good night Mr. Mayor. Thanks for the party."

The chair scraped against the ground as the mayor left. Abigail forced herself not to squirm under Thomas' gaze. She was embarrassed. Not for herself, she cared less what the mayor thought of her, but for Thomas. Tonight was his night, his celebration, and she almost caused an unnecessary scene.

"I'm sorry that—"

"Let's go do something." Thomas interrupted her, light returning to his eyes. A dangerous, wild, searing light.

"What did you have in mind?"

In their conjoined hands he ignited another burst of fire. The heat tickled against Abigail's palm. "We haven't played on the roof in a while."

Blue fire revolved around Thomas' wrists. The flames twirled up his arms, around his neck, and over his torso. He lowered the fire's temperature to keep his cut off shirt from burning, to keep his skin perfectly pale in the gorgeous moonlight above. The hot air billowing from the blaze whipped his raven hair around him. The blue shine reflected off his emerald eyes. He molded a fireball in his hands as if he played with freshly fallen snow instead and carefully crafted it into a tight, smooth sphere. He tossed it into the air several times. Easily catching it and sending it back. He took a pitcher's position and launched it across the roof. The fireball extinguished before it reached the edge with a puff of blue sparks and smoke.

All Abigail could smell was the woodsmoke that was so distinctly Thomas.

All Abigail could see was the silhouetted body covered in indigo fire that was so distinctly Cinder.

The last time they threw fireballs across this roof she had fallen.

Fallen off the roof. Fallen off the tightrope between hero and villain. Fallen so dangerously close to a burning sun. She fell for a villain.

She shook her head. That was a long time ago. For the sake of their life together, the flame villain had died. Cinder was no more. Burned to ashes. Like a phoenix, Thomas returned to take his life back.

Tonight, was a brand-new game of catch on her roof.

Abigail lit her cherry-red blaze atop a fingertip to guide her across the roof. The spinning exhaust hubs were a dangerous inconvenience in the dark. One wrong step would cut open her bare foot.

"Do you miss it?" Thomas asked when she stood near him. He snapped his fingers and sent another burst of blue fire into the air. The flames curled above him before drifting back to his waiting palm.

"I ignite all the time at work." Abigail pinched a piece of the blue blaze off his hand, and it morphed her red flame purple before the blue took over completely.

"Lighting fires wouldn't be the best thing at my job." His voice rivaled the emptiness of a deserted shopping mall; cold, unused, eerie.

"Good thing you can do more than just start them."

Thomas looked at her through the fireball he held in his hand. His image broke apart and reformed several times as the fire crackled between them. He handed the blue flame toward her. "Toss a few with me?"

Forming a glove around her hand, Abigail grabbed the fireball from him. She took several steps backward and asked, "Did you do this a lot growing up?"

"With baseballs," Thomas answered. He effortlessly caught the fireball when Abigail lobbed it toward him. Plucking it from the sky as if it were a falling star.

"Easier or harder than this?" Abigail fumbled the ball as it sailed back to her.

"Harder. Without the consequences of dropping it, I didn't have a reason to be good."

"I take it you didn't play little league?"

The fireball lit his crooked smile as he caught it. "Was forced to play lacrosse after getting into too many fights playing hockey."

"Didn't melt the ice?"

"Only to increase my speed." Thomas created a second fireball and tossed it with the first. The orbs burned as dangerous as the gleam in his eyes.

"I was in band." Abigail caught both fireballs, the blue light filling her vision. She infused them with her red flames, changing the blue fire to cherry-red before tossing them back. "They just needed the extra body, so I never learned the instrument. Just the marching."

"What did you pretend to play?"

"Trumpet."

"I think my high school days were better than yours." Thomas turned the fireballs back to blue and launched them across the roof.

"I wouldn't go that far." Abigail caught the first fireball with her cloaked hand, but the second was a direct hit against her side. She snuffed the fireball in her hands and patted the flames that tore into her clothes. Her T-shirt flaked away with the flame. Cold air prickled her hip bone and belly button.

Abigail created a new ball in her hands, but Thomas was at her side before she could throw it. He snuffed the cherry-red blaze away with his right hand and clasped their hands between them. He offered his other hand to her, his gaze daring her to take it. She did, his dares had lost their edge a long time ago, but the gravity of his stare did not. She held his hand for several heartbeats before she could look away from his crooked smile and examine it. In her hand, his fingers were normal. The inky black stains were gone.

"If absorbing fire stains them," Abigail started, the pieces falling together.

"Starting fires cleans them." Thomas finished with a grin.

Chapter Ten

Abigail leapt out of bed the next morning. Her phone's promise of a ten-minute snooze was betrayed by the alarm being silenced completely. The panic of finding clean clothes momentarily chased away the groggy grips of tiredness that pulled at her. An unavoidable side effect from staying atop the roof far longer than necessary last night. She found yesterday's jeans, a pull-over hoodie, and a pair of mismatched socks. The outfit would suffice until Abigail could change into her Avalon costume at the Hero Relief Center.

She mashed her feet into a pair of sneakers without untying them and tossed everything she might need into her purse hanging off a kitchen chair. It normally took Abigail an hour to ready herself before leaving for work. Today she managed it in four minutes. So long as she left in the next two minutes she'd be back on track, and no one would know she overslept.

Abigail was almost out the door when she felt it. The fuzzy sweaters growing across her teeth. The sensation on her tongue almost made her gag. She breathed against her hand and the accompanying bad breath did. She turned back into the apartment; her dental hygiene warranted an extra minute of the time she barely had. The bathroom door was shut and steam sneaked out around it. She didn't have time to be polite. And it wasn't like she hadn't seen it all before.

Without knocking, Abigail opened the door and froze.

Thomas stared at himself in the mirror. His hands gripped the counter tightly. The steam fogged up the glass. In his reflection, the moist residue left familiar markings along his face. A scar of fog ran the length from eye to chin.

The image stole Abigail's breath away just as the thief who used to wear the scar would have.

Thomas' attention snapped away from his mirrored self and he smiled at Abigail through the reflection. Abigail thought she saw the scarred reflection smirk before he wiped it away. "Hey babe."

Abigail forced herself to inhale. "I needed to brush my teeth."

She looked around the bathroom but didn't find any more ghosts. Her heart rate settled down and a blush crept over her nose. She must have more sleep dust in her eyes than she realized. She rubbed a knuckle inside the corner of her eye trying to remove anything before she could conjure up another fake image of Cinder.

"Bashful this morning?" Thomas teased, stepping away from the sink and her toothbrush. "I would have thought you'd be used to seeing me naked by now."

Abigail's blush deepened but she didn't tease him back. Guilt bit at her mind. Her mind had jumped to *him* so quickly. She smothered her toothbrush with mint paste and washed the nasty taste out of her mouth. Once done, she kissed Thomas. She grabbed onto his hands so he couldn't disappear and kissed him again.

"Don't you have some sidekick to boss around?" he asked.

"I'm getting there." Abigail released him. "I'll see you later. Be safe at work."

Thomas shoved her out of the bathroom. "I'm the safest person in the city. San Arbor's very own Avalon is watching over me."

Abigail's wide yawn popped her ears. She rubbed the spot just under her ears and swallowed down another yawn. She should have grabbed the extra-large cup from the cart vendor, but when she weighed being groggy against finding a private moment to relieve herself of the

32 ounces of coffee, the bathroom break won. The small, three gulp coffee did little to remove the fog in her head or the dust in her eyes.

Whenever her eyelids fluttered shut, she saw Thomas' grin behind his blue flames. The soft glow of the moon at his back. The infinite blackness of the sky, the infinite green of his eyes. Everything replaced the glimpse in the steam. She focused on him now and not the villain he was forced to be. The Thomas in her memory did terribly good things to her insides.

"Jeeze, Avalon," Lancelot said over his shoulder. Two pigeons eyed him as he walked too close to a discarded French fry. "Up all night with that secret boyfriend?"

"There is no secret boyfriend." Abigail muttered through a third, and hopefully, final yawn. "I just grabbed two straws by mistake, you know that."

Most of San Arbor had bought into her excuse. The tabloid magazines shifted away from the mystery of Avalon's date and currently focused on the reconstruction of the Grand Hotel and Mayor Benton's party. Despite the lack of paparazzi at the event, several cell phone photos had been sold to the press, and moments of the night flashed around Abigail. The moments deemed worthy enough for the print editions didn't compare to the private ones she held inside her mind from the same night.

"You don't have to lie to me, Avy."

Abigail stopped beside her sidekick. The downtown street was empty besides a few delivery cars dropping off what she expected to be early lunch orders. She didn't want to lie to Lancelot, but she had to. She needed to keep Thomas safe and away from the media and other heroes. It was better that Lancelot stay in the dark about the situation just like the press.

"Be a good sidekick and check the logs." Abigail instructed, ignoring any more statements regarding straws, slushies, or secret boyfriends. If their identities weren't at stake, Abigail would declare her love for Thomas atop the highest roof top.

Lancelot pursed his lips. "Anything else, your majesty?"

"Make it quick," she added with a grin.

After scrolling through his phone, Lancelot reported, "No updates from the HRC. The others are doing fine. Nothing on the scanners or from DaVodi. Looks like you may have an easy day, sleepy head."

"Isn't it my job to give *you* shit?"

"I never saw that in my contract."

"Come on." Abigail turned around. "Let's finish the block and head toward the courthouse."

"Think there'll be trouble?" Lancelot asked, skipping to her side.

"I don't want there to be, but lunch time usually draws a crowd of outside eaters, and you know how unpredictable a crowd can be."

"When did you stop seeing the normality in the world?" He used his powers to move a crumpled soda can from the sidewalk into a trash bin across the street. "People could just be enjoying the weather, you know."

Abigail gripped his shoulder and forced him to look at her. "Just because you're not paranoid doesn't mean people aren't out to get you. In our profession, playing safe is always better than playing sorry."

"I do think I saw that in my contract." Lancelot smiled and Abigail allowed it to ease away her grim demeanor. "Next office day, do you want to train with me?"

Abigail removed her hand and jabbed him lightly against his chest. "Getting rusty?"

"I've got a few new moves I want to try." Abigail felt the psychic tap on her shoulder and still fell for it, glancing to look at the empty street behind them. "They're all about misdirection."

"I can't wait to lay you out."

Lancelot smirked. "I'll be ready for you, baby."

"Do not call—"

The gut punching *squeal-crash* of two metal bodies colliding echoed through the street. Abigail whipped her head to the four intersections surrounding them but found them all accident free. Her body lifted off the cement and floated up to Lancelot as he hovered above the street. The methodically planted trees below rustled as psychic waves rippled over them.

"Two streets over," Lancelot explained, looking over the buildings.

"How bad?" Abigail kicked her feet to speed up her ascent and reach the same height as her sidekick, but he still hovered ten feet ahead of her.

"Not sure, I can't see it yet."

Abigail saw the crash once they floated over the Imperial Building. A four-door sedan was T-boned halfway into a minivan that was bent around a light pole. Smoke bellowed from the vehicles. Black rubber burned into the street from the sedan's attempt at braking.

It was very bad.

Abigail turned her communicator to the city-wide frequency. "Two vehicle collision on Jefferson and Ninth, back side of the Imperial Building. Avalon and Lancelot are on the scene."

A voice replied immediately. "Paramedics are being dispatched."

Abigail addressed Lancelot and the frequency, "We'll contain the scene until they arrive. Keep everyone calm, but don't move any of them."

"If they're dying?" Lancelot asked.

Abigail switched her communicator off. There were moments when the rules of heroes had to be broken. "We break protocol if we can save them."

Lancelot lowered them in front of the impaled minivan. Abigail saw the whites of the driver's eyes. They shook and couldn't focus on one thing for more than a second. Steam rose from the engine of the sedan and seeped into the minivan, fogging the windows. Worse than the sight was the smell. The disgustingly sweet scent of gasoline was everywhere. Abigail looked under the van and saw the liquid oozing from the undercarriage of both vehicles.

It was a time bomb. One misplaced spark would send them all ablaze.

"Ma'am." Abigail straightened and addressed the woman in the minivan. Her face bled from where pieces of the broken windshield had cut her. A pile of glass sat in her lap. More pieces dangled from her skin. "Ma'am can you hear me?"

She started to shake her head, then stopped. Her face turned ghostly white, the blood against her skin becoming dark. She thrashed under the seat belt, but it and the pressure of the sedan against the back of the seat kept her imprisoned. "The kids. In the back! Are they okay?!"

Abigail rounded the van and yanked the passenger door open. Dark fumes poured out of the opening, and she found three tiny children strapped inside booster seats. The one strapped on the side of the collision wasn't conscious. His tiny head leaned against the hood of the sedan penetrating the minivan, but his chest continued to rise. She smiled at the two other children. It was bright, and it was false. Blood pooled around another boy's ear where his head must have bounced off the side of the door. His bottom lip quivered. The girl looked through Abigail. The shock of the accident shutting her small mind down. Tears fell silently down her face and onto her pink Merlin T-shirt.

Abigail turned back to the driver, "They look okay. Are you hurt?"
She looked down. "I think I'm cut."

"Nothing that can't be stitched up." Abigail remained calm despite seeing more patches of blood soak into the driver's blouse. She stepped away from the minivan and tapped her earpiece. "I've got multiple injured in the van, a woman and three kids. One unconscious. ETA on that ambulance?"

"Four minutes," the same voice from before responded.

"We've got gas too. I'm going to pull the kids."

"Negative Avalon. Not without neck collars."

Abigail gritted her teeth and turned off the communicator. She exhaled deeply through her mouth and nose, almost depleting her oxygen supply. She could not ignite here. She could take zero chances of an accidental spark. She heard the faint wail of approaching sirens. They sounded so far away it could have been a gust of wind instead. She joined Lancelot at the sedan. Its driver lay slumped over the steering wheel. Glass punctured his forehead in a deadly crown. Lancelot met her eyes and shook his head. Blood dripped from two of his fingers where he failed to find a pulse.

Abigail swallowed hard. "The bus is coming."

"Not for him." Lancelot replied. Abigail admired his professionalism. Her stomach still threatened to turn over at the sight of a dead body. "Let me move this car out of the way."

"There's a kid pinned to it. I don't know what will happen if the car is moved. He's not responding."

Lancelot tapped off his earpiece, his question directed only to Abigail. "Can we grab the kids if the other side door is accessible? That gasoline puddle is growing."

"Yes, but the light pole is in the way."

"I'll move both cars off the pole. Will that work?"

It had to. "Do it."

Abigail returned to the driver of the minivan. She refused to look at the driver's red shirt. She swore it was orange when they arrived. "We're moving the cars. Just hang on. I need you all to look at me."

The minivan sighed as pressure was removed from one side. The hood rattled as three tons of mangled steel and plastic rose a few inches off the pavement. The woman's breath sped up and she gripped the steering wheel.

"Are these your kids?" Abigail asked.

Keep them talking. It was rescuing 101.

The woman shook her head, then answered, "I'm their nanny."

Abigail strained to hear the ambulance, but the sirens sounded farther away.

"I need to call their parents." A sob shook the woman's chest.

"You can at the hospital." Abigail glanced up. Lancelot hovered above the vehicles with his hands outstretched toward them. His arms shook as he pulled the mass away from the bent light pole. A scarlet line of blood spilled from his left nostril. Inside the bend of the pole, dark wires twisted under the cracked outer casing. A flash of bright light slipped through the wires. As quick as it occurred, it was gone. But the sudden flash meant everything.

The beautiful spark was a death sentence.

"I need the power cut!" Abigail shouted into her earpiece, fumbling to turn it to the correct frequency. "Lance, stop!"

The cars stilled before floating to the ground. The metal heaved back onto each other. Lancelot landed next to her, wiping his nose with the back of his hand. "What's wrong?"

Abigail pointed to the light pole. Thankfully, it didn't spark again. "The wires are hot. I saw a spark. These cars may be the only thing keeping the power box together."

The sirens roared louder. They were a chorus of chaos coming from every direction. Underneath them, Abigail heard one of the kids crying. Red light flooded the scene as an ambulance turned onto the street.

"I'll move the gas." Lancelot stated simply. He was in the air before his commander could tell him otherwise.

Abigail flagged down the ambulance. The paramedics inside leapt from the bus with impressive speed and gathered their tools from the back. Abigail followed at their heels feeling as useless as a bull in a china shop.

"There's four inside the van," she forced herself to annunciate, following the paramedics to the wreck. "Three kids and the driver. The man in the car didn't make it."

"Stay back," one of the medics said. "Let us do our job."

Abigail froze on the sidewalk. The only thing she could do was not be in the way. In her mind, the minivan morphed into a coffin with three tiny lives taken by flames. The fire powers she loved her entire life had turned into a potential weapon.

Perhaps they were always that way.

She watched the paramedics enlist Lancelot's help in removing two of the kids in the van. Once they were in neck collars, he floated them to the back of the ambulance. Both the boy and girl giggled as Lancelot made silly faces at them. The paramedics retrieved the third kid and driver and transported them to the ambulance on a gurney. They left as a second ambulance arrived to collect the sedan's driver. His body was unceremoniously enclosed in a black bag and loaded into the bus. The lack of sirens when they left was just as loud as the ones that screamed when arriving.

"So much for a slow day," Lancelot said as he approached Abigail. He wiped his hands on his pants and the blood smear was a sickening contrast against the blue stripes. Abigail wasn't sure who the blood belonged to, but his nose had stopped bleeding.

"There should've been something more I could've done."

Lancelot grabbed Abigail's hand before it formed into a fist at her side. "We did what we could. Unless you can reverse time there was nothing else."

Abigail sighed. "Your nose. Did you hit yourself?"

"Give me a little bit more credit than that, I did make it into San Arbor's best hero company after all."

"Doesn't explain what happened." Abigail allowed his energy to combat her sour mood.

"I haven't moved something as heavy as two cars before, I think it was my power overextending." Lancelot shrugged as he finished his theory. "I used to get nose bleeds a lot when I first developed my powers."

Abigail tried to picture what a young Lancelot looked like, but, in her mind, he didn't look very different than the man who stood across from her. She had to remind herself he wasn't a boy. He was a hero, and a good one.

"You did great today." Abigail meant it. Her sidekick kept impressing her. She was glad to have him at her side, baby blue pants and all.

"Today's not over, boss."

The sound of an explosion reminded them of that. Lancelot ducked, covering the back of his head with his arms. Abigail searched above them for any signs of the blast.

Once the sound dissipated, Lancelot hovered up to get a better view of the city. "What was that?" he called down to Abigail.

At the second blast, Abigail smelled smoke. In her bones she knew exactly what it was. "A fire."

"I see smoke!" Lancelot mentally plucked Abigail from the street and elevated her to his side.

Lancelot flew them to the source of the smoke. They both shielded their faces as they passed through the thick wall of it. Below them, a fire had ruined the first floor of a commercial building. The front window display of cookbooks, knitting kits and cardboard character cutouts were easy fuel to sustain the blaze. Abigail examined the building and understood the blast occurred from three windows shattering after failing under the pressure of the heat. The first floor would have been burned beyond recognition if a team of heroes wasn't already on the scene.

Abigail hadn't imagined the earlier swarming of sirens. A firetruck sporting a large three on the side was parked in front of the building. Its red lights bathed the street in red and white. Two hose lines were dragged into the building while an aerial ladder hung parallel over the roof. The dark smoke faded as they got closer.

Lancelot lowered them next to Chief Bridgett Warren.

"We're here to help, if we can." Lancelot said in Abigail's pause. She squinted through the smoky windows searching for Thomas.

"Showed up a little late," the chief answered. "We've got it under control."

"We were working an accident a few blocks over."

"Are all your people safe?" Abigail butted in.

Chief Warren looked at Abigail. "They're fine."

The fire truck's winch whirled as it retracted the hoses. Purvis and Thomas emerged from what remained of the entrance. Abigail's heart soared and she sighed. *Alive and smoking.* Thomas exchanged a fist bump with Purvis as they neared them. He tossed a lazy smile to Abigail before reporting to his chief.

"All clear."

"That bookstore needs a major clean up, though." Purvis jabbed Thomas' arm. "I'm glad we're not the ones doing that."

"Paper is so easy to burn." Thomas looked at Abigail. Sweat and swagger clung to his face. "Hello, hero."

"Hey, yourself." Abigail kept her arms tight at her sides in fear of pulling Thomas into her and refusing to let go. "We should stop running into each other at disasters."

Thomas grinned. It was more incredible than her memories. "I heard ladies like a man in uniform, is that true?"

"Sanders." Chief Warren ended the conversation. "Get this truck loaded. Purvis, get Maddox off the aerial."

"Avalon, we should get back to HQ." Lancelot issued his own commands.

Restrained by their babysitters, Abigail and Thomas traded a final look before separating back to their public lives that shouldn't intertwine.

Abigail didn't return to her office when she and Lancelot arrived at The Hero Relief Center. Her sidekick quickly tackled the media personnel on the phone who had been on hold for the last hour waiting for the heroes to return from the car accident. She delivered him a chocolate bar from the vending machine, mouthed *I owe you one* and vanished before anyone else wanted an interview. Abigail still wore her bright and bubbly media smile, but she realized it was more exhausting now than it was when she was a sidekick. She didn't mind handing off that part of her responsibility to Lancelot.

She slipped into an employee bathroom, pulled her mask around her neck, and washed her face and hands. Both were surprisingly clean after an afternoon of heroics. Her reflection frowned at her. She hadn't been very heroic at either event. Her wonderful flames kept her power-less. Useless. Stuck on the sidelines.

She twisted the tap off too harshly and the handle loosened in her grip.

"Get over yourself," Abigail muttered, reattaching the handle. "Lives were saved, your job was done."

Even if she wasn't needed at either rescue.

Abigail exited the bathroom with the destination of a training room in mind but paused outside a room filled with computers and numbers. The door was propped open, and she couldn't help but be drawn in by the conversations of the crime analyst team. She tucked herself inside the dimly lit room.

"We should send this report upstairs," one analyst with a rubber duck printed tie said. "It could be a pattern."

"I think you've seen too many dramas, Justin." Another analyst laughed. "This is just a coincidence at best."

Justin slapped his computer monitor. "I don't believe in coinci-dences. These numbers don't lie."

The other analyst leaned over to view the computer screen. "I'm sure there's an explanation. You should call SAFD before bothering King Arthur about something you only have a hunch about."

"What are you looking at?" Abigail asked, peering over Justin's other shoulder to see the data. At the mention of the San Arbor Fire Department, she could no longer just listen.

"Justin thinks there's something—"

Justin interrupted his friend, "I just noticed that over the last few weeks there's been more fire related incidents in this section of the city." He leaned back so Abigail could see the map better but continued talking. "I know you discovered that crime ring a few years back by seeing a similar pattern."

Abigail smiled but it didn't reach her eyes. "You're right, but my data was gathered over several months. Keep an eye on this, but I wouldn't say it's more than outdated fire codes and bad luck. You should call SAFD, though. Maybe they can send their investigators and the building owners can start updating. What company oversees this section? Does your computer show you?"

Abigail recognized the street names. She recognized the sandwich shop on the corner she'd shared numerous lunch breaks at. She still gulped when Justin confirmed her thought.

"It's Ladder Company 3, Avalon. They've been seeing a record-breaking number of fires recently."

Chapter Eleven

That night, soot-stained boots and scuffed sneakers were piled outside the apartment door. The carpet inside was miraculously stain free from the two inhabitants' flames. This made Abigail happy. When she did decide to move, she would receive at least a part of her security deposit. The dark marks on the patio made years ago, however, would definitely cause a deduction. Watching the man who was to blame for them drink a decaf coffee on the porch made Abigail happier than any security deposit return.

Alive and smoking, just as he always promised. A promise he'd been making a lot the last few weeks.

"You're staring." Thomas commented, setting his mug on the ledge. The city burned in the colors of sunset behind him.

"You're easy to stare at."

Thomas smiled. "What're you thinking about?"

"Have you noticed all the big fires have been happening on your shift?" Abigail blurted out. The analyst team's discovery hung around her like muggy air before a summer's storm. The sooner she released the rain the sooner the world would dry out. "Your area and your shift."

"It has felt pretty busy." Thomas shrugged, Abigail's frantic question having little effect on him. "Must just be a coincidence."

Abigail frowned and Thomas chuckled. His nonchalant mood prickled her.

"Are you really worried about me, babe? I'm fireproof, remember?"

"We all have our limits." A nasty handprint-shaped scar had been hers. At one time, a heroic explosion had been his.

"A little house fire isn't going to lay a finger on me."

"These haven't been little house fires. These have been some serious blazes. Way more than San Arbor is used to seeing."

"It's a good thing they have a super on their force, then, right?"

"Tommy, I'm serious. Things are dangerous. If they find out you have powers without being registered, they could take you." Abigail remembered the determined look on the mother's face as she clutched Lillian in her arms; remembered how wild and feral the mom became to protect her own. Even in the face of two superheroes.

Abigail knew the lengths she would go to protect Thomas.

"Doubtful the way the mayor talks about me," Thomas pulled her mind away from the memories. His light-hearted tone tried to rub against Abigail's darkening thoughts until they sanded down to match his. "He's called me twice since the party wanting to know if I've given his offer any thought."

Abigail refused to let the conversation get sidetracked. Crossing her arms, she pierced Thomas with a heated stare.

Thomas hooked his arm around her waist and pulled Abigail into him before she could wiggle away. "I worry about you too, you know? But I won't ask you to hang up your cape."

Abigail's mouth parted like a fish. She was unsure which statement to address first. "I'm not asking you to quit your job. And I'm fireproof too."

A dark smile flashed across Thomas' mouth before the darkening shadows of the sunset snatched it away. "You're not bulletproof, though."

Abigail fidgeted with her fingers. The bruise and healing puncture wound on her knee was an easy reminder that she wasn't immune to other types of damage.

"I know what's waiting for me inside the buildings I run into." Thomas' voice was surprisingly soft. The rumbling thunder of it trembled against Abigail. "There's no telling what kind of call you'll get, and one day it could be something too much for your flames. Fires don't scare me Abbs, losing you does."

Abigail melted in his arms. Her fireproofing still immune to Thomas. "I never wanted to make you worry about me."

"I think you picked the wrong career for that."

"What would you have me do otherwise?"

Thomas answered quickly with a brilliant grin. "Grow snow carrots with me on the mountain side. We'll open up a little stall on the side of the road and sell them overpriced to tourists."

"You've thought a lot about this," Abigail chuckled.

"There's some boring days at the firehouse too, gives me time to think."

"When the days aren't boring, when you can't think of farming, will you promise me you'll be careful?"

Thomas sighed dramatically but gave into her demands. Like he always did. "Of course, babe. I promise I'll call my favorite hero if things get over my head."

"I love you."

"I love you." Thomas said it like a promise. "Do give the vegetables some thought, though."

"Do snow carrots even exist?"

Thomas shrugged. "You'll have to come back to the mountain with me and see for yourself."

The kitchen timer rattled on the countertop, and Abigail instantly regretted doing laundry first thing in the morning. She rolled off the couch, her impromptu nap stiffening her limbs, silenced the alarm and jogged to the laundry room on the bottom floor and switched the load. The jog shook the remaining drowsiness the accidental couch nap left, and she filled the laundry basket with the next load. Laundry was one chore that always evaded the hero, and now her morning off would be filled with fabric softener, folding shirts, and untangling dryer sheets from pant legs.

She could only hope the HRC called her for backup.

On the return trip to her floor, the smell of laundry soap was replaced with warm maple syrup. It made Abigail's stomach gurgle. In place of the ticking kitchen timer on the counter was a takeout spread of pancakes, sausage and questionable-looking scrambled eggs. Thomas was completing the spread by pouring orange juice into two cups.

Abigail left the laundry basket by the door and joined him at the island. "I was wondering where you went."

"We never have eggs." Thomas teased, returning the juice carton to the mostly empty fridge. He tossed the checkered takeout bag from breakfast into the trash can.

Abigail selected a paper plate with the most appealing pancake stack and drizzled syrup over the entirety of the breakfast. Thomas claimed the second plate and followed her to the couch. He pulled the coffee table closer to them so he wouldn't drop anything on the carpet.

"Did you watch the news yet?"

Abigail frowned. She wasn't *that* predictable, but she did change the station to Channel 9. It was hard not being connected to San Arbor when she wasn't in a mask. The HRC would call her in if something big happened that required her powers, but it never hurt to be informed.

"I'll just watch the weather report."

"You don't have to lie to me." Thomas stole a sausage link from her plate.

Abigail quickly snatched one of his before focusing on the news report. The graphic in the screen's corner depicted a firetruck with flames behind it. She turned the volume up seven points.

"San Arbor fire crews are still battling a fire that started twenty minutes ago at a local business on Hopple Street."

The graphic morphed to a live feed after the anchor read the prompter. Two firetrucks from Ladder Company 6 were running point at the store. A window shattered on the second floor and dark smoke whipped wildly about as cherry-red flames chased behind it. Abigail swallowed her bite, but it didn't settle in her stomach well.

"Six is a smart team," Thomas commented beside her. "Their chief's been fighting fires longer than you've been alive. Kind of bummed we're not out there. The layout of that building would be cool to work in."

Abigail eyed him, her mouth hanging slightly open.

Thomas chuckled around a bite of pancake. "You can't look at me like that. I know you get the same way when you're on the bench and your team is running without you."

"That is so not the same."

"Would it be the same if I wore a mask?"

Abigail dropped her gaze to her soggy pancakes. The syrup penetrated the cake and separated the dough. Her mask and his shield shouldn't be any different. They both served San Arbor, both protected the city's people, and both felt the itch when they couldn't do their jobs. But, somehow, her Avalon mask felt safer than the metal shield he kept inside his wallet. Abigail knocked her knee against his.

"I don't mean to be so…"

"Motherly."

"Concerned." Abigail growled her correction but whispered her next admittance. "I just don't want to lose you again."

Thomas knocked his knee back against hers, but much softer as he tried to avoid her injury. "If you never give up on me, I won't go anywhere that you can't come too."

His conditions almost made Abigail laugh. He was outrageous if he thought she could ever turn her back on him. From the first second they met, deep down she knew they were connected somehow. At the time she didn't expect it to be as nice as breakfast on the couch and whispered *I love you*s in bed. Abigail was addicted to Thomas. She knew that as much as she knew how her flames felt against her skin.

Maybe even more.

Abigail grabbed his hand and kissed his knuckles. The staining had completely vanished, and velvet skin pressed against her lips. "I'm not going anywhere, Tommy. I promise."

"Then neither am I."

They finished their breakfast in comfortable silence and continued watching the news. Besides the fire, the city was safe. The Knights on duty were having an easy morning. Abigail's afternoon patrol could mirror the still morning, or something big and bad could terrorize the city. She would make sure San Arbor remained standing regardless of the day. The news concluded with an aerial shot of the Ladder 6 truck and crew. The local store was saved and would be back in action after some interior rebuilds. Employees from the diner across the street were waving the first responders over for breakfast and coffee. Their checkered uniform shirts became pixelated on the screen.

Chapter Twelve

When Abigail arrived at the HRC later that afternoon, Lancelot was pacing the lobby floor. His blue cape fluttered behind him as he turned on his heel when he reached the end of the room. Shannon wasn't at her post behind her desk, so the only audience to Lancelot's anxious walk were the four large portraits hanging on the back wall. The black and white photos showcased the Hero Relief Center's main heroes. Abigail remembered the day her photo joined the wall. The pride that squeezed her heart when the poster was first hung was intoxicating. Avalon, the Dragon Slayer. Abigail, the hero.

The whirl of the automatic door signaled her arrival.

"There you are!" Lancelot's boot squeaked against the tile as he changed his course to her. "We've got to go."

"Go where?" Abigail swatted away the psychic touch as it wrapped around her arm, but she was still lifted off the ground and floated to Lancelot's side.

"There's a fire and—"

"Where?" Abigail unrolled a spare mask she pulled from her jacket pocket. Blue jeans weren't her preferred crime fighting wardrobe, but she doubted there was time to change.

"Seventh and Vine."

"Downtown. A restaurant?"

"Alexander's," Lancelot answered, levitating them to the staircase. His psychic abilities would float them to the roof quicker than the elevator. "There's studio space above it."

"How bad?" Abigail knew the answer. For her to be called in it would have to be an inferno.

"Just starting." Lancelot exited the stairwell three floors too soon, and they flew down the hallway toward Abigail's office instead of the roof. "But SAFD is handling two other fires right now. Quinn wants us there, A-sap."

Abigail swallowed hard. She started disrobing before they made it to her office door. She set her focus on pulling on Avalon's costume. The quicker she was dressed, the quicker she'd be on the scene. She tightened her mask and reminded herself they were both fireproof. Thomas would be fine. "Where are the other fires?"

"Across the city." Lancelot answered, staring at the ceiling.

"Arson?" Abigail realized he was trying to give her as much privacy as he could. "I'm dressed, by the way."

"I don't know." Lancelot grabbed her wrist and levitated them with his telekinesis. They flew to the staircase and finally headed for the roof and their jumping off point. "We'll have to figure it out after we save the day."

Abigail knocked her knuckles against his. "Let's be heroes."

San Arbor mourned the temporary death of the Twin Leaf Bar for a week. News crews documented the rebuild and a reopening ceremony was set with red ribbon and oversized scissors. San Arbor wouldn't know what to do if the city lost its oldest downtown restaurant. Alexander's was serving customers when the city's roads were still compacted dirt. Dust and flower blossoms blew in with the hungry guests as often back then as they did now.

The red and gold curtains hanging in the windows vanished between wisps of smoke. Angry red flames flickered inside the door daring someone foolish enough to come inside. More smoke plumed from the second story windows as the fire invaded the rest of the building.

Studio spaces full of paper and art supplies would be a quick meal for any fire.

"Drop me there." Abigail pointed at the small fire truck parked on the sidewalk. "Check the windows for people inside the upper levels. I'll radio with information."

Lancelot nodded and set Abigail at her desired destination. Without the extra weight, his flight speed increased. Abigail's hair whipped around her as Lancelot shot up to the second story. He flew around the windows and fire escapes as a blue blur.

"Fill me in." Abigail walked toward the nearest firefighter before her feet touched down.

"The blaze started near the front of the building," the woman answered. The volunteer tag was as polished as the truck company badge pinned next to it. "The hostess called it in about fifteen minutes ago. SAFD is split between the two other—"

"Your only job is this one." Abigail interrupted. "Have you completed initial search and rescue?"

"Yes, but—"

"Lancelot is doing a sweep upstairs. Clear out your guys. I'm going inside for the secondary search." She didn't wait for a confirmation from the firefighter. The flames called her home. She was the one foolish enough to accept its dare.

"Avalon!"

Abigail turned, the heat from the fire scratching her back, and stared back at the firefighter.

"We'll have the hose ready for you," the woman declared.

Abigail gave her a thumbs up and ran into Alexander's. Her mask turned on and lit her path inside the building. The 1920's inspired decor was melting as the fire ate away the history of the architect and the restaurant.

"Hero Relief Center, call out!" Abigail shouted as loudly as she could before radioing Lancelot. "I'm inside. Water is coming soon. Find anyone?"

"A few," Lancelot was quick to reply. "Bringing them down now. Do you need me in there with you?"

A small blast erupted in front of Abigail. She shielded her face with her forearms. Flaming strips of tablecloth rained around her and singed her hair. "Negative. Make sure the gas has been turned off. I'm headed to the kitchen."

The radio clicked off, and she called into the building again. No one called out to her, so she ventured deeper into the back. The employee coat closet was destroyed, the manager's office was in ashes, and the metal kitchen pass table was glowing red hot. Abigail followed the destructive path as if the fire had been expecting her and left the trail as a welcome mat.

"Hero Relief Center, call out!"

The red-hot path led to the kitchen. The double doors swung wildly as the hot air billowed in and out of the room. The metal and molten hinges dripped onto the carpet. Abigail pushed them open, the intense heat an afterthought against her fireproofing, and scanned the room. The charred path led to a treasure after all. A waitress was stuck in a corner. An empty fire extinguisher was clutched in her arms. Vengeful flames crept across the chemical coated floor toward her.

"I'm coming!" Abigail shouted. "Hang on!"

Abigail raced across the flames, her feet snuffing footprints into the floor with each step. She reached for the waitress' hand and hauled her into her arms. The waitress replaced her death grip around the extinguisher for Abigail's neck. Breathing through the smoke and flames was easier than the vice grip of the waitress.

"It's going to be okay," Abigail promised. "We're getting out of here."

"Gas is off," Lancelot's voice shouted inside the earpiece.

It didn't stop the explosion.

The sudden heat wave slammed against Abigail's back. Her skin prickled as the air expanded around her. Her fingers sparked red in the moment before the blast, anticipating the imposing flames. She shot out of the kitchen with the new fire rushing for her and tucked herself around the waitress to keep her covered. They landed halfway in the dining room, crashing into a burning table. The waitress screamed against Abigail's ear.

Abigail scrambled off the table and patted out the fire tearing through the waitress' uniform. Bright red and blistered skin snarled through the fabric. Once the fire on the waitress was out, Abigail rocketed to the door, her flames propelling her quickly through the main floor until she could run outside. She set the waitress face down on a gurney that waited for them. Her burned skin was a disgusting contrast against the white pad below her.

"Soak it!" Abigail yelled at the firefighters, her ears still ringing from the blast. Shattered glass crunched under her boots.

The volunteer woman shook her head. "Your partner is still inside."

Abigail blinked. "Lancelot?"

"He flew in after the explosion."

"Lancelot!" Abigail shouted into her earpiece. "Lance, where are you?"

The line was dead silent.

Abigail ran back inside Alexander's. Lancelot's name tore through her throat. The dining room was a storm of smoke and cinders. The cloud rotated in on itself, consuming the room. She struggled to find the kitchen, her mask pin lights bouncing wildly against the smoke.

Every dark spot on the floor could have been a body. Abigail engulfed her hands and snuffed the blazes she could. She overpowered the flames until they submitted to her own, but it wasn't fast enough. The restaurant kept burning. A chunk of the ceiling collapsed. Lancelot was still lost.

"Lance!"

Kicking down the door to the employee coat closet, Abigail plunged her hands into the layer of ash on the ground. Her fingers knocked into something hard. Fearing a femur bone, she was ecstatic to only find a metal chair leg in the debris. Another section of the roof crashed down in the main room and shook the floor. Tiny embers flew through the door and illuminated the closet. In the corner, a heap of clothes held Abigail's attention. Despite the low light, the blue and white stripes of the fabric clutched her heart and restricted it from beating.

She kicked through the debris and collapsed at the pile. There was nothing there but items left by the fire. The charred fabric dusted away in her hands, but Lancelot wasn't inside the blue shawl. More dark smoke invaded the room, and Abigail returned to the restaurant. The tables and chairs were all gone. The restaurant was breaking down. The fire was taking everything. It was trying to take her sidekick.

Abigail thought she imagined it at first, but she heard it again. The faint calling of her name. She followed it like a wayward ship to a lighthouse. The melting kitchen doors appeared in the smoke, and she somersaulted through them trying to avoid the molten plastic and steel that fell like rain. A costumed form lay face down on the floor phasing in and out of the billowing smoke.

"Lancelot!"

Abigail grabbed him by his charred puffy shirt sleeve and turned him over. His cheerful face was pale, his lips quivered, his eyes stared at the empty space above him. A crisscrossing of black ran from his fingertips to his elbow crooks and spilled across his chest. The flesh was destroyed and melted. Abigail swallowed down the smell of burning flesh. The smell was worse than the sight.

For the flame hero anyway.

Abigail grabbed Lancelot's face and forced him to look at her. "We're getting out of here. Can you move?"

Lancelot lowered his gaze to his outstretched arms, but Abigail yanked his chin and forced his attention to her. "I think so," he answered.

Each word scraped against his throat. His mouth and nose were covered in soot. If the fire wasn't going to kill him, the smoke in his lungs would.

Abigail scooped him into her arms. She focused all her flames to the bottom of her feet and shot them out of the restaurant like a mint in a diet cola bottle. Glass ripped through her hands and arms as they soared through the lobby windows. The sidewalk was scorched in a three-foot radius from her landing. A gurney rolled toward her to accept Lancelot, but Abigail didn't want to lower him.

His burned arms. His pale face. The cough and rasp in his voice. His tattered hero costume. The tremble in his chest. It felt like only her holding him was keeping Lancelot in one piece. The moment she released him, he would flake away in a snowstorm of ash and soot. She forgot how fragile one of them could be.

"You dumb kid," Abigail scolded, finally lowering him onto the gurney. Her arms would ache from carrying two adults in one rescue, but she'd worry about that tomorrow. Blood dripped onto the sidewalk where window glass tore into her arms and hands. She would worry about that tomorrow, too. "What were you thinking?"

"I heard the explosion," Lancelot said over the rush of water around them as the fire fighters blasted the building.

Abigail walked alongside the gurney as the paramedics steered it toward the ambulance. "You're not fireproof."

The paramedic stopped Lancelot's reply. "You shouldn't talk, sir. You need oxygen."

The paramedic strapped an oxygen mask over Lancelot's dirty face, and Abigail said, "I'll meet you at the hospital."

"You can ride with us," the paramedic offered, loading the gurney.

Abigail hopped into the ambulance.

Chapter Thirteen

The waiting was the worst. Abigail was never good at it, but it was unbearable this time. She sat pressed in a corner of the emergency room lobby with her hands sanding together and both feet bouncing against the floor. Each bounce of her foot matched a tick from the second hand on the clock in front of her. She'd been waiting for over two hours and was just as in the dark as she was when they arrived. At least when they arrived, Lancelot was still with her. She had no idea where he was once the paramedics wheeled him past the door and she was told to "sit and wait."

She had no idea what his condition was. She had no idea if his burned body passed out on the gurney would be the last time she saw him. If the horrid screams that pierced her ears would be the last thing she heard him say.

The double doors pushed open, and a nurse called someone's name. The same nurse had been calling other people's names the whole time. A man raised from a seat and followed the nurse into the sealed off emergency room. Abigail fought the urge to force her way after them. She fought the urge to find Lancelot on her own.

Her flames were useless here.

Abigail gave up mentally trying to speed up time by glaring at the clock and tried to distract herself by watching the television bolted to the wall. A newscast was starting up, and the familiar theme of Channel 9 let Abigail take a stable breath.

After the anchor's scripted greeting and preview of the weather to come, the first story loaded up and the Ladder Company 3 truck came into view. A factory with tall stacks on the far end burned. Two aerial ladders were suspended above the blaze and showered the building with water. Dark smoke continued to pour through the roof.

"Fire crews are still battling the fire at San Arbor's Textile Factory," the field reporter shouted over the noise of the scene. "Initial reports say the fire started in the rear of the facility but spread quickly due to the fabric housed near the area—"

The reporter ducked and the camera collapsed on its tripod as the factory's second story windows shattered away. A wave of red fire pulsed from the new openings.

Sparks crashed against Abigail's hands and mouth. She needed to be there. She needed to protect Thomas, protect her city, but she was trapped inside the hospital. Thomas was fireproof. He would be fine. She couldn't say the same about Lancelot right now.

Her city and her partner needed her.

She was trapped.

Abigail walked across the room and turned off the television before the images on screen made her do something reckless. Turning away from the screen, Abigail found the other waiting guests watching her. No one protested her turning off their only source of entertainment. She assumed her costume had something to do with that. She tried to smile, failed, and returned to her seat.

The door squeaked open again, and the nurse called, "Um, Lancelot family?"

Abigail leapt from her seat and ran to the nurse who pulled up her clipboard like a shield. "Is he okay?" Abigail blurted out.

The nurse ushered her pass the door to the hallway on the other side. "He's been removed from the ICU, which is good, but he's still in recovery. You can sit with him, but he needs to rest."

"Is he okay?" Abigail repeated harshly. She tasted sulfur on her tongue.

The nurse gulped, and Abigail should have regretted her growl. "His O2 sats have improved, and his burns have been treated but he has a long recovery ahead of him. He'll most likely be recommended to a plastic surgeon for skin grafts." The nurse stopped outside a door. "Are you sure you want to see him? See him like this?"

Abigail blinked, unsure if she heard the nurse correctly. "Of course, I do. I want to be there with him."

The nurse opened the door and Abigail entered Lancelot's room.

The brightness of the overhead lights clashed painfully with the whiteness of the room. The white blinds on the windows and white curtain pulled around the bed didn't help, either. There was nothing in the pristine room that could distract Abigail from Lancelot's beaten body. Her eyes were drawn to the burns sneaking out from under the gauze around his arms and chest. She couldn't look away. She wouldn't. Not when he sustained them under her watch. The IV machine plugged into him chirped periodically. Abigail hoped the high pitch sound was a good thing. The numbers on the display made little sense to her.

She was tired of seeing heroes in the burn unit.

Abigail kneeled at the side of the bed. Unsure of what to do, unable to do anything as she was face to face with his injuries. The smell of burnt flesh overpowered the clean smell of the room and gripped her throat. The nurse wheeled a chair next to Abigail and left without a word.

A heavy pit formed inside her stomach. It was the same feeling she had seeing Volcanic in a similar state four years ago. She was glad Lancelot was able to block his face from the fire, at least he didn't have half his face covered in gauze. The nurse said he would heal. Volcanic's burns lasted for years until they were finally able to be removed. She guessed he had been repaired with skin grafts the same way Lancelot would have to be.

Abigail settled into the chair, bringing her knees to her stomach to try and settle it. Both situations felt like her fault. Her flames didn't cause the burns, but her actions put both heroes in a path heading for the fire. She wished she could absorb fire like Thomas instead of only creating the blaze. Lancelot wouldn't be stuck in this bed on a morphine drip if she could.

Too many times Abigail had been pushed to the sidelines because of her fire. She didn't doubt her mask, she knew her resolve to be a hero was strong, but there had to be another way to use her flames. A better way to do her job.

She retrieved her phone and updated the other Knights on Lancelot's condition and location. A prompt reply from Merlin let Abigail know they'd be there soon. A second message buzzed its incoming, *Alive and smoking*, and ushered a sigh of relief from Abigail. But the feeling was minute compared to the endorphins flooding her system at finding Lancelot's doe eyes watching her. They were hazy under his mask, affected by the morphine pumping through him, and it took him a few seconds to focus on her.

"You dumb kid." It was all Abigail could say.

Lancelot smiled, her scolding having zero effect. "I didn't know you'd be here."

"I rode in the ambulance with you, remember?"

Lancelot scrunched his face trying to. "I must have passed out."

Abigail pulled her chair closer to the bedside. The scratching sound of chair legs against the floor pushed the ambulance ride out of her mind. Passing out was a peaceful understatement. The paramedic put him under to stop his screaming. Lancelot pretended it didn't hurt until the doors closed, and Abigail had believed him, until the bus pulled onto the road with Lancelot and his pain hidden inside. "What were you thinking? Going in there?"

"You weren't out, and I heard the explosion and I—"

"Are not fireproof," Abigail reminded; her voice was as cold as the room's floor. "All of our training together to handle fires, what is your number one rule?"

"Listen to you."

She ignored his dopey smile. "Don't run into the building."

"These kind of itch." Lancelot looked away from Abigail to fiddle with the gauze closest to his elbows. He scratched at the wrapping until his fingers slid underneath and brushed the burn. Lancelot winced.

"Don't mess with them." Abigail pulled his hand away.

When he absent-mindedly reached for the wrapping again, Abigail grabbed his hand and held it against the bed. The hospital blanket was also itchy. She desperately wished there was something comfortable in the room for him. The morphine dripped another drop into his IV.

"I swear I turned the gas off," he said. "Avy, I swear I did."

"I know you did." That was rule three. Eliminate any gas connection.

"Then what caused the explosion?"

"I don't know," Abigail admitted. "Leftover gas in a tank maybe, or some condensed canister in the kitchen. We'll worry about that later. I'm sure there's a full report waiting for us at HQ."

Lancelot chuckled but it didn't sound like him. The joyful bounce of his voice was replaced with a thick and raspy sound. "Think you can take care of that paperwork for me, boss?"

"Just this once, sidekick." Abigail patted his hand as softly as she could, fearing the marred skin would crack like an egg. "Do you need anything? I can get the doctor?"

"Just tell me I didn't miss dinner."

"No one's brought food by, so I think you're safe."

"Good. Call me crazy, but I love hospital food. When I was a kid, I faked being sick after my tonsils were out just to stay an extra day. Think they'll give me ice cream, again? It's the only thing I ate for a whole week. It was awesome."

Abigail listened to Lancelot reminisce about his chocolate ice cream desires until the door squeaked opened and the other Knights walked in. Excalibur's armored body hardly fit through the door, and the balloons he carried wrestled with the frame until all ten of them were inside. Baby blue ones to match Lancelot's pants, and yellow suns cheering him to *get better soon!*

"Woah!" Lancelot eyed the balloons, then the Knights. "You guys came to my birthday?"

Merlin frowned and checked the machine readouts. They must have made more sense to her, because after her examination she pressed the call button to the nurse's station.

"Doctor said he'll be okay." Abigail joined King Arthur in the middle of the room. His refusal to wear a mask made him stick out, the easiest to target but the most feared of the Knights. "His arms will heal."

"Good." King Arthur sighed, and then shook his head at Lancelot's state. The sidekick was making Excalibur sing happy birthday to him. "Walk me through the situation."

"We're not sure," Abigail started. "I'm hoping the report from SAFD will help, but after the gas was cut there was an explosion inside. We missed each other, and Lance flew in to look for me."

"Dumb kid."

"That's what I said."

"I'll make sure we have their report before the morning."

"I'll get it figured out." Abigail promised her team.

The door opened again and admitted a nurse. It was the same kind-faced woman who checked on Lancelot an hour ago. Three pink pens pierced her bun. She froze a moment when her eyes landed on King Arthur. She didn't move again until he smiled at her.

"How's he doing?" the nurse asked, grabbing the clipboard from the counter.

"Too well," Merlin grumbled. "This drip is too loose. He thinks it's his birthday."

Lancelot pulled a balloon string so the sun on the other end bumped repeatedly against the ceiling. "Birthday cake, birthday cake," he sang to no one. "Birthday cake all for me."

"His birthday was months ago." Merlin completed her diagnosis.

The nurse checked the morphine drip but didn't change it. "He'll be in a lot of pain otherwise. We need Lancelot to sleep so he can get better."

Abigail was amazed to see anyone stand up to Merlin. She wondered if this nurse had super abilities of her own.

"And that is what we want too," King Arthur said before Merlin could react. She stepped into a corner of the room. Her pointed hat created a dark shadow across the bed. "Thank you for your work."

"It's just my job." Her voice squeaked as she addressed him. "If he needs anything, call the station."

"Ice cream if you have any," Abigail called before the nurse exited the room.

Excalibur finished tying the balloons around the room, away from Lancelot, and joined the others. "He'll be here for a while."

"He shouldn't be alone, either." King Arthur replied. "HRC will send someone."

"I'll stay until then." Abigail decided. "They can come in the morning before I'm due at work."

"You've been here all day."

"He's my sidekick." *He's my responsibility.*

King Arthur eyed her for a moment before giving in. "Alright. But Mitch will pick you up so you're not riding the bus like that."

"I don't know, King," Excalibur interrupted. "Heroes on the bus might make a good picture."

"Or a terrible panic." Merlin said behind King Arthur's back. "Why else would a hero be on public transportation except to catch a bad guy."

"I could show we're just like everyone else," Abigail agreed with Excalibur. She would have agreed with anyone if it got her out of seeing grumpy Mitch first thing in the morning.

"But we're not," said Merlin.

"Mitch will be picking Avalon up." King Arthur ended the discussion. "Do you need anything before we leave?"

The grip around her heart tightened, and Abigail guiltily jumped at the offer. "Would you keep an eye on Lance for a minute? I need to make a phone call."

"Sure." King Arthur nodded. "See if you can grab yourself an extra blanket while you're out."

Thomas answered on the second ring of her phone call. His deep voice was an instant comfort from the day, and Abigail leaned against the snack machine she huddled with in a hallway alcove. *Alive and smoking* confirmed.

"Hey babe, out saving the day?"

"It's saved for now." She smiled into the phone's receiver. "I'm not coming home tonight, though. I'm staying at the hospital to watch over Lancelot. He got hurt pretty bad today and I don't want him here alone."

Thomas didn't respond right away. Abigail didn't expect him to. Ever since his accident, Thomas avoided hospitals like a bull avoided slaughterhouses. "Sounds like a shitty place to spend the night."

"I know, but he's my teammate."

"You don't have to explain it to me." Abigail heard the patio door slide open on his end of the line. "Saw you on the news today. What happened?"

"Restaurant fire, we got everyone out, but Lance got caught in an explosion. His arms and chest are burnt bad. Smoke inhalation, too."

"It was a good day for fires." Abigail didn't share his sentiment. "We had two on shift."

"Two? I only saw the factory fire."

"The fire jumped across the street," he explained. "A flame on a breeze, we got them both out."

"Four fires in one afternoon," Abigail chewed the inside of her lip. "That's four too many."

"You doubting me now?" Thomas chuckled. "If I count right, we're 3-1 today."

"Only because you didn't call us to any others." Abigail easily played his game.

"You only have one fire hero." Abigail imagined his smug grin, and the shrug of his shoulders. The image was home, and for a moment she forgot where she was.

"We could have two, you know."

"I told you babe. I'm leaving all the masks to you. I'll fight fires the human way."

"Until you absorb them."

Thomas laughed. "Fingers are all clean tonight. Try again."

"I love you, and you're crazy." Abigail smiled again; things were too easy with Thomas. Her mood improved instantly. "You have an incredible gift."

"You're the only one who sees it that way. I love you, too."

"Movie tomorrow night?" Abigail asked before he could hang up, desperate to keep their conversation alive for just a moment longer.

"Let's throw in dinner too," Thomas agreed.

"Something besides popcorn?" Abigail faked a gasp.

"I think it's going to be a special night. Goodnight, Abbs."

Chapter Fourteen

Lancelot was still asleep when the HRC agent relieved Abigail the next morning. His body was as motionless as the moment he passed out the night before, the ice cream half eaten and dripping down his chin. He hadn't stirred when Abigail removed the ice cream cup and dabbed the chocolate off his face. The nurse promised it was just the morphine that kept him so still, and not the threat of rigor mortis. The expert opinion didn't help Abigail sleep any easier. She checked on Lancelot every time she twisted uncomfortably in the chair.

Which seemed to be about every half-hour. The sunrise pierced between the blinds all too soon, and Abigail eyed the hospital bed to find a way to squeeze both their bodies onto the mattress. The crisscrossing of burns stopped her. Any extra pressure against them would be painful. Instead, she watched the subtle rise and fall of Lancelot's chest. At least he was able to sleep through the night.

Sometime after the sunrise began, the door handle jiggled. Abigail scrambled around the bed to put herself between Lancelot and the door. The nurses always knocked between their comings and goings, even if the light rap didn't fully wake Abigail from her rare moments of REM. Abigail wouldn't let this intruder harm her sidekick. Fire sparked between her thumb and pointer finger as she rubbed them together.

A casually dressed man entered the room and gulped seeing the smoke rise around Abigail. "It's just me, Avalon. The HRC sent me to relieve you this morning."

Abigail straightened and smiled. "Sorry about that."

"How's Lancelot doing?"

"According to the nurses, he's going to be okay." Abigail looked down at him. She wanted to believe the nurses, but it was difficult when all she saw was his cauterized body.

The HRC agent handed Abigail one of the large coffees he wielded. "What do you think? Fire's more your specialty, anyway."

The agent didn't see the snarl forming on Abigail as he looked at Lancelot asleep in the bed. She forced it down. It was just a question, not an accusation. "He'll be in pain for a while."

"We're parked in the employee lot." The agent looked back at Abigail. "There's a media storm out front."

Abigail sipped her coffee. "We should see about getting Lance moved somewhere else."

"I heard President Samuels is working on adding a hospital wing at HQ. I saw a budget plan for it."

"Strange he hasn't done that sooner."

"Usually, you guys are too super to get hurt."

Abigail felt another pang in her chest from the second statement that wasn't meant to be an insult. Usually, they're too super to get each other hurt. "Let me know if anything changes."

"I will," the agent said and settled into the chair for his watch.

The car ride back to the Hero Relief Center was silent. With grumpy Mitch at the wheel, Abigail didn't expect a warm welcome. He looped the car around the hospital, and Abigail saw the hungry swarm of paparazzi outside the main entrance. She gritted her teeth. Lancelot needed peace and quiet and those cameras offered neither. She'd do whatever she could to get the new medical wing constructed at the HRC faster.

Once in her office, she stripped off her day-old costume and showered away the soot trapped on her skin from the fire. The overly clean scent of the hospital was replaced with the overly clean scent of industrial grade soap. Her hair dried in a static burst around her head and begged to be treated better. Abigail brushed it down with her fingers, made a silent promise she would, and donned a clean costume.

As promised, the report from the Alexander's fire was on her desk. Whoever delivered the document placed it neatly onto her desk's mound of other reports, and the folders blended in together. Abigail made a mental note to get organized, again, and opened the file. The report was a copy of the handwritten account, and the frayed edges from the original paper skewed the copy. Abigail tried to pick the imperfections away, but the copy remained as it was delivered.

The San Arbor Fire Department's report didn't help as much as Abigail hoped it would. Their investigators didn't mention the explosion as a notable factor in the fire. The blast was wrapped up with the initial damages. Lancelot's burns wrapped up with the initial injuries. Abigail chewed the inside of her cheek but signed off on the document. The explosion was just her bad luck then. A grease vat could have burst under the heat, or a compressed cooling unit in a freezer, a hundred spray cans of cream, anything could have erupted. She wrote *lance needs fireproof cape* in a thick Sharpie marker on the front of the file and tossed it into the empty seat across the desk.

Deciding to do something productive, she organized her desk by stacking all the other files on top of each other into one towering stack and made another promise she'd go through them later. Pages of old cases peaked from the cream-colored folders and the occasional picture corner folded around the edges in protest. Abigail yanked her broadsword out of its scabbard and ran her drills in the open space. With each block she willed a call from someone with an update on Lancelot's condition. With each overhead strike she willed the speaker to go off on a call. With each snap kick she willed the Knight on patrol to trade places with her. With each turn of her feet, she willed something to happen but all she did was run her form until she slipped in the sweat that streaked the floor.

Abigail was still terrible at waiting.

Abigail was met with zero news when her shift ended. There were no more attacks on San Arbor. The police didn't require a hero's help. The patrolling Knight did not switch her places. The budgeting committee ushered her out of their board meeting while they discussed finances. Her day felt wasted despite the ache in her muscles and her clean office. She traded her Avalon costume for her day clothes, faded blue jeans and a T-shirt from a local record store, and descended the elevator to the lobby.

The report on the Alexander's fire still claimed her thoughts. It weighed uneasy in her mind. Something didn't sit right with the details. She recalled the little data that was scribbled on the report as the elevator opened on the lobby level. Something felt missing, a piece of the puzzle deliberately left out. Perhaps she just wished there was something more that could justify Lancelot's injuries besides an accident. If there was something to blame, then there was something to fix.

Something or someone she could remove so it could never happen again.

Abigail stopped when she approached the door. Her bag threatened to slide off her arm. On the television screen in the lobby, the news report displayed a horrid picture of Lancelot. He was asleep inside his hospital bed, head hanging lazily to the side and his green gown looking like a rag. Abigail's hands began to smoke. The image was taken from the outside of the window of the room. She saw the HRC agent's shoes in the corner of the shot where he must have been sitting. Someone snuck this photo.

The image faded to the news anchor whose voice was muted, but the subtitles didn't hide his enjoyment of the story. *It is unknown at this time if Lancelot of the Round Table Knights will continue his hero career,* the subtitles read. *San Arbor citizens are asking if he is even fit for the position if he can be defeated by something as small as a fire. At Channel-12 we have to ask, are the Round Table Knights as super as they want us to believe?*

Abigail sighed heavily, forcing her frustration and ability to ignite out of her system. The news cast switched to a press conference with Mayor Owen Benton and her anger returned as cherry-red sparks fell to the tiled floor. She could hear his voice in her head as she read the subtitles. *What were the heroes even doing? San Arbor Volunteer Fire Department had the situation under control while the Knights were doing who knows what inside. It's difficult to trust the fire controlling one when she let her own teammate get burned up. These superheroes need to leave the hero work to San Arbor's real—*

Heat boiled inside Abigail. Steam pushed between her lips like a roiling kettle, and she spat a string of blue fire at the mounted television. The melted plastic and electronic components plopped onto the floor in steaming heaps. Her arms still shook violently at her sides.

"Shannon's not going to be happy about that tomorrow." Excalibur tried to joke behind her.

Abigail growled. "I'll bring her the TV from the break room."

"What got you heated up?"

Abigail turned. The rest of her aggression momentarily disappeared seeing her old boss outside his metal suit of armor. If being a weapons master didn't work out, Excalibur, who went by the name Aaron outside his mask, could easily have a job as a running back on the San Arbor football team.

"Benton," Abigail answered. "The whole world. Did you know someone snuck into Lance's room to take a photo of him all banged up?"

Excalibur nodded. "He was transferred right after the photo went viral."

"Transferred? Transferred to where?"

"An HRC safehouse with a nursing staff to watch him. He can recover there without all the noise. He's safe there."

"Why didn't anyone tell me?" Abigail wanted to stomp her foot. "I could have helped protect him."

"That's exactly why," Excalibur answered, and held up a hand to stop Abigail from interrupting him. "It was King's decision, and I agree with it. You blasted a TV at the mention of it, can you imagine what you'd do if you caught the person taking the photo?"

Abigail hated the image that flashed in her mind, but she didn't deny it. "Do I get the address to the safe house?"

Excalibur nodded. "I'll send it to you, but you have to promise you won't go over there tonight. Lance needs his rest. The nurse had him pretty sedated when I saw him last."

"I promise." Abigail made a cross over her heart, and for good measure added, "I couldn't go tonight anyway. I have dinner plans."

Excalibur smiled and shoved her toward the door. "Good! Go be normal for an evening."

"We can't be normal," she reminded him.

"But we can have our secret identities. I'll see you tomorrow."

The lingering thoughts of the fire, of Lancelot, of Benton, of the media vanished when Abigail saw Thomas standing inside the restaurant. He wore a suit jacket and stained blue jeans that should have looked tacky, but Abigail still melted when he caught her staring. She became putty in his hands when he pulled her close and kissed her hello. The waitress cleared her throat twice before they could follow her to their table.

An Italian CD played on loop on the overhead speakers. A second waiter circled the dining room ready to refill any water glasses with his twisted spouted bottle. The fake ivy plants hanging around the arch ways needed dusting. The single candle burning between Abigail and Thomas dripped wax onto a saucer already covered in seven different colors of wax. Abigail watched the fire reflect in Thomas's eyes, and she found it hard not to submerge herself in their emerald wastelands.

Thomas covered her hand with his own, and his touch broke her self-induced trance. She blinked until his crooked smile came into focus. "You stare any longer and I might catch fire, babe."

His smile was infectious. "It's just so good to see you again."

"Come on, it was barely a day." Thomas blushed slightly. "Don't tell me you're a clinger."

"If I was, don't you think you'd know by now?"

"I'd hope so."

Abigail peeked at the menu. "What made you want to come here?"

"I like the way it looks." Thomas waved at their waiter as he circled back toward them. "Heard their champagne was good, too."

"This is a big change from slushies and popcorn."

"We'll still get those." Thomas ordered two flutes of champagne from the waiter. "I'm just keeping you on your toes."

"I don't think you can surprise me, anymore."

Thomas grinned. "I'm hoping I can once more."

Abigail was about to tease him, but her cellphone interrupted the reply. She removed it from her pocket and silenced the unknown number. She sat it on the tabletop, and it vibrated again against her water glass. Flipping it over she saw the same number flash across the screen.

"Important?"

"If it is, they'll leave a message." Abigail glared at the phone as it rang a third time.

Thomas grabbed her hand. He rubbed his thumb over her knuckles. They were wrapped in brown tape from her crash through the window yesterday. Abigail watched him, waited for him to say something. He didn't speak, he didn't move, not until the waiter returned with two flutes. The champagne's bubbles popped excitedly between them.

"Abigail, you mean the world to me, and I—"

Abigail's heart jumped into her throat but was squashed back down as her phone vibrated again. She snatched it from the table and snarled into the receiver.

"Is this Avalon?" a frightened voice asked on the other line.

Abigail pulled the phone away and really looked at the number. Her HRC extension flashed alongside the number. "Who's calling?"

"I'm Lancelot's nurse. You were his emergency contact." Abigail began to place the voice. She saw the pink scrubbed nurse with the pens in her hair from the ER room. She must be the one assigned to him at the safe house. "Things are getting worse, and we will have to intubate—"

"What?" Abigail pulled her other hand from Thomas needing both to hold the phone. Gravity seemed to intensify around her. "But he was fine, he just needed rest."

"That was the best case scenario, but injuries can always change. I need to know—"

"I'm on my way." Abigail stood and bumped the table, sloshing their drinks over the edge of the glass. "I'm sorry," she apologized after ending the call. For spilling the drinks, for stopping her dinner, for not rescuing Lancelot sooner, for everything.

Thomas sighed but it ended with a dark laugh. He swallowed his champagne in two gulps and joined her in the aisle. "You'll never stop surprising me, babe. I'll grab us a ride and meet you out front."

Abigail dumped a handful of cash on the table not caring if it was enough for their bill and dashed to the front door. She was unwrapping a spare mask from her pocket when a black motorcycle sped in front of her. Thomas flipped the helmet's visor up and patted the remaining strip of seat behind him. Abigail tucked herself as close to him as she could and wrapped her arms tightly around him.

"Where'd you get this?"

"Parking lot!" Thomas shouted over the engine roar. "Didn't think you'd care."

She should have, but she knew this stolen bike would be quicker than any legal transportation at the moment. "Go West! We need to get to Mulberry Road."

Chapter Fifteen

The motorcycle's kickstand was barely on the ground before Abigail jumped off the back and ran to the safe house. The two-story house matched the others on the sleepy cul-de-sac loop. The four different locks on the door did not match the rest of the neighborhood's minimal security system. Abigail inputted the last code and the door finally opened.

Her eyes darted around the unfamiliar house. The modern decor didn't fit with her pounding heart. The silk flowers in the vase should have been sharpened knives, the shag rug between two couches should have been covered in blood. Every unknown shadow was a killer coming for Lancelot. From the stairs she saw the glow of lights. She launched herself up them two at a time.

"Nurse! Nurse!" Abigail shouted into the hallway. "Where's Lance? Where is he?"

The same nurse from the hospital emerged from one of the upstairs bedrooms. Her hair fell around her face and her eyes mirrored Abigail's panic. The red on the nurse's hands was the disaster she was searching for downstairs. The devastating scent of burned flesh crashed into Abigail like a tidal wave.

"Go."

Thomas' low rumbling voice brought Abigail back to the ground. Her feet could move again. She moved the nurse out of the doorway and found an unconscious Lancelot on a bed. The gauze around him was removed, and a sickening mixture of black and red discoloration painted his arms and chest where the burns had worsened. It looked like his skin was replaced with molten rock. The machines hooked to him screeched alarm codes.

The door shut behind her and trapped the severity of his condition inside the room with her.

"You have to save him," Abigail said to the nurse, but it was Thomas who stood across the bed from her. The motorcycle helmet hid his face.

He reached his hands over Lancelot's body and blue smoke poured out of his fingers. The smoke encased Lancelot's damaged arms. Abigail watched the miracle in awe. The smoke pulled the burns away leaving pink flesh underneath. Thomas' fingers accepted the burns, and it inked all ten of his fingers a dark purple.

"I should have done this the moment you told me." Thomas' voice sounded far away as the helmet muffled the sound.

"It's dangerous." Abigail replied unable to look away from her sidekick.

The blue smoke crawled across Lancelot's chest removing his burns like an eraser. It seeped into his mouth and nose and absorbed the internal damage. The more Thomas healed, the larger his staining became. The inky darkness stretched over his palms and up his wrists, the monitors hooked into Lancelot quieted down as his oxygen levels raised.

"I'm counting on you not to tell anyone."

Abigail assumed Thomas was smirking under the helmet, but it was hard to be certain. She could only nod. The blue smoke returned to Thomas' outstretched hands and Lancelot inhaled deeply. "You're incredible."

Thomas didn't reply. Abigail only saw her reflection in the helmet's visor. A fist beat against the locked door followed by shouts from the nurse. The miraculously healed Lancelot between Abigail and Thomas was unexplainable. Abigail didn't have the power set capable of doing anything like it. Thomas wasn't supposed to have powers. Unregistered abilities would be a fast ticket downtown to the SAPD. A permanent ticket away from her.

"The window." Abigail whispered.

"I'll meet you at home."

Abigail waited for the motorcycle to start up before unlocking the door. The nurse pushed her away and checked on Lancelot. After examining his body and the machines, she turned to Abigail with awe, shock, and anger all fighting for room on her face. Her bloodied hands looked ready to clamp around Abigail's neck.

"I had to." Abigail tried to fit the entire situation into one explanation.

"But how?" The nurse looked back to Lancelot's pink arms.

"I can't tell you, and I need you not to tell anyone either." Abigail took the nurse's hands, ignoring the wet stickiness pushing between their joined fingers. "Please, this has to stay between us."

"I have no way to explain this medically."

"Then don't."

"I need to write something in his medical report."

"Then lie."

The nurse sighed and pulled her hands out of the hero's grip. "I'm only agreeing to this because if you hadn't done whatever you did, he would be dead. His lungs were failing."

Abigail swallowed hard. Superheroes weren't supposed to die. They were supposed to be invincible. But, if that was the case, why did Lancelot look so small wrapped in a flowered quilt? The bed dwarfed him. The shadows made his face look something more skeletal than man. His soft eyes looked mushy and unfocused. His feeble fingers wrapped around Abigail's hand, but he didn't have the strength to hold on to them.

"Hey Avy."

Abigail dropped to her knees, fighting the urge to pull him into her arms. He had been so close to death, and she had never known. If it wasn't for Thomas, she would be looking at a corpse.

"You're going to be okay," she declared, but tears still prickled her eyes.

"I knew I would be."

"He still needs rest," reminded the nurse.

"I won't fight that," Lancelot grinned. "I feel like shit right now."

"You should sleep," Abigail said. "You'll feel better in the morning."

"Will you be here?"

Abigail tucked a matted strand of hair away from his eyes; his skin was cold. "I'll be waiting for you at HQ. I'm going to have to do all your paperwork while you're here."

"Maybe I'll stay a few extra days, then."

Abigail returned his smile. "We'll miss you if you do."

Lancelot turned his head to find the nurse. "I don't think guilt tripping me is good for my health, right?"

The nurse looked away from the monitors. "If your condition keeps improving like this, I think you'll be fine."

Lancelot sighed and turned back to Abigail. "Guess I'll be seeing you at work, then."

"Don't say it like it's a bad thing." She squeezed his hand. "Go to sleep. I'll come see you tomorrow."

"Thanks for saving me, hero." Lancelot released her hand.

Abigail lingered outside his door until he fell asleep. She waited a few more minutes watching his healed chest rise and fall. He still looked too close to death. Eaten alive by the very thing she cherished.

Chapter Sixteen

It was cold when Abigail exited the safe house an hour later. Her T-shirt did little to ward off the chill partly created by the night and partly by her mind. She would need a backup plan in case the nurse couldn't keep quiet. Thomas would need an alibi in case the investigation ever pointed in his direction. In a perfect world, Lancelot's recovery would be cited as a miracle and be left alone, but this world was not perfect, and people would demand answers.

Perhaps the chill was the reason Abigail found the fire so easily. Drawn to the heat like a lovesick bug to the zapper-lamp. Both drawn to a thing screaming disaster in their faces. It was a small house on the top of the street that burned. The for sale sign pounded in the yard welcomed strangers to their "new home!" while red flames dancing behind the first-floor windows turned away potential buyers.

Abigail ran up the driveway and kicked the door in. The sound of the wooden frame breaking was devoured by the roaring fire. The minimal furniture pieces left for house showings turned to cinders. Adrenaline surged through her veins and supercharged the hero's abilities. She shot flames from her hands and overpowered the rogue ones licking up the dining room table and couch cushions. The house fire was smothered after a few minutes and Abigail wandered inside, waving black smoke away from her face and looking for the start of the fire.

This was real hero work. Not locked in an office waiting for her patrol day or a request from San Arbor.

Something metallic caught her attention in the corner of the living room. The gunmetal exterior twinkled in the dying coals surrounding it. Abigail nudged the small box with her shoe before leaning down to better examine it. The metal sides started to melt but otherwise the device was intact. Through the smoldering holes, Abigail spied something that didn't belong in a realtor's open house: a tangle of wires wrapping around a chunk of rock. Abigail sniffed the box and her nose scrunched at the smell of manure.

This fire was no accident.

She exited the house, calling the non-emergency line to the HRC and reported her findings. Next, she called Thomas who answered on the third ring.

"Do you still have that bike?"

"Would you arrest me if I said yes?"

Abigail heard traffic through the receiver. "I'd ask you for a ride."

"Where to?"

"HQ." She walked down the driveway cradling the phone against her shoulder. She continued to examine the metal box in her hands. "I think I'm onto something. About the fires. Have you seen anything to make you suspect arson?"

Thomas took a moment before answering, "Nothing that I've seen, but a different department handles that."

"I found a contraption that smells like a farm. I'm going to have Merlin examine the core inside. I'll bet twenty bucks it's ammonium nitrate."

"Where are you?"

"Still on Mulberry, walking toward the lights at the intersection."

"I'll be there soon."

Thomas arrived before the HRC could send their investigators, but Abigail didn't wait for them. She held the most important piece of evidence and waiting around for a cleanup crew wasn't going to help. She placed the contraption inside the saddle bag on the bike and nestled herself around Thomas. He revved the engine, and the tires screamed against the pavement before speeding onto the main street. His pale hands looked out of place steering the black handles, but he expertly commanded the motorcycle downtown and onto the lawn of the Hero Relief Center.

Once stationary, Thomas flipped the helmet's visor up as Abigail retrieved her box. "Can I take a look at that?"

"I don't want your fingerprints on it."

Thomas stared at her with his mouth slightly agape. Half a word struggled to escape.

"I just don't… It's just a precaution." Abigail's palms sweated. "I don't want anything to accidently point to you."

Thomas slowly grinned and his unspoken word turned into a snicker. "Your prints are okay, though?"

"I found it, of course my prints would be on it."

Thomas crossed his arms. "Doesn't that break some kind of chain of custody?"

"Probably." Abigail silently cursed herself for disobeying her own training. She hoped it wouldn't have a negative effect on her or her team. "I'll sort that out later once we figure out what it is."

"Can I assume you won't be home tonight?"

Abigail tried to smile. "Not if I want to solve this case."

Thomas looked up at the dark corporate building behind them. "Are your friends even home?"

"Someone has to be."

"If you need a ride home, you know who to call."

Abigail tried to kiss him through the helmet but only managed bumping into his nose. "I don't think you should be driving this anymore."

"I think a certain hero will let it slide." Thomas smirked.

Abigail leaned in again and after a successful kiss, she said, "I'll see you tomorrow. I promise."

Thomas nodded, flipped the visor back down, and sped away on the stolen motorcycle. The possible fire accelerant in Abigail's hand made turning a blind eye to him easy, and she entered the HRC. The side door accepted her passcode, and she rode the elevator to the eleventh floor. The overhead lights powered on as she crossed the motion sensors, but the floor was otherwise dark and quiet. Without her Avalon costume and sword, she almost felt like an imposter stalking the empty floor. Abigail stopped at Merlin's office and, unsurprisingly, found it empty.

She'll be here in the morning. Abigail told herself and retreated to her office. The lack of Merlin and her intense knowledge on all things chemical did delay Abigail's plan, but she'd make sure everything else was ready before morning. She powered on the computer at her desk and opened all the reports on the recent San Arbor fires. She'd comb through all the data, find something she missed, connect the accelerant to them, too.

Abigail didn't factor the last two days of negligible sleep, and as she read over the digital reports her eyes grew too heavy to tell the letters apart from each other. She was asleep, drooling on the folder of old reports, before she finished reading the Twin Leaf Bar report.

The dreamscape crumbled around Abigail's subconscious avatar. A maskless Avalon directed traffic as the buildings around the intersection burned in brilliant purple flames. Twinkling embers formed a crown around her head while others burned through the hoods of cars. The dream was a disaster, but the sleep was peaceful, until the hand on her shoulder shook her a second time and dissolved the space completely.

Abigail jolted up. Her head bashed against her chair in a panic to remember where she was. Dim daylight streaked the floor from the office windows.

"If you were evicted there are better places to sleep than here."

Abigail focused on King Arthur perched on the edge of her desk. He removed his hand from her shoulder and smiled. It was as bright as the sunrise. Both hurt Abigail's eyes and she ran the back of her hand across them.

"What time is it?"

"Almost seven."

"Is Merlin here yet?"

"No," King Arthur answered. "Is that why you stayed here all night?"

Abigail shook her head. "I found something in a fire last night. I wanted her to look at it." She handed King Arthur the device. The scent of manure rushed her senses awake like she inhaled ground coffee beans instead. "I'm pretty sure it's an accelerant."

King Arthur examined Abigail's crucial piece of evidence. "It looks just like the others."

"The others?" Abigail's heart skipped.

"The other incendiary devices." He spoke so smoothly, like the news wasn't currently shaking Abigail to her core.

"There were more incendiary devices? Where?"

"The last few fires."

Abigail glanced at her computer screen. The reports were still opened. "There was nothing from the SAFD. How did they miss them? How did you know?"

"They didn't miss them." King rotated the device as casually as a child would a toy. "The switches were found during their overhaul phases. I just made sure they stayed out of the reports."

Abigail gasped. "You stole them?"

King Arthur laughed dryly. "It's not stealing if they don't remember having it."

"You used your powers."

"Of course."

"Why?"

King Arthur sighed, lowering the incendiary device to the desk. "The heroes are under attack by the mayor. If we're not on top of everything, then this life of ours will be over. If Benton turns San Arbor against us, then what do you think will happen to us?"

Abigail was silent.

"'Xcal would be fine, I'm sure. He's done a great deal to keep his identity a secret. Lancelot and I would face some difficulties, but our powers aren't as flashy as others. We'd be able to lay low, move cities if needed. Think of you and Merlin. What do you think would happen if the media didn't have eyes on two individuals with such *dangerous* abilities? When the city stops trusting us, we become dangerous. To them, anyway."

Abigail was quick with her response. "If they learn we're hiding evidence from the first responders then they won't trust us. That was part of the ordinance, we all work together."

"If the arsonist is caught, why does it matter who did it?"

"It shouldn't matter."

"Exactly, but we don't have the same luxury of keeping our jobs if we don't get them first. All eyes are on us, Abby. You want to keep being a hero, don't you?"

Abigail swallowed hard. She felt stuck between a rock and a hard place. King Arthur's sunshine-powered smile was too sweet. It soured her stomach. "Can I see the full reports?"

"Of course." King Arthur smiled wider and patted her head. "I need my fire expert on the case."

"Then why didn't you tell me sooner?"

King Arthur was immune to her growl. "I was going to after Alexander's, when the switches became a pattern, but you were distracted."

"This same device burned Lancelot?"

King Arthur nodded. "There were five total, six counting this new one. Think you can figure it out?"

"Of course."

"I'll have the reports printed for you today. You can start going over them after your patrol." King Arthur stood but didn't leave the intimate space. Abigail felt trapped between him and the wall. "I don't have to remind you to keep my decisions secret, correct?"

Abigail nodded, then said aloud, "Of course not, sir."

"If it truly bothers you, I can undo my mind manipulations. Make everyone remember what they really saw." King Arthur sounded predatory; his sharp fangs trained for Abigail's throat. Leaning down, his threat continued, "I'd have to restore the memories of those officers from the First Financial Bank, too. If I had to restore the memories at SAFD it would only be fair for me to do the same for SAPD, don't you think?"

Abigail swallowed down the memory at the bank where a body bag zipped closed over the man she killed. It was in self-defense. She knew that. But Benton and the city wouldn't be so sure. Her flames were dangerous. If King Arthur wanted to, he'd make sure they appeared monstrous and murderous.

He'd use them to burn her life to the ground.

"It doesn't bother me, you're just protecting us," she lied, finding it hard to breathe inside the cage he constructed.

"Exactly." King Arthur finally stepped away from Abigail. "I'm glad you see it my way."

Chapter Seventeen

The third seat on the left of the Round Table was empty. The missing body weighed heavily in Abigail's mind. The silence around the seat, the lack of the squeaking bolts and muffled rolling of wheels, only amplified the feeling. Every natural tug on Abigail's hair pained her. When a curl fell over her shoulder, she reached out for the familiar sensation of Lancelot's ability but found nothing. The coldness that followed the realization was arctic compared to the usual chill of his psychic touch. Her sidekick remained hospitalized. Recovering from the burns she couldn't protect him from.

Her sidekick. Her responsibility. Her failure.

The Round Table meeting continued around her. A box of doughnuts circled through the Knights and President Samuels. A cardboard tray of coffee cups with the matching logo of the doughnut shop followed. The breakfast was either a current sponsor of the HRC, or a kind gesture from a co-worker. Abigail didn't know, and she didn't care. Her breakfast remained untouched. Her coffee cooled in her unnaturally warm hands. Her mind couldn't focus on President Samuels' opening remarks.

All she saw was Lancelot's burned body. The craters in his chest. The charred remains of his arms. The blackness of his hands. The violent red of his face. The inhumane screams he unleashed in the back of the ambulance. It didn't matter that Thomas healed him. She couldn't seem to hold onto that image of him.

Lancelot knew the dangers of becoming a hero. Every Knight signed the same waiver. Every hero knew the risks. They were all fools in believing a mask could protect them.

Abigail reflectively reached for hers, two fingers resting against the red material around her eyes. The thin fabric contained a thousand microchips, she would never understand how they worked. The ends tied together into a cute bow on the back of her head, housing a proximity sensor and the power supply to the microchips. She remembered the first time she put the mask on. The pride she had for herself, the excitement to do good, the thrill of being a hero.

She was there when Lancelot suited up as a Knight for the first time, too. He was young, full of the same excitement. She was proud for him. The seat on her left hadn't been empty since that day.

Her sidekick. Her responsibility.

"You ready?"

Abigail blinked her vision back into focus. The meeting had ended. The room had emptied. All but her, the last doughnut and Excalibur. A folder sat on the table before her. She flipped to the first page and didn't understand any of the information on the page.

"What is this?"

"Plans for the department redesign, what Samuels was talking about?" Excalibur's incorporeal voice trickled through his helmet, but the chill was lost on Abigail. She'd grown use to the metallic sound a while ago. "About the new medical wing?"

Abigail peeked at Lancelot's chair. She could picture him leaning back, feet on the table, doughnuts and coffee floating around him. Unburned and safe.

"Avalon, you're not listening."

"I keep seeing Lance." Abigail turned to the ironclad Knight. "I missed the whole meeting. I'm sorry."

Excalibur's medieval helmet tilted down as if he were frowning. "He's going to make a full recovery. You remember what the doctors said, after his turn-around he's going to be fine."

It was still hard for Abigail to picture Lancelot's healed skin. The damages came to her mind far too easily. "He shouldn't have gotten burned to begin with. I was with him, and I couldn't protect him."

"Lancelot made the decisions to break protocol and put himself in that position." Excalibur raised a hand, silencing Abigail so he could continue. "You pulled him from that fire, you have to know he would've been worse without you there."

"He wouldn't have been there in the first place if I wasn't there."

Excalibur laughed once. "That kid wants to run into trouble as much as you do. It's what makes him a good Knight. It makes you a good Knight too, Avalon."

Abigail snuck a final look at the empty chair. "I'll feel better when he's back. When I catch this arsonist."

"That's the Dragon Slayer I trained."

"What'd I miss from the meeting? Besides this?" Abigail tapped the medical wing folder.

"Patrol routes. I hope you're not too independent to be working with your old boss again."

Abigail smiled. "Should I grab the phone to post live updates like old times too?"

"I'll make an intern do that." Excalibur pulled Abigail from her chair and guided her past Lancelot's empty one.

San Arbor was peaceful. People inside the residential district stopped Avalon and Excalibur for photos and autographs more often than to report trouble. The peace could be attributed to many things. The crime rates for the city had been decreasing since the Call To Action ordinance passed and The Round Table Knights became San Arbor's only hero corporation. The presence of two heroes on the street helped deter would-be criminals. The sun shined brilliantly so there were few shadows for filth to hide in.

Abigail wanted to chase leads on the arsonist. She wanted to explore the other incendiary devices King Arthur kept locked in his office. Abigail wanted to destroy any doubt in her head that could lead her into thinking he wasn't a good hero. He was doing what he had to to protect them. Just as she would do whatever she needed to protect the city.

Instead of doing any of that, Abigail posed with Excalibur and a small boy while his mother took their picture. Ensuring the trust of the citizens was every bit as important as hero work despite the lackluster feel of it. Excalibur made sure no fan was left empty handed. He quizzed the boy about his school and asked him about his favorite subject. Abigail admired him for his dedication. She was also grateful for the constant distraction keeping her mind off Lancelot.

She knew he would love a day like today, though.

"Avalon, check this out!"

Abigail promised she'd recreate this perfect day for him after he fully recovered.

"What's up, boss?"

Excalibur turned his bulky form to reveal a group of young women. By the uniform two of them wore, they were from the neighborhood high school. The third member of the group caused Abigail to grin. She didn't wear the matching tan khakis and maroon polos as her friends. Her uniform was replaced by a handmade version of Avalon's costume. The girl wore it all; the dark pleated skirt, the red chest plate, the golden gauntlets, and the beautiful red mask tied into a bow.

"Wow!" Abigail said excitedly. "You look amazing."

"She even has a foam sword at home," one of the other girls stated.

The mini-Avalon nodded but didn't meet Abigail's gaze.

"What's your name?" Abigail asked.

"Melissa."

"It's so cool to meet you, Melissa." Abigail used her media voice, bright and cherry, but meant every word.

"You're my favorite Knight."

"Ouch." Excalibur joked behind them.

"Thank you." Abigail ignored her boss. "Your costume looks amazing."

"You like it?" Melissa looked up at Abigail, straightening her back to better present the outfit. "I made it myself."

"You made this?" Abigail asked in disbelief. She'd seen Avalon Halloween costumes downgrade the outfit into a tunic dress, and even the HRC approved merchandise didn't always get the dragon emblem right on the chest plate. Melissa's could pass for the very one Abigail currently wore. "It's incredible."

"My mom taught me how to sew so I could make it."

"You should've heard her complaining about the costumes in stores," chimed one of the other girls. "Melissa kept saying she could make a better one."

"She definitely did," Abigail said. "Can I get a picture of you?"

"Of me?" Melissa's head shot up with surprise.

"Well, *with* you," she said. " 'Xcal can take it."

"I would love that!"

Abigail slid her phone from her boot and handed it to Excalibur, then pulled her sword from its sheath and held it out toward Melissa. "You said your sword was at home, would you like to hold mine?"

Melissa accepted the blade as easily as Abigail first had from Excalibur. She gave it a small twirl at her side and readied it in front of her. She looked like an action figure.

"One final touch." Abigail blew against the tip of the blade and the sword ignited in blue fire. "It won't go pass the hilt."

If Melissa feared the flames, she didn't show it. She looked over her shoulder and shouted at her friends. They quickly snapped a few of their own photos.

Abigail stood beside Melissa, mimicked her stance with a cherry-red fireball in hand and they both smiled at Excalibur.

"I want to be just like you," Melissa said while Abigail extinguished her sword and returned it to the sheath. "I can't breathe fire, but I want to be a hero too. Your flames are so pretty, and nothing scares you. You're so cool."

"You don't need any special powers to be brave," Abigail replied kindly. "It's a good heart that makes a hero, not the powers."

"A cool costume does help." Excalibur joked behind Abigail.

"I like yours just fine." Abigail told Melissa. "It was amazing to meet you."

"I think I'm supposed to say that."

Looking into the bright eyes behind the mask, Abigail knew she needed this more than the kid. She would continue to be a hero. Abigail would become a better hero every time she donned her cape. If San Arbor didn't need her, she knew at least one kid needed Avalon.

"I hope to see you again."

"Oh my gosh, I do too!"

Abigail followed Excalibur down the sidewalk, a wide smile cracking her face in half. Inspiration surged through her. Her steps seemed lighter. She skipped ahead of Excalibur and uploaded the photo to her social medias. A moment after the upload completed, a social media app's user @KnightLancelot gave it a big thumbs up.

Today was turning into a perfect day.

"Seems like you needed that," Excalibur commented.

"I think I did."

"I'm happy we chased that funk off of you," Excalibur chuckled. "It was starting to stink."

Abigail slapped his shoulder, but the armored knight wouldn't feel it. The pair continued down the street. They passed a mini mart, jumped over a puddle in front of a carwash, waved to a pair of kids sitting on a fire escape. Abigail returned a silly face from a toddler inside a car at a stop light, and turned down a street marked by a fast food joint offering toy heroes with every kid's meal.

Every part of San Arbor was beautiful. From the high-rises of downtown, the nature preserve, the bar district, the residential clusters, the historical center, every piece inspired Abigail to be better. While she dreamed of being a hero, she never imagined serving a city like this one. Her dreams hardly left her township four hours away. Abigail knew her younger self who ran through her neighborhood in a bath towel cape would be proud of the hero she was today.

She would continue to be a hero that both could be proud of.

Turning off a different street, she saw the danger before anything else. The colorful art gallery signs and the outside display of dresses from a clothing store distorted in her peripheral vision. She zoned in on the smoking box truck outside a deli. The back door was shut but gray smoke steeped out the tiny openings along the track. Someone exited the deli holding a fire extinguisher. The driver of the truck jogged to collect it.

Sparks fell from Abigail's fingers as she saw the situation unfold before the driver could set the first domino into place. He struggled with the extinguisher and granted Abigail a few extra seconds.

"If they open the door, the truck will flood with oxygen and explode."

"Go!"

Abigail sprinted forward at Excalibur's command. The sidewalk bubbled under each step as she used her flames to propel her. The people couldn't hear her shouting. The driver readied the extinguisher while the other prepared to open the door. The padlock dropped to the ground. The door was shoved open.

Abigail tackled the man away from the door just as a fireball flew out of the back of the truck. Red flames reached into the sky as more flames tumbled out of the box truck. Burning pieces of cargo rained down in the parking lot. Both Abigail and the man slid along the pavement before coming to a stop. The man's arms were red and gnarled. The injury clawed around the side of his face. Despite the man's dark mustache and twenty extra years, Lancelot's face flashed in front of Abigail.

His scream echoed in the back of her mind and deafened the fire behind her.

"Avalon!" The cold metal of Excalibur's glove pressed against her cheek and shocked Abigail away from her memories. "Avalon, stop the fire."

Abigail released the man to Excalibur and found the box truck driver trying to kill the flames with the fire extinguisher. He wasn't close enough to the source for the foam to be effective. It only created a slippery puddle on the asphalt. Abigail took the extinguisher from him and jumped into the truck. The flames greeted her like an old friend as the fire snaked around her limbs before meeting the resistance of her fireproof skin and costume. They left her for the easy cardboard consumables left in the truck.

Once inside, putting the fire out was easy. Abigail emptied the extinguisher and the chemical scent of the foam mixed horribly with the singed smell of deli meats and cheeses. The deli would have to wait for a new delivery. The product inside wasn't even suitable for pigs. She snuffed the remaining flames with her own and in minutes the terrible blaze was gone. Abigail was about to leap out of the box truck when something stopped her.

She picked up the tiny black box from behind the wheel casing of the truck. It was tangled with several wires ripped up from the floorboard. There was no denying the gasoline smell creeping up from the hole, or the sickening scent of manure clinging to the remains. The charred exterior of the box flaked away in her hands. The fire and the extinguisher had destroyed it, but Abigail knew what it was.

An incendiary device.

Abigail dusted her soot-covered gloves together and left the truck.

"I have no idea what happened," the driver tried to explain. His eyes bounced between the two heroes and the burnt truck. "How can something like that just start smoking?"

"Looks like there's a mechanical issue by the left tire," Abigail lied. "I could smell gas while inside. Is this an older truck?"

"Yeah, but a reliable one."

"I'd get it looked at." Abigail concluded her diagnoses and walked over to the man she tackled. He sat on the curb and didn't look at all like someone who had burned their arms and face. "Sir, can I give you a ride to the hospital?"

"I don't need one."

"Your burns?"

"These?" The man rotated his arms for Abigail to see. They weren't burned as she feared; the man's arms were discolored by road rash. Blood, gravel, and skin mixed over his arms, but the wounds looked superficial. "Got them from our fall. I appreciate you saving me, but next time can you knock me into a mattress or something?"

Abigail wasn't sure if the man was trying to joke. His mustache hid any emotion she tried to read from his face. "I'll pass your suggestion along to the boss."

The man sent her off with a nod, and Abigail returned to Excalibur. She remained silent while he finished his wellness checks and farewells. The moment their backs were turned to the deli, Abigail jogged across the street.

"What's the rush?" Excalibur caught up to her on the opposite sidewalk.

"We need to report back to King," Abigail whispered. "This wasn't an accident. I found an incendiary device."

"Like the others?"

Abigail almost lost her footing on the curb. "You know about the others?"

She couldn't tell what expression was under his helmet. She desperately wished he wasn't wearing it.

"King pulled Merlin and I aside this morning to fill us in. Told us you found one at last night's fire. That he found one from Alexander's but wasn't sure what it was until your discovery. It was a lucky break you were at the housefire to make the connection."

"Yeah." Abigail swallowed. "Real lucky."

Excalibur tapped on his communicator. "I'll call in a heads up." He was silent as he listened to the radio. "King and Merlin are at a call now. Another fire."

"And another switch, I'd bet."

Chapter Eighteen

It was hard for Abigail to look at anything but Lancelot as he sat across from her. Three days ago, his arms were darker than the midnight sky. The damaged skin resembling molten rock and the pain she knew he felt would've been unbearable without the morphine drip. Now the burns were just a memory, a bad dream that couldn't have been real. Lancelot's arms were completely normal now, the baby-pink flesh healed and hardened into what it was before the Alexander's fire. The miracle was still a secret, the healing credited to some higher power, but Abigail knew without Thomas her sidekick would've died.

"Hey? Avalon?"

Abigail blinked, looking away from Lancelot's perfect arms and found his head cocked to the side across the desk from her.

"Are you feeling okay? I've asked you like a dozen questions and you haven't said anything."

"I… I wasn't listening. I'm sorry, Lance. What's up?"

He chuckled. "If I didn't know better, I'd say you don't want me back."

"That's so not true," Abigail smiled. "It's just hard to believe you're here already. Are *you* feeling okay?"

"I feel great, Avy." Lancelot flexed his arms theatrically to prove his point. "Seriously, whatever happened at that safe house, I feel amazing."

"Just don't run into any more fires, okay?"

"I'll try not to." He snapped his fingers. "That reminds me, I had an idea for a tag-team move for us. Can I show you later?"

Abigail tapped the desk between them. "We really need to find a lead on this first."

Two more fires were set in the last three days. A laundromat was left in ruins as the dryers reacted to the heat and exploded leaving two injured, and an apartment leasing office on the South side was set ablaze in the middle of the night. The same accelerant device was found at each crime scene, and the San Arbor Fire Department still didn't know about them. Abigail felt dirty running the case in secret, but her choice had already been made.

Not by her.

The quicker she caught this arsonist, the better she and her city would be, and the less lies she'd be responsible for.

"There's not really a pattern to them," Lancelot commented while flipping through the case files. "The places don't make sense either. It's everything from a bookstore to a factory, to a little diner. It doesn't make any sense."

"Either these places mean something to the arsonist, or they're just easy targets."

"A lot of these fires started in the daytime when people were there. I'm surprised no one has seen anything yet."

"The incendiary device. It could have a timer."

"I wish we had one that wasn't so burnt up. Has Merlin found anything useful?"

"Just what the fuel is," Abigail sighed. "She's running purchasing orders on the type of manure right now."

Lancelot stretched his arms high above his head, then strummed them against the desk. "Maybe we'll find something useful outside. Want to search the crime scenes again?"

"We've been there enough this week." Abigail answered but didn't look up from the files spread around them. She ran her hands through her hair.

"We could get lunch while we're out."

"I'm not hungry."

"Dinner then." Lancelot burst out. "I want to take you to dinner. Tonight."

Abigail slowly looked up. Lancelot was blushing but did not look away from her. "What?"

He reached across the desk, slipping his hand around hers. His hand was clammy, but it held onto hers tightly. "I'm asking you on a date, Avalon."

"Lance, no."

"I've checked the contract," he quickly defended. "It's not against company policy. It'll be fun, I promise."

"Lance, I'm in a relationship." Abigail pulled her hand away. "With someone else."

His blush darkened. The pinks of nervous love turning to the reds of embarrassment. "Why didn't you say anything? I wouldn't have asked if I knew."

"I didn't tell you for the same reason you don't know my real name," Abigail explained. "I have to protect my family. It's a secret identity, remember?"

"But we're a team."

"We are, but it's easier this way. When your year with us is over, you may be recruited to a different company, or to a different city."

"You'll tell me your name once I'm a hero?"

Abigail admired his undefeated smile. "Maybe."

A cloud of silence encased them. The flipping of files and scratching of pens created an awkward soundtrack for the shot down sidekick. It was a lot easier for Abigail to keep her eyes on her own work now. Suddenly, the lingering psychic touches and teasing made sense. She felt foolish for not seeing Lancelot's real intentions. She hoped she hadn't led him on in some way or given him the wrong impression.

"Is it the firefighter?" he asked after a few minutes, his voice sounding as if he were chewing rocks.

"I wouldn't tell you if it was."

"If it is, you should bring him in for the case. I bet someone like him, who's seen a lot of fires, would see something we're missing."

"What did you say?" Abigail looked up.

"Just that someone with a better understanding of arson could see something else?"

Or someone who had a better understanding of crime and villainy.

"Lance, you're a genius! Of course." Abigail leapt up, knocking several files to the ground. As she rounded her desk, her cape threatened to knock several more to the floor.

"Where are you going?" Lancelot levitated the files before they crashed onto the tile.

"To see an old friend."

"Should I come?"

"Not this time," Abigail paused at the door. "Keep looking over the files, please? I want someone here in case Merlin finds something about the devices."

And she thought some separation today would help them return to their normality.

Lancelot frowned, lowering the messy files back to the desk. Pages and photos dangled from the folders. "We're going over the combo move when you get back, though."

Abigail was about to shake her head but couldn't deny his pout a second time. "Fine. It better be cool, though."

"Don't worry. It's *hot*."

The house of retired hero Volcanic hadn't changed since Abigail last visited. Its small frame was still stuck between two taller buildings which blocked the light and removed the need for curtains. The front porch still had terracotta flowerpots with no flowers on either side of the stairs. The perfectly laid black shingles matched the perfectly hung black shutters, and the tiny front yard was cut exactly to the neighborhood standards. The last time Abigail had been here she carried a tiny chocolate cake and bottle of wine from the convenience store the next street over. Kenneth had been surprised to see her then, surprised she knew it was his birthday, and surprised that she even cared.

He looked just as surprised to see her on his porch now.

"Hey boss." Abigail smiled sheepishly; perhaps she should have brought another cake. "Hope you don't mind me dropping by."

"Is everything alright?"

Kenneth still towered over her. Even in her heeled boots, Abigail was four inches below his nose. Streaks of gray weaved inside his short hair, and his permanent scowl hadn't lessened in his retirement. Every gruff thing about him was a strange comfort to Abigail. After all the years, she still looked up to the hero that gave her the first chance to succeed.

"I was hoping you could help me with a case."

Kenneth raised an eyebrow. The eyebrow that had been burned off years ago after Cinder's attack. The eye below it was as pristine as the brow. The skin around it healed, and the eyelid repaired. Beside the dark smudge under it, Abigail could almost forget the gruesome injury ever occurred.

"The all-mighty Relief Center needs my help?"

"You were the best," she reminded.

Kenneth huffed. "I still am. Volcanic's solo numbers haven't been beat."

"Yet." Abigail grinned.

"Inferna would have a better chance."

"I like to think she hung up her cape with the big man, too."

"What's the case?"

"Can we talk inside?"

Despite Abigail changing into her civilian clothes and taking an extra bus between the office and Kenneth's house, she suddenly felt exposed on his front porch.

"Coffee's in the kitchen."

Kenneth stepped back into the house, and Abigail followed him inside. The interior was exactly like she remembered: cold, modern, and void of familiar items. The refrigerator didn't have magnets, the dish towel was a forgettable checkered pattern, and the bar stools were uncomfortable.

"If I didn't know any better," Abigail said as Kenneth poured her a cup of coffee. He kept it black, matching his, and placed it in front of her. "I'd believe you were just renting this house. There's not a shoe out of place, or picture on the wall."

"I have a skyline photo of San Arbor in the living room." His defense shut down any room for negotiation. "What about this case has you stumped?"

"It's an arson case," Abigail explained. "The fires the last three weeks have all been connected by an accelerant device. There's no apparent motive or connection with the targets. That we can see, anyway."

"Three weeks? The Jolt Station fire?"

"I don't think it's connected. The fire department said a faulty train engine started it, and there weren't any devices found." That King Arthur told her about, anyway.

"What's SAFD say? Their arson department is one of the best, if I remember right."

Abigail busied her hands by taking a scalding gulp from the mug. Her jet-black tongue didn't feel the heat, or the burn, but she couldn't deny how awful the lie tasted. "They handed it over to us."

"No suspects?"

"Not even a guess. If there's been any evidence left behind, the fire or water destroyed it."

"Sounds like you're looking for a ghost."

"A fire-starting ghost?" she snickered at the mental image. It was a Halloween costume gone wrong.

"Would that be so strange?"

Abigail shook her head, suddenly sobering. In their world, nothing could count as too strange.

"You need more information," Kenneth declared.

It wasn't the answer Abigail hoped she'd get coming to her old mentor. Volcanic always had an answer for everything, and on the rare moments he didn't there wasn't much that stood in his way to find it. The defeat tasted as bitter as her drink. She was back at square one and could only hope something new was discovered at the HRC while she was out.

Kenneth spun his mug on the counter slowly. He said his next words even slower. "How is he? Tommy."

"Excuse me?" Abigail's heart jumped into her throat and heat creeped over her cheeks.

"I know he's back in the city." Kenneth sounded nervous as he tip-toed through his thoughts. "Working with the San Arbor Fire Department. I know he came to see you, too."

Abigail swallowed, but her dry mouth didn't improve. "How do you know all of that?"

The dark past of Thomas Sanders was known by three people. Himself and the two superpowered individuals sitting at Kenneth's kitchen counter. Abigail would never expose what Thomas had once been, but she couldn't say the same for Kenneth, who helped create his villainous identity and whose gruesome injuries came from the ex-sidekick's flames. It was getting hard to breathe. Abigail's skin prickled as her fire readied to defend its master. If it came to a fight, Abigail wasn't sure she could beat Volcanic.

Kenneth took a breath and the room seemed to shrink. "He came to see me. The day before your hero announcement."

"Why?"

"To apologize."

Tearing her gaze off of her mug, Abigail looked at Kenneth. "What?"

"He showed up at my door, apologized for attacking me, and healed me." Kenneth rubbed the smudge under his eye. "I didn't know he could do something like that. Four different surgeons told me it couldn't be done, that the burns were too close to my eye and any attempt could blind me. He fixed it in minutes. Just peeled the damn thing off like it was a Band-Aid."

Kenneth spoke each of his words with factual accuracy. He didn't dwell on any details or offer his opinions on it.

A surge of pride for Thomas rushed through Abigail. "He's incredible, isn't he?"

"He also asked if I would let him see you." Kenneth added quickly. "I told him no."

"Why?" Sparks bit between Abigail's fingers and the coffee mug.

"He's dangerous, Abigail. I see it in his eyes, in his movements. He acts like he's hunting something."

"You don't know Thomas," Abigail defended. "Not anymore. He's different."

"So, he did find you."

"We're living together."

Kenneth sighed. "You have to be careful. Promise me you'll be careful."

Abigail placed her hand over his. Both radiated enough heat to boil the liquid in the mugs on either side of them. "Cinder is dead. Thomas is good, he's a hero. The mayor is trying to make him the face of the fire department. He's not the boy you trained anymore, but he's a man you should be proud of. He deserves that much from you. This second chance."

Kenneth exhaled deeply through his nose, his breath blowing across the top of Abigail's hand. "You're not the girl I trained anymore either, are you?"

She shook her head.

"Will you tell him I saw his Jolt Station rescue on the news?"

"You could tell him yourself? Come over for dinner."

Kenneth shook his head. "I can't."

"You can't or you won't?"

Kenneth pulled his hand out from under hers and focused on his coffee. After several sips, he lowered it back to the counter. Abigail watched his face, desperately trying to read his thoughts but coming up empty. She had a hundred questions and feared he wouldn't have the answers to any of them. She tried asking anyway.

"Have you seen him since he healed you?"

"Not in person."

"He didn't have that ability when he was Wildfire?"

"If he did, he never said anything."

"Do you think it came from the accident?" Abigail knew it was a long shot. It made little sense that the same blast that super charged his flames would grant Thomas the ability to heal burns.

"Stranger things have happened."

"He's the reason I can breathe the blue flame." Abigail stuck out her tongue, and Kenneth flinched at the marred flesh. "I wonder if I'll be able to heal, too?"

"Do not attempt it," Kenneth said. "If that power came from the accident, I don't want you anywhere near that size of a blast."

Abigail found his concern sweet, but pointless. She currently sat inches from the cause of that accident. One bad sneeze and she could be turned to ash.

"I'm sorry it took me needing something to see you. You should consider coming to dinner. Soon."

Kenneth smiled. It was so rare a gesture his face took a moment to adjust to the shape. "After you solve this case, I'll treat you. Your boyfriend too."

The word looked like it hurt coming from his mouth, and it made Abigail laugh. "Deal."

They finished their black and bitter coffee in familiar silence. While working as his sidekick, they shared infinite black and bitter coffees at their office. Kenneth was the one who convinced her to ditch the cream and sugar, saying neither helped the effect and would only weigh her down after a couple of years. Volcanic and Inferna became as recognizable a name as the chain coffee shop that appeared on every street corner. Abigail captured her hero title without her old sidekick moniker, but she knew his training and advice was part of the reason she made it that far. After he retired, Saves the Day hero company scrambled to produce a new number one hero, but couldn't compete with the Round Table Knights.

"You didn't come here just for coffee. What else is bothering you?"

"What?" Abigail asked.

"This conversation could have happened over the phone," Kenneth explained. "You didn't even bring any files concerning the case. I assume HRC has secure phone lines."

"They do, I don't know why I didn't call." Abigail pushed her mug across the counter. "Guess I took the opportunity to come and see you."

"Remember the psyche class we were forced to take?"

Abigail scratched the side of her head. "Honestly, I don't. You do?"

"It was to better understand your partner. Apparently, Saves the Day thought I needed the extra help when they signed you on." Kenneth's tone changed from annoyance to sincerity. "I won't force you to tell me anything, but you know I'll be here if something is troubling you."

Despite the steely look of Kenneth that once won him the contest of "most villainous looking hero," Abigail felt more inclined to trust him than the silver-tongued King Arthur. But she couldn't reveal the threat of King Arthur. Kenneth was no longer a hero, and Abigail didn't need protecting. She'd win this battle on her own.

She'd keep Kenneth safe, because if King Arthur could destroy her reputation, then he could easily do the same to Volcanic.

"What's troubling me is that I haven't seen you in years and we're just talking about work. I still have a lunch break to take, want to join me?"

Chapter Nineteen

Although Abigail hadn't cracked the arson case that afternoon, her spirits were high as she stepped off the bus and returned to HQ. She stayed longer with Kenneth than she planned but remembering shared missions and filling in three years over just one cup of coffee was never going to cut it. Abigail crunched on two peppermints before entering the main lobby to hide the taste of beer on her breath. *It was just one with lunch*, she rehearsed her defense in case anyone got close enough to notice.

Seeing Lancelot still seated in her office surprised Abigail. He had his own desk, his own office and yet he remained at hers. She would always be glad to see the young Knight back in action, but she wasn't glad to see him in the same place she left him in. Especially after he announced his feelings. He didn't look up from his self-assigned task of organizing the files on her desk.

"Hey Lancelot." She tossed her coat onto the chair across from him.

Abigail forced herself to sound cheerful, dipping into the charisma she reserved for interviews. She would make sure their partnership didn't turn awkward after his earlier confession. Still, she wished they could've started a new day and locked the moment into yesterday. She could pretend to be happy and excited for interviews, so she would pretend not to notice any thick air between them.

"Hey Avy." Lancelot refused to break his concentration on the files. They floated into three stacks in the center of the desk. His hands moved as if he conducted an orchestra, or something else more beautiful than the stacks of paperwork. Half of which Abigail knew could probably be stored away by now.

"What are you still doing here?" Abigail moved to the edge of the desk, watching the final folders magically fall into their new places. "It's getting late. I thought you had tonight off?"

"I don't know how you stay focused with all these papers laying around." Lancelot looked up and winked, clearly not feeling any leftover nerves from earlier. "Plus, we're going over this combo move."

"You're really set on this move, aren't you?"

"We can call it the Fire Bubble."

Abigail shook her head. "That doesn't sound too heroic."

Lancelot finished his mental stacking and stood from his seat. "Just wait until you see it."

Abigail dropped her gaze away from him. She would do better about prolonged eye contact and any unnecessary physical contact. She took a step back from him and gestured at the stacks of files. "How am I supposed to find anything now? I knew where everything was."

Lancelot chuckled, not buying her concern for a second. "They're still in order." He pointed to each stack as he listed off their purpose. "These are your active cases, the ones on top are the ones you have to finish and submit to President Samuels. These are things that could relate to the arson case, and this one is random criminals you have files on."

Lancelot reached for the first folder on the criminal stack. It was the thickest in the stack with edges turned brown from how often it was opened over the years. Abigail swatted his hand away. "I'm so over looking at files. Show me this Fire Bubble."

Lancelot smiled, whatever he wanted to show her in the folder became an afterthought. "I'll change and meet you in the training room."

Abigail watched Lancelot stretch across from her in the training room. His training suit looking like an expensive two piece from some overseas fashion catalog, despite her wearing the exact same outfit. He widened his stance, his hands outstretched, and his face stupidly eager to receive the fireball Abigail crafted in her hands. The flame sphere sparked as she compacted the energy. Bright red embers trickled onto the floor. Constructing the projectile weapon churned her stomach.

"Are you sure you want to do this?" she asked for a third time.

"Positive." Lancelot answered. "I've been practicing. Send it over."

Abigail gritted her teeth, hoping he would have changed his mind, and tossed the fireball toward her sidekick. Before impact, it froze in the air. The fire orb twisted against an unseen force between the hero and sidekick. Abigail approached her fireball and examined it. A rainbow shimmer wrapped around the sphere containing the blaze inside. Lancelot moved his hands to the left, and the smokey sphere followed them. The fire inside slowly collapsed in on itself without any oxygen.

"Cool, right?" Lancelot looked at Abigail. "I can't believe it worked so well."

"You didn't know if it would work!"

Lancelot delivered a sheepish smile and shrugged. The sphere shifted up and down to match his shoulder movements.

"What are you going to do with it?"

"Nothing." Lancelot moved the ball in front of Abigail. "I just needed to make sure I could control it. Will you get rid of it?"

Abigail frowned. Fire wasn't something she could simply *get rid of*, especially her blaze. She cupped her hands together and the remaining flames tumbled into her palms as Lancelot removed his forcefield. She sanded her hands around the sphere until it snuffed out with a puff of smoke.

"My idea is to create a pocket around us, with the fire on the outside," Lancelot said, talking with his hands. "We can use it as a shield. Not just for us, but for people too."

"Like the waitress."

Lancelot nodded. "Exactly."

"It's a good idea, nice thinking Lance," Abigail admitted. "But how's this a combo move?"

"I guess it's really not." Lancelot scratched the side of his face. "I just wanted to work together."

Abigail clapped his shoulder, but then quickly dropped her arm. "Who else can shoot fireballs at you?"

He smiled, "We're a great team."

Abigail summoned flames to her hand. "Get your shield started. I want to go slow in case there are any holes."

"Why? If I get burned again, can't you fix me?"

Abigail stared at him, her fire dripping onto the ground. "We don't know how you healed."

"Sure." Lancelot wiggled his eyebrows. The move was supposed to be playful and charming, but it only made Abigail's stomach cramp. "Whatever you say, Avalon. But I'm going to believe what I think I—"

"You're wrong." Abigail cut him off. "Whatever you're thinking, you're wrong. A miracle saved you, that's it. You have to be careful around fire, do you understand?"

"Yes, ma'am," he sighed. "Will you toss that thing already? Shield is up."

Abigail chewed the inside of her cheek before making her decision. Lancelot waited expectedly for her attack. This was a fifty-fifty shot of being an incredible idea that could help a lot of people, or an easy trip back to the hospital for Lancelot. His new skin just lost the pinkness and returned to its normal hue. Abigail couldn't be responsible if it turned molten again. She exhaled deeply, and the fire in her hands shrank with the loss of oxygen. She lobbed the flame like a softball.

The fire cascaded over Lancelot after hitting the invisible bubble around him and slid to the floor.

He grinned wildly at the success. "I'm good!"

Abigail sighed with relief and tossed another fireball. The shield held strong, and the assault did little to its structure. Each ball crashed into the bubble and sizzled to the floor like rain over an umbrella. Abigail felt like she was throwing handfuls of pasta sauce rather than her flames. She stepped closer to Lancelot and asked, "How's the temperature inside?"

"A little hot, but not bad." Lancelot whipped the back of his hand across his sweaty forehead.

"Ready for something stronger?" Abigail tapped her finger against the shield. It rippled from her touch, and she finally saw how big it was. Lancelot stood at the center of a six-foot hamster ball.

Lancelot moved his hands in a circle around him. The psychic sphere shimmered between them. He nodded.

Taking several steps back, Abigail inhaled deeply through her nose. She tasted sulfur in her mouth as her tongue sparked against her teeth. She spat a breath of blue flame at Lancelot. The flames ripped through her mouth. The impact of the Dragon's Breath knocked her sidekick and his bubble back several feet. Thick blue smoke filled the training room, and Abigail lost sight of him.

"Lance?" she called, moving through the smoke. "Lance, are you okay?"

A cough answered somewhere in the smoke. She turned in a circle trying to pinpoint the sound, but the area remained obscured. Her skin prickled as an invisible touch brushed her arm. The smoke suddenly cleared in front of her and created a tunnel with Lancelot on the other side. His styled hair fell around his face, but he looked okay. He looked alive, but smoking.

"I'm still good," he assured, walking through his mentally created tunnel to meet her. "My shield broke when I fell, but I'm good."

Abigail grabbed one of his arms and made sure he wasn't burned. She released him and said, "I'll try to hit you harder next time."

He laughed. "If you eat a lot of peppers, do you get hotter?"

"What?"

Lancelot blushed and busied his hands trying to fix his hair. "I was going to ask you that tonight, at dinner. If you said 'yes.'"

"It's not food related," she answered and took a step to create more space between them. "Let's try again. I want to see if your bubble is truly covering all sides of you."

Lancelot removed his hands from his hair and made another circular motion around them. As the psychic tunnel collapsed, the blue smoke filled the vacuum with a *whoosh* until it crashed around an invisible wall. The smoke encased Abigail and Lancelot and rolled around them like a dark ocean. Lancelot pushed and pulled the shield around them, tightening and expanding the bubble, and the smoke moved with similar elegance.

"Does that answer your question?"

Abigail walked around him. She ran her fingers along the space where the smoke refused to enter. A hum of energy tickled her fingertips. She wondered what else Lancelot's ability could do. Right now, it felt limitless. She summoned a cherry-red blaze in her hand and tried to force it through the shield. The barrier held strong; ripples of rainbow light pulsed around the fire as it shrunk in her palm.

"I'd say this is pretty successful."

"I want to try it under water next." Lancelot lowered the shield, and the smoke tumbled around them. "But I don't know how I'm going to filter out the air."

"It's only good for short usages." Abigail noticed he panted to catch his breath, noticed how small the fire in her hand became without a steady food source. "I still don't want you blindly running into fires."

"I'll only go where you tell me." He sealed his promise with a smile.

Several hours later, Abigail hung her smoke-infused training suit in the closet in her office and returned to the jeans and T-shirt she arrived in. Also hanging inside the wardrobe was her Avalon costume. Abigail adjusted the sleeves so it better fit on the hanger. The thick material was soft against her fingers. *I'll be back tomorrow*, she thought with a chuckle and wondered if she was feeling what some police officers felt when they couldn't take their patrol cars home after their shifts. It was probably for the best. If her timesheet didn't dictate when she was in costume, Abigail knew she'd never willingly strip away the alter ego.

If she had it her way, she'd never be without her mask. She'd be a hero at all hours of the day.

Her apartment complex was quiet when she returned that night. The new doorman was gone for the evening. The lobby was cold and empty. There was no strip of light coming from under her apartment door. None of this surprised her, though. Her watch ticked closer to midnight with each of her steps. She quickly settled on a sandwich for dinner, the quietest thing she could make, and gently slid her key into the lock.

The apartment should've been dark, but as she opened the door, she witnessed shadows jump across the walls. The smell of woodsmoke assaulted her nose. Her eyes watered from the sudden heat wave push-ing into the hallway. She didn't see the fire, but every cell in her body was on edge. Something was burning. Abigail shut the door, locking herself and whatever was foolish enough to be in her apartment with her. She followed the shadows toward her bedroom where a blue light streaked out from under the door. She grabbed the doorknob and actually felt the heat on the brass. She ripped the door open, and the heat intensified.

In the center of the room, blue flames twisted inside a metal trash can like a tiny tornado. The vortex stretched upwards to the blackened hand hovering above it that dropped things into the center. The flames chomped down greedily on the offerings. It made Abigail think of a starving dog finally finding scraps of food. Strips of paper vanished in seconds, pieces of cloth bloomed into a brilliant flash before disintegrating, indigo flames snaked up shoestrings before falling back into the trash can. He loomed over the pyre with his shadow stretching over the walls. It flickered as violently as the fire did, but he stood with an unshakeable resolve that made the tiny fire look as dangerous as a forest fire. Without any more fuel, the flames inside the trash can leapt into the outstretched hand and curled around his fingers.

Without thinking, Abigail grabbed his hand. The blue flames attacked her unprepared skin before jumping back to their owner. Abigail winced. No matter how strong she was becoming, these violet flames still burned her. She squeezed her blackened hand so her nails bit past the pain and tore into her palm. She searched his face for answers.

She only found the stormy green eyes of a villain. His scars may have been gone, but Abigail recognized the chill clawing down her spine while she drowned in Cinder's fathomless stare. She opened her mouth to speak, but nothing came out.

Thomas yanked his burning hands and himself away from her in a panic. He fell back onto the carpet and scrambled backward until the bed stopped him. His fire burned angrily between them inside the trash can, blue tendrils of flame snaked over the rim. He balled his hands into fists, extinguished his flames and cradled his hands to his chest. Even in the low light, Abigail saw them. There wasn't soot on his hands like before. They were charred. They matched the fresh burn on her hand. They would have matched the scar that once wrapped around her throat, or the ones that once covered his face. The darkness had stayed with him all this time.

"You're scarred." The accusation she made was a punch to her own stomach, and Thomas flinched as if she punched him, too.

Thomas swallowed. Abigail saw his jaw move as he tried to say something. What came out was raw and cracked against his teeth. "I don't know what's happening to me."

Abigail's feet moved the second his voice cracked. Her arms outstretched to catch him if any more of him broke. She moved beyond the harmless burning trash can to his side of the room and sat down. Their knees bumped together as Abigail trapped him between her and the bed. "What's happening *here*?" she asked gently, hoping an easier question would open the door to harder answers. Abigail feared the answer to what was happening to *him*.

"It felt good to burn things," he admitted in a whisper, refusing to look Abigail in the eye. "Ever since the night on the roof, it's been like an itch." He ignited a tiny blue flame atop his scarred finger; the shadows it created did horrible things across his face. "I feel complete with it. Like I've been lying to myself, hiding it away."

"That's dangerous." Abigail whispered back. Her tiny bedroom felt cavernous.

"You don't think I know that?" Thomas snapped, and the flame expanded atop his finger. He didn't speak again until the flame calmed down to its original size. "I can't just light things on fire."

"Dangerous for you." Abigail corrected her statement. "If anyone saw you ignite, they would take you. They could connect you to…" she didn't finish her sentence, fearful if she said it out loud then it could condemn him. *They could connect you to Volcanic's attack.*

He turned his gaze from the flame to her. His crooked smile felt like home. "You walk in on me setting a fire in your bedroom and you're worried about the government taking me? Babe, your priorities are so bad."

"I can get new stuff, never a new you. Whatever this is, we'll figure it out."

"Sometimes I think I take advantage of your loyalty."

Thomas wrapped his other hand around his burning finger and snuffed out the flame. Soft darkness encased them.

"I loved you as a villain," she reminded him. The darkness made it acceptable to admit, acceptable to remember.

Thomas found her hand in the darkness. His fingers brushed against the burn, and he loosened his hold. Thick blue smoke danced between them, smelling of the woodsmoke that reminded Abigail of a weekend spent in the mountains. Abigail's hand cooled as Thomas dragged his index finger over each of her fingers to remove the damage, the darkness, the pain.

"Would you have married that villain?" Thomas sounded braver in the darkness, some of the rumble returning to his voice.

Abigail blinked several times and her eyes adjusted. His ever-present smirk was gone. Thomas wasn't joking. The ache in her hand was distant. "What?"

"This would have been better at dinner, but lately it's been hard to get you alone. I want you to marry me, Abigail."

"Are you serious?" Abigail felt her heart stop.

"Deadly." Thomas collected her left hand and slid a golden band over her ring finger. "I'd like to stop carrying this thing around with me all day."

"How long have you been doing that?" Abigail ran a thumb over the ring. A gemstone scratched against her thumb, but she couldn't make it out in the dark.

"About a month."

"That's a long time to change your mind."

"This minute waiting for your answer feels a lot longer."

Abigail smiled, the darkness hid it, but her voice could not. "Of course! Thomas, of course I'll marry you!"

She leapt into his lap and wrapped her arms tightly around his neck. His stubble scratched her cheeks.

His whole body relaxed around hers.

His lips crashed onto hers as his relief washed over them both. Tears pricked the edges of Abigail's eyes, and she squeezed them shut. She pulled Thomas closer against her, refusing to let anything come between them. He hungrily kissed her, and Abigail realized she never felt more wanted than how Thomas made her feel. This entire apartment unit could erupt in flames and Abigail wouldn't care so long as she kept him in her arms.

Tonight, the case, the arsonist, her sidekick's quest to get himself hurt, and her boss' manipulations burned away under Thomas' touch. Tonight, there was only them. Tonight, they were only human.

Chapter Twenty

Files relating to the arson case flooded the kitchen island and threatened to slip into the sink full of dirty dishes. A map of San Arbor crinkled between two chairs where it was pinned on the floor. Pens lay in ruin on top of the files. Loose sheets of handwritten notes disappeared under folders. Sticky notes clung desperately to their positions. Abigail brought the documents home, thinking that examining them with a new scenery would shake something loose.

But her full attention was on the ring wrapped around her finger. She loved the way the weight of the gold band forced her hand down. She ran her thumb over the sapphire raising from the center. The rough stone snagged against her thumb. It was beautiful. Abigail twisted the band and watched the light catch and reflect off the jewel.

Her tiny kitchen-office was lost to her as she fidgeted with the ring. Her mind distracted with what it represented. The promise of forever, of a life together with the person she loved most of all. She finally understood the giddiness at the end of sappy romance movies. The weightlessness at the end of books. The tremble her uncle described about his knees at his wedding years ago.

She thought she ought to call someone to share the news with. Her mother should've been Abigail's first call, but then she'd have to explain Thomas and the lightning fast approach of their relationship. Perhaps she should start with them meeting before announcing their engagement. The last thing Abigail wanted was to hear her mother's snide remarks of her moving too fast when all she wanted to do was share a life with Thomas. Surely, her mother could believe in soul mates.

"Morning babe."

Thomas' kiss against her cheek surprised Abigail, and it pulled her from her thoughts. Not even gravity could stop the smile that claimed her face at seeing him. She hoped the rush of endorphins never stopped. She snatched his hand before he could get too far away.

"Good morning, fiancé."

He grinned. "Like how that sounds?"

"I do."

"I do too." Thomas kissed the top of her hand and then gestured to the paperwork. "What's all of this?"

Abigail dropped her gaze to the mess of files. "My current assignment."

"Is this about the recent fires?" Thomas grabbed her coffee mug with his free hand and took a sip. He frowned at the cold temperature and ignited his fingertips to heat the mug. The embers faded when steam poured from the top.

Abigail nodded. "It's my job to find the arsonist."

"Arsonist?" Thomas repeated. "You suspect just one person?"

"Yeah, we're pretty sure the same person is responsible for all of them."

"How do you know the fires are connected?"

Abigail reluctantly released Thomas' hand and found a photocopy of the incendiary device. "Remember that device I found on Mulberry? Turns out more were found at each of the other fires. It did contain an accelerant."

"I'm glad I didn't take that bet." Thomas examined the photo. "Our guys haven't said anything about this."

"It's, um, HRC only. Your fire investigators handed it over to us." Abigail heard King Arthur's threat in the back of her mind. Thomas began to launch one eyebrow into his shaggy hair, so she asked another question before he could. "Do you recognize it?"

"It looks impressive, whoever made it knew what they were doing."

"What do you mean?"

Thomas returned the photocopy to the table and ran his scarred finger across the image. "These charred edges. Most poorly made accelerants act like a bomb and explode. This one slow burned. What was the timer like?"

"I don't know if there was one." Abigail admitted. "Merlin is still taking them apart. We only find them after they've burned up, so it's been hard to piece them together. We know what the accelerant is, but that's about it."

Thomas leaned over the counter to look at everything. He examined every sheet of paper, every handwritten note, every photocopied report. When he raised his head up, his nose brushed Abigail's and he stole a quick kiss. "I'd have your wizard look at a thermal timer. I think your arsonist has this set to unleash under a certain temperature."

"How can you tell?"

Thomas shrugged. "Fire science training."

Abigail fished for a pen and sheet of paper from the pile and scribbled down his theory. From the corner of her eye, she watched Thomas dump her old coffee in the sink and toast a piece of bread with his hands.

"It felt good to burn things."

Abigail looked between her feet to the San Arbor map. Ladder Company 3 had been called to half of the connected fires. Thomas had been near the others before the blazes began. Abigail rubbed her hands up and down her arms, the ring snagging across her skin.

"Ask me."

"Ask you what?" Abigail looked up, her heart booming in her ears.

Thomas swallowed his bite of burnt toast. "What you're thinking about."

"Did you start these fires?" The question repulsed Abigail. She felt like she chewed on a handful of poison dart frogs. She wished she was ingesting the deadly amphibians instead of accusing her fiancé of arson.

"No." Thomas dusted his hands over the sink. "I'm playing with fire, but I didn't start those."

Abigail felt guilty for even thinking about it. Cinder was dead. He had to be. She focused on the note for Merlin. The sapphire stone distracted her again. She didn't think she'd get any real work done with it shining in her face. She looked up and found Thomas staring at her.

"I'm not mad you thought it was me."

Abigail blushed. "I am."

"Just means you're a good hero. You won't play favorites with your fiancé."

"I'll always play favorites with you." She meant it to be a joke, but she knew the truth.

Thomas chuckled. "I'd hope so."

Abigail wished she could get lost in his crooked smile for the rest of the day, but as the clock on the microwave ticked closer to eight, she knew she was running out of time. She needed to catch the arsonist. That's what a good hero would be doing.

"Want me to drive you to work?' Thomas asked, noticing the time himself. "I told Maddox I'd help him stain his deck today. HRC is on the way."

"No, it isn't." Abigail began stacking her files together and shoving them into her briefcase.

Thomas shrugged and admitted, "Maybe I just want to drive you to work then."

"On that stolen bike?"

"Embarrassed?"

Abigail pinned him with a look that did little to dampen his mood. "*Concerned* about being caught with stolen property."

"I'll give it back," he smirked. "Maybe."

"Today."

Thomas tossed his hands up in defeat. "Okay. I'll park it somewhere and call in an anonymous tip."

Abigail flattened her hair down as she walked into the Hero Relief Center. The ride over whipped her curls into a frenzied mess of static and volume despite the helmet. She was surprised she didn't find a twig or bird lodged somewhere in the mess. After slipping into her Avalon costume, Abigail knocked on Merlin's door. She was greeted with the sour smell of animal poop when she entered.

Merlin, equally stunning in a lab coat as her hero costume, watched a liquid bubble inside a beaker. She adjusted the Bunsen burner, and the flame scorched the bottom of the glass. The smell of manure was quickly replaced by fairgrounds, and Abigail desperately wanted cotton candy.

"What are you working on?" Abigail asked, inhaling deeply to savor the sweet smell.

"Science," Merlin replied but didn't answer. She scribbled into her notebook and then killed the flame. The smell faded away.

"Have you discovered anything new about the incendiary devices?"

Merlin shook her head, turning away from her experiment. "Tracking down shipments of the manure isn't going well, either. Anyone at the nature preserve could have access to it. The grounds are treated twice yearly with the stuff. Four of the seven stores that carry lawn care products supply the stuff too. It's a common blend so I can't easily track the brand."

"I may have something that could help. Do you still have the switch?"

Merlin pulled the half-burned switch from her coat pocket. It felt so delicate in Abigail's hands. She thought one ill-timed sneeze could turn the thing to dust.

"If we're still thinking there's a delay start with it, and since there's no timer on it, do you think it could be a heat sensor that triggers it?"

Merlin stared blankly at Abigail until a sly smile curled her red lips with amusement.

Abigail fumbled over the rest of Thomas' theory. "Shouldn't the device have been destroyed in the explosion, too? Does that mean it's made more professionally than by someone new to this?"

Merlin took the device back from Abigail. "A thermal sensor would explain why it didn't ignite before the fires initially started. It would need to heat up."

"It would give the arsonist time to get away," Abigail added.

"Would it also explain why it didn't start the fires?" a male voice asked.

Abigail jerked her head and found Lancelot in the corner of the lab examining Merlin's impressive bookshelves. They extended from the floor to ceiling with a maintenance ladder propped against the shelves to access the highest books.

Lancelot returned the book he was flipping through on the shelf and joined her. "You talked to your firefighter, didn't you?"

Abigail blushed and glanced to Merlin who was busy focusing a micro camera over the device. A digital image appeared on her computer. "I didn't talk to anyone about the case. That would be against protocol."

Her mouth dried at the lie, and she prayed Lancelot would drop it.

"Come here." Merlin's command distracted Lancelot, and Abigail followed him to the computer with a silent sigh of relief. "See this?"

At first Abigail didn't. The inside of the device looked like a tangled mess of dirt, metal, and ash. Merlin used a pair of tweezers to point at a strip of reflective red lining. Most of it had burned away but about half an inch of it remained untarnished.

"A thermal sensor?" Lancelot asked.

"I believe so." Merlin stepped back. "Avalon, will you test it?"

"What are you looking for?" Abigail asked, but already ignited her fingertip.

"Any kind of reaction." Merlin readied her notebook. "Burn slow."

Abigail pressed her finger against the red strip and slowly increased the temperature of her blaze. After four minutes of a steady increase the device remained lifeless.

"Maybe it's broken?" Lancelot sounded hopeful. "It could only have one charge in it, or something?"

"Or it needs more heat."

Abigail matched Merlin's knowing smile. She pulled her flame away from the incendiary device and breathed blue fire into her palm. The flame quickly obeyed and settled on the top of her finger. When she touched the blue flame against the sensor it shrieked in response. The red strip glowed but without any fuel it powered down.

"Thermal ignition." Merlin nodded while writing in her book. "Incredible."

Abigail shook out her hand and the blue fire dissipated. "Will this help you track it down?"

"Not the manure, but this is a big clue to have."

"Does only Dragon Breath light it?" Lancelot looked up from the device.

Abigail's breath caught, but thankfully Merlin rescued her a second time.

"It's the temperature that causes the reaction," Merlin said. "Dragon Breath does burn extremely hotter, but regular fire will reach that temperature given enough time. It supports Avalon's theory of an escape plan."

"King's going to love this!" Lancelot excitedly announced. "Let's get the fire department in here so they can—"

"Let Arthur handle that." Merlin didn't look up from her notes.

Abigail's heart broke. It broke at Merlin's intense loyalty to their secretive leader. It broke at Lancelot's loyalty to the law that was currently lost to their team. Would her sidekick still look up to King Arthur if he knew the truth?

"Avy?"

Abigail looked away from the incendiary device and focused on Lancelot. "Sorry, what?"

"Patrol, remember? Are you ready to go?"

She smiled. "Let's be heroes."

Merlin stopped them with a snap of her fingers. "If you run into any fires, go to the back first. That seems to be where these switches are left. Think like the arsonist. The incendiary device will be close enough to the fire to heat up, but in a place where it won't immediately catch fire."

"You got it." Lancelot delivered a thumbs up.

"We'll report if we see anything." Abigail pushed Lancelot out of Merlin's office, and they headed to the streets of downtown San Arbor, a new sense of vigor overflowing inside Abigail's blood stream.

Chapter Twenty-One

"Are you seeing this?" Lancelot asked.

"It's hard not to," answered Abigail.

Ahead of them, two additional sets of arms pillaged the inside of a minivan while the original set picked at their owner's teeth. The extra four arms extended from the woman's sides just under the original ones, which were made of flesh and looked like the rest of her. The extra sets were created from a thick fog and possessed the ability to phase through the minivan's windows without triggering any alarms.

The villain was definitely hard to miss. The power set was something Abigail hadn't seen before. She didn't know what else the fog arms were capable of. Gruesome images flashed inside her mind of the ghostly appendages phasing through her chest and ripping out her heart. Abigail didn't want to find out if that was possible.

"Let's end this quickly," Abigail whispered to Lancelot. "Grab her arms with your telekinesis, and I'll rush her from the back."

"Which arms?"

"All of them."

Lancelot nodded but remained in place. His powers were far less flashy than Fog Arms, but Abigail didn't need any grand show to know they were working. Abigail trusted Lancelot. Her sidekick wouldn't let her down. Without any prompting from him, Abigail ducked toward a green SUV and crept behind Fog Arms, who counted a handful of change collected from a center console.

Fog Arms grunted, dropping the nickels and dimes as her arms constricted around her. She struggled against the invisible hold, and Abigail leapt forward. The woman whipped around and faced Abigail, her expression stunning the hero. Usually, when she leapt toward criminals and villains, they would look fearful or at least surprised, but this woman sneered at Abigail. Annoyance painted every inch of this woman's face. Even though her real arms were pinned to her sides, she lifted her fog arms and gripped Abigail's midsection before she could pull her sword. The fog arms tossed Abigail onto the asphalt, and she rolled across the ground until the trunk of a car stopped her. Thankfully the parking lot was empty of cameras, civilian or media, that could have caught her embarrassing tumble.

"Lancelot?" Her single word contained a dozen questions.

"Are you okay?" his response buzzed through Abigail's headset.

"I thought you had her." Abigail returned to her feet and eyed Fog Arms, who turned her full attention to Abigail. The villain hadn't moved, but her black arms twisted like snakes.

"I *did*. Her other arms must not be affected."

Abigail didn't like the uncertainty in his voice. Lancelot's powers seemed to be unstoppable. The limitations only created by his own lack of experience. "Lock her feet to the ground if you can."

After a moment Lancelot said, "If they're real, they're trapped."

Abigail approached Fog Arms. The villain tried to pick her foot off the ground, but it refused to budge. Fog Arm's sneer collapsed when Abigail knocked her knuckles together creating a shower of sparks.

"Let's not make this ugly," she said to Fog Arms. "You're going to return everything you took."

"I don't think so."

Four dark and smoky arms rushed for Abigail. She completed a series of tumbles and flips that would make a gymnast proud and escaped their grip. She fell back into the body of another car and rolled beneath it to avoid a pummeling from the four fists. Regardless of their makeup, the appendages had solid mass to them. Abigail still felt the pressure against her ribs where the hands had first grabbed her.

Abigail popped up on the other side of the car and yelled across the hood at Fog Arms, "Is that your only trick?"

As an answer, the four arms snatched at Abigail's hair and mask, and she barely ducked away in time to avoid a demasking. One hand did fist into her hair and yank her head hard against the side of a door. Abigail shook the ringing from her ears and darted away another car's length.

"Too easy," she taunted.

"Avy, what's your plan?"

Abigail rolled to the side of a pickup truck before answering Lancelot on their comm link. "Testing her range. There has to be a limit, right?"

"I guess so, but what if it's not as short as you think it is?"

Abigail ignored his caution. "When she reaches it, I want you to strike. A blow to the back of her head ought to be enough."

Abigail scurried around the truck and ducked to avoid two of the incoming arms. A third grabbed at her ankle and Abigail spun on her heel to dodge. The fourth hand punched hard against Abigail's thigh, applying the force of all four arms. She crumbled to the ground and all of the hands raised up, ready to slam down. Abigail took a rapid breath and spat a plume of Dragon's Breath into the arms. All four foggy appendages dissipated for a moment. Abigail grinned. If the arms were composed of fog, then heat would evaporate them. In the cover of smoke, she tucked herself behind a car. She grabbed a discarded Styrofoam cup and rolled it across the parking lot aisle. The four arms pounced on it with wild reflexes. Abigail inhaled deeply and spat a cloud of blue fire against them. Her theory was correct. All four arms faded to outlines of darkness, but once the flames were gone, they returned to their shape.

"Do that again," Lancelot requested inside her ear, "I'm going to strike now."

Abigail bolted down the aisle away from Fog Arms, loudly smacking her boots against the pavement to catch her attention. She rounded a light post and exhaled a mighty breath of fire onto the outstretching hands. They trashed violently under the heat. She took a breath through her nose and continued the assault until Lancelot spoke again.

"She's down and out. Crowd's here too, by the way."

Abigail wiped her mouth with the back of her hand. A bit of soot clung to her skin from her lips. "I'm calling SAPD. We'll need a collar to keep her contained. Is she cuffed?"

"Yeah, but I'm not sure how much that'll help."

"It'll help the public stay calm."

Abigail crossed the rows of cars back to her sidekick and the crowd of about fifteen people forming around him, despite his continued warnings to stay back. Several cell phones were already recording the scene. One teenaged boy live-streamed to his followers; his broadcast speculated on why the woman became such a troubled villain. He was on a theory involving an abusive partner when Abigail tasted sparks in her mouth. Each of his words heated her frustration more.

"Are any of these vehicles yours?" Abigail asked, blocking the crowd's view of the unconscious Fog Arms. Committing petty crime or not, she didn't deserve to be gawked at like a zoo animal.

"Uh, that one is." One man pointed to a nearby car.

"Several of these vehicles have been rummaged through," Abigail addressed the crowd. "SAPD is enroute, please give your statements to them."

"What about her?" a woman asked, keeping a small girl hidden behind her legs.

"She will be detained and tried."

"But you caught her," said another person in the crowd. "Do we really need to pay for a trial when you caught her in the act? Seems like an easy sentence to me."

There was a murmur of agreements to his statement. Mayor Benton's accusations from the night of Thomas' party suddenly held a weight Abigail wasn't happy about.

"Every person in San Arbor has the right to a trial." Abigail reminded with authority.

"But she's a villain!"

A chill ran down Abigail's spine. The crowd of citizens in front of her suddenly looked venomous. "She still has the same rights as you, and us."

Fog Arms floated off the ground and the crowd gasped and scrambled backwards.

"Didn't mean to scare you," Lancelot smiled. "It's just me."

Lancelot lifted his hand up and down and Fog Arms mirrored the motion. The crowd calmed down and several members even caught his infectious smile.

"How about I clear the area for you, so you can check your cars? How far away are the police, Avalon?"

"Couple of minutes," Abigail answered, but her attention was locked on the live streamer who continued filming the woman. He was now enlightening his followers that he didn't think any villain should have a right to a trial.

"—power corrupts absolutely and if you start to use your powers for evil then what's going to stop you from turning absolutely evil?"

"Right, Avy?" Lancelot squeezed Abigail's shoulder and forced her to look away from the teenager.

"What?"

"We better move our captive to the front so SAPD can collect her easier?" he repeated patiently.

Abigail looked around. Fog Arms still floated above them. The crowd still waited. The teenager sill recorded. Her hands smoked at her sides, the dark wisps revealing her hidden feelings. She forced a smile. "You're right. Good idea, Lancelot."

She followed him away from the crowd to the end of the aisle. Lancelot lowered Fog Arms to the ground and turned to Abigail, wringing his hands together.

"Are you good?"

The quick answer was yes, of course Avalon was good. But the truth was she wasn't. The crowd had been quick to condemn Fog Arms just because she was a villain. Abigail frowned; she had been quick to condemn criminals in the past, too. Thankfully, Abigail didn't have to explain the prickling in her blood stream to someone who wouldn't understand her plight, as Merlin chirped inside their linked communicators.

"Wrap up whatever you're doing," she instructed. "I found where the manure is being sent. We're all meeting there."

"Go," Lancelot encouraged Abigail. "I'll wait for the police."

Abigail shook her head and tapped her earpiece. "Merlin, we have a villain detained and are waiting for transport from SAPD. We'll be there as soon as we can."

The address Merlin delivered sent Abigail and Lancelot to a dirty street between dirtier buildings. The first-floor windows were either boarded up or broken out, and almost every front door sported a big red X spray painted across the plywood boards to prevent entrance. Only three cars were parked along the sidewalk; two wearing faded yellow boots on their back tires, and another had a stack of parking tickets pinned beneath a window wiper.

Despite the sense of abandonment, Abigail felt watched. She glanced up to the upper windows expecting to find someone staring at her, but she only found shadows. It didn't help comfort her.

The target building sat at the end of the road. A two-story house that was probably sought after when first constructed now lay crooked on its foundation. The wraparound porch looked too dangerous to step on, and one of the columns supporting the porch's roof featured a nasty crack running down the side. Another red X on the front door marked the home as condemned.

"This doesn't look like the safest place to build a bomb," Lancelot commented.

Abigail shared his thought. "Maybe the manure is just delivered here. It could be transferred somewhere else."

"Is the mail man allowed to make deliveries to condemned houses?"

"I'm not sure the deliverer is part of the United States Postal Service."

"Evil runs together, got it."

Abigail shook her head. "That's not really what I was trying to say."

"Let's see what King's found." Lancelot waved his hand to catch the attention of the other three knights examining a cellar door.

Abigail followed her sidekick with the same prickling sensation along her skin she felt when leaving the parking lot. Excalibur clapped her on the shoulder when she was close enough, and the heavy motion snapped her away from her frustrating thoughts. She smiled up at him, but the fake grin turned sincere looking into his gray helmet. She didn't know why she always thought he smiled behind the mouth guard, but the thought was enough for her.

"Hey boss," Abigail said. "Has anyone gone inside?"

"Not yet," Excalibur answered.

"I don't think we need to." Merlin pointed across the weed infested backyard. "Any idea why that shed is bolted?"

Calling the backyard building a shed was an understatement. It was more like a small barn. The gray painted exterior was brighter than anything else on the street, and its steel panels looked about twenty years newer than the house it sat behind. Its addition was most likely the newest renovation on the whole street.

"That looks safe enough to build a bomb in," Lancelot adjusted his earlier statement.

King Arthur was already halfway across the yard. "Let's get inside."

The five Round Table Knights surrounded the simple door and the series of padlocks attaching it to the wall. Merlin tugged on the largest of the three locks.

"A little welding will do the trick," she said to Abigail.

Abigail stepped up to the locks like she was stepping up to bat, except her aluminum stick was replaced with a thin line of red fire blazing from her pointer finger.

"Hold on," Excalibur stopped her. "I want to handle this."

"Lock picks aren't a type of weapon." King Arthur eyed the twin picks Excalibur produced from his pocket.

"You're right, but I don't need my ability to use them." Excalibur settled himself at the locks and started picking the top one. "I taught myself how in college. I thought it would make me cooler."

"Did it work?" Merlin asked, but she didn't seem interested as she leaned against the shed.

A soft *click* answered for the knight, and Excalibur moved to the second lock. This one proved more difficult and took Excalibur several minutes to unlock. Abigail was ready to push him aside as he broke his pick in half at the final lock, but he had an extra in his pocket and the last lock fell to the ground.

"Cool, or what?" he asked the group.

"Pretty cool," Abigail answered, eager to get inside the building.

"Lights up when we get inside," King Arthur said to Abigail, stopping any further discussion of Excalibur's street credit. "Lancelot, shield up as well. I don't know what we'll find in there."

King Arthur pushed open the door. Abigail's curls tugged at her ears as Lancelot's force field extended past her and shielded the front of the group. The dim room turned sunny under the two fire balls Abigail summoned in her hands. The scent of manure weighed heavily in the air. Abigail tried breathing through her mouth to avoid smelling it, but the scent had stained the air and she could taste it now. On one side of the long, tube-shaped interior, plastic wrapped containers of the size of yard mulch lined the wall, while the other half of the building was constructed into several rooms blocked off by sheets hanging from clothesline.

"Homey," Merlin said.

"Spread out," King Arthur instructed.

Merlin examined the stacked containers, her red dress kicking up dirt and dust moats as she did. She gave King Arthur a nod after examining a wrapped package.

Excitement filled Abigail. This was the place. She was closing in on the arsonist. They would find something to connect them here, they'd find out who they are, and they'd catch them. This would finally be over. San Arbor would be safe again. Abigail set to investigate the rooms. In the first one made of blue sheets, she found a cot and drool-stained pillow. She grabbed a pair of jeans from the floor and checked the pockets. Besides a couple of fast-food receipts paid for with cash and two nickels, the pants did little to aid her investigation. Abigail dropped them to the ground and wiped her hands against her skirt. Everything in the place smelled like cow droppings.

Abigail scrunched her nose and checked the next room. This one promised to be more helpful. A folding table sat in the center of the space under a pair of industrial lights. She twisted on the power supply, and light glinted off several incendiary devices on the table. Half were completed and half were still in their infancy stages. There was at least a dozen in total. At least a dozen more planned arson attacks. Abigail exhaled to prevent accidentally sparking near one.

"I found the switches." Abigail exited the makeshift room. "This is definitely the place."

From the center of the room, Lancelot asked, "I'll call DaVodi so he can collect the evidence."

Abigail watched King Arthur's face twist from annoyance to political. "Don't. We don't want to tip off the arsonist if he comes back before we find him. All those squad cars wouldn't be good hanging around here."

"Oh, right." Lancelot glanced at the other knights, attempting to hide the embarrassment on his cheeks.

Abigail felt bad for her sidekick. He didn't know King Arthur was keeping the information on the devices a secret. "Lance and I can head back," Abigail said to King Arthur. "We'll run house records and see who owns the property."

"I'm not sure that'll be necessary." Merlin pointed to her ear then back toward the building door. A car shifted into park on the street. Muffled music turned off, and a car door slammed shut.

"Hide," King Arthur quickly directed. "Lancelot, get ready for a capture. Merlin, Avalon, it's too dangerous in here for your powers. Keep them off."

Abigail nodded and ducked behind the curtain of the bedroom. She peeled the sheet slightly off the wall to see into the main room. Lancelot stood to the side of the door giving him the best advantage to grab the person when they entered. The other knights vanished behind various items. The path from the street to the shed wasn't long, but Abigail felt like she waited ages before she heard the outside locks clank against the door.

"Something's off," a voice said. "Marco knows better than to leave these open. Marco?"

A man entered the shed and called again for his friend. Half his head was shaven, and a coiled snake tattoo replaced the hair. It looked fresh and parts of the skin were still raw with blood and ink. He returned his attention to the cellphone perched between his shoulder and ear.

"Let me call you back." The man ended his call and stored his phone. "Marco, you here?"

Lancelot used his foot to shut the door. The sudden sound caused the man to spin around, but Lancelot locked him in a bear hug before he could get away. The man thrashed against Lancelot.

King Arthur exited from his hiding place and cleared his throat. "Man with the tattoo? Calm down."

The man slumped against Lancelot as the will to fight evaporated away. He grumbled something in coherently and glared at King Arthur. He looked as dangerous as the poorly inked cobra on his skull.

The purple shine dissipated from King Arthur's eyes. "Get him outside, Lance. We'll take him to DaVodi."

"I didn't do anything!" snapped the man inside Lancelot's arms. "I was forced to do all this! You don't have anything to connect me!"

Merlin laughed and gestured to the manure. "I can't wait to hear how he talks himself out of this."

"It never is their fault, is it?" King Arthur replied. "Think there's any juror that would buy his sob story?"

"Or lawyer who'll pull the insanity plea?"

"My client isn't smart enough to do something like this," King Arthur mocked.

While King Arthur and Merlin talked, Abigail saw the twist on the man's face. He began to snarl. Not at Lancelot who held him back, but toward King Arthur and Merlin who belittled him. He didn't break King Arthur's command to calm down. His next action was one of pure focus. He was calm, but he was mad. The man reached into his pocket and removed something that looked like a bike handle.

Abigail smelled the sulfur. She knew exactly what he held. She knew exactly what he was about to do.

"Stop laughing at me!" warned the man.

Abigail leapt from behind the curtain just as the man tossed the bomb at King Arthur. She shouted for her boss to get down, but her feet were moving faster than her words. With her feet propelling her with fire, she tackled King Arthur to the side, laying herself over him as the shed shook from the blast.

It was over too soon to be a normal bomb. There wasn't a blinding flash, nor a deafening ringing. Abigail looked over her shoulder and saw a sphere of smoke and sparks hovering a foot off the ground. Merlin's outstretched hands oozed with foam and dripped onto the concrete floor ahead of her, but she stared at the contained blast in disbelief. Lancelot's hands were outstretched ahead of him in tight fists. A line of blood dripped down both nostrils.

"Avalon?"

Abigail tore her gaze away from her sidekick and to King Arthur who was pinned beneath her. She scrambled off him and helped haul him to his feet. "Sorry sir, are you okay?"

"I imagine I am because of you." King Arthur smiled at her, and for the first time in a while it reached his eyes. "Nice work."

"He's clean," Excalibur called out. He cuffed the man's hands together even though his head lolled over his shoulder in unconsciousness. "There won't be any more blasts."

Chapter Twenty-Two

The news of the captured arsonist traveled faster than any of the fires he actually started. Two news vans arrived with the police cruisers when transport came for him. Abigail could visibly see a vein throb against King Arthur's throat at their arrival. She didn't need any command to help Excalibur contain the scene before the Knights left. Merlin constructed a temporary barrier between the officers and the media so they could have privacy while their detectives conducted their investigation.

When the Knights of the Round Table returned, the front lawn of the Hero Relief Center was crawling with media crews. The reporters crowded around the car before Mitch could turn off the ignition. Abigail barely heard his grumbling over them. Several camera flashes broke through the tinted windows.

"Avalon, will you handle this?" Merlin asked, already positioned to exit the car on the opposite side of the crowd where an employee door was already opened for them. "You've always been the best at it."

The compliment didn't feel authentic, but Abigail agreed. The media was part of the job. "Sure thing."

Merlin smiled; it was one of the few Abigail received from the wizard, and she exited the car. For all his bravery, Excalibur was quick on her heels.

"Tell them that we'll release a full statement after our joint investigation with SAPD," King Arthur instructed. "Keep your answers short, and just ease any concern they have."

"Will do."

Lancelot looked away from the window. "There's a lot of them out there, I should stay on the ground with Avalon."

"That's fine, go ahead and get things started."

Lancelot pushed opened the door and the outside noise rushed into the cab like a windstorm. King Arthur reached across the seat and pulled the car door shut. Abigail's hand rested instinctually on the hilt of her sword as just the two of them remained in the tight quarters.

"About the incendiary devices," King Arthur said. "I want you to tell them this was the first time we've seen them. Tell them we found the lead based on a large shipment of manure flagging one of our data-bases."

"You want me to lie to all these people?"

"I want you to keep us all safe. Remember our past conversation?"

Abigail nodded. She wished she didn't remember the not-so-subtle threat her boss tossed around lazily in her office.

"If all these people find out we've been keeping secrets, then eve-rything we've worked for is over."

"I just wish we didn't have to lie. In future events."

King Arthur smiled and patted her knee. "I do too, it's a nice dream to have. But, Abigail, we don't do this to just keep ourselves safe but also San Arbor. The police force isn't fireproof. I'd hate for them to rush into places they shouldn't be."

Abigail swallowed her rebuttal. She knew King Arthur wouldn't care that she thought everyone being prepared would be safer. "Do we have a record of the flagged database? I know once I say something about it, DaVodi will want a copy for the report."

"Merlin is drafting it up now." King Arthur opened the car door again. Flashes of light bounced around the interior. "We didn't nick-name you Dragon Slayer for nothing, get out there and destroy this beast."

"The media," she corrected, exiting the car. "I'll take care of the media."

The car pulled away, Mitch taking the highest profile Knight away from the madness, and Abigail prepared herself for the gauntlet. In her delay, Lancelot distracted the crowd and currently entertained Monica with Channel 9 News by mentally juggling her press badge, microphone, and notepad. All three items floated back to her arms as Abigail joined him.

"You're getting good at that," she greeted Lancelot, squeezing herself into the camera frame with him.

"I can teach you sometime."

"I don't have your telekinesis."

"I can juggle with my hands too." Lancelot pretended to juggle invisible balls and drew a small laugh from the crowd.

Abigail went to shove his shoulder but changed her hand's trajectory to tuck a curl behind her ear instead. She turned to Monica and the other reporters. "I take it you have some questions."

Several microphones were shoved under Abigail's chin.

She cleared her throat. "A full statement will be released after our investigation with San Arbor PD is completed, but there is one suspect in custody for the arson attacks on the city."

"Are they powered?" someone asked.

"They don't appear to be, but all precautions are being made to keep everyone safe."

"What led you to the house?"

"A large shipment of manure flagged one of our databases," Abigail answered. Catching a questioning gaze from Lancelot, she spoke quickly so he couldn't interject. "We thought it was weird and wanted to check it out. You can imagine our surprise when we got there."

"Manure?" asked a reporter who wore a San Arbor Community College badge around his neck.

Lancelot answered, "The kind with high levels of nitrogen and other elements that can be used in the creation of explosives."

"What other elements?" asked the young reporter as he scrawled down every word Lancelot said.

Lancelot smiled at the Channel 9 camera. "I can't be listing off a bomb making kit on a news report, now can I?"

The crowd chuckled. The young reporter blushed a shade just lighter than a tomato.

"Does owning a few bags of manure legitimize the arrest of anyone these days?"

Abigail caught the eyes of the elder woman who asked the question. "No, but the over 50 pounds of it does warrant someone to be a person of interest."

"Not to mention the bombs also found, right?" Monica asked, her eyes on Lancelot.

"Avalon knows more about that."

"We do not believe them to be bombs," Abigail spoke slowly. She waited to ensure everyone had heard her and jotted down their quotes. She couldn't afford to backtrack in her lie. "There were several incendiary devices found at the scene, yes. SAPD are still going through the scene and collecting evidence."

"Can you tell us anything more about the devices?"

"Not at this time. This is the first time the Round Table Knights had seen them. We don't even know if they were used in the arson attacks."

"Is San Arbor safe now?"

"San Arbor and her citizens are always safe with us protecting you," Lancelot said.

"Us, along with the other first responders in the city," Abigail added. "As we mentioned, a full statement will be released once we know more. Now, if you'll excuse us, Lancelot and I have more work to do inside."

"See you later." Lancelot lifted himself and Abigail off the ground and floated them to the roof of the HRC. He launched into his own questions when they landed. "What was that down there, Avy? What database?"

"Orders from King." Abigail kept her back to Lancelot and walked to the roof door. She couldn't chance him seeing the lie on her face. Abigail was certain she looked as guilty as she felt. "Don't worry about it."

Despite lying to the media, despite lying to the police department, despite lying to Lancelot, Abigail was ready to celebrate the capture of the arsonist. The man caught at the shed hadn't been convicted when she left the Hero Relief Center, but she thought it would only be a matter of time until he was. Even though he claimed not to have started any fires, the evidence created a big and flashy arrow pointing directly at him. There would still be weeks' worth of investigations, the media would still run the story like crazy, and she was sure the Knights would still have their fingers in the case, but Abigail could finally breathe easily now that the criminal was caught.

The looming threat of King Arthur started to subside as well. She completed her assignment, she caught the bad guy and continued to lie to the media, so now King Arthur had nothing to hang his threat on. The death of the criminal would remain her secret.

Her evening continued to get better as she smelled the campfire scent of Thomas as soon as she stepped inside the restaurant lobby. She maneuvered around a family of five waiting for a hostess at the desk and spotted Thomas lounging on a bench with his arms draped over the back.

"Hey babe," he greeted while getting to his feet.

The country music overhead faded, the two adults requesting children's menus faded, their kids fighting over the small pack of crayons faded, the taxidermy bull head above the door faded, everything faded except Thomas. Abigail pounced onto him, almost knocking them both back onto the bench. He returned her kiss and gave her a second one for good measure.

"You're in a good mood."

Abigail lowered her feet back to the floor, but Thomas refused to let her go any further than the space created inside his arms. She didn't want to be anywhere else.

"We caught the arsonist," Abigail whispered. The lobby was deserted now that the family was gone, but she refused to take any chances of someone hearing her.

His face dropped. "What?"

"We caught him! Well, SAPD has someone in custody for the fires, but we're pretty sure he's the guy. We tracked him to this shed, registered in his name, full of manure and incendiary devices."

"Damn fool."

"What?"

Thomas blinked. "The guy's an idiot. For keeping everything in one spot."

A confused chuckle fell from Abigail's mouth. "You seem a little upset about this."

"I just thought he was a professional." Thomas' crooked smile returned. "The guy looked so good on the reports you showed me."

"Everyone slips up eventually." Abigail shrugged.

"I wouldn't."

"Sure," she laughed. "The internet is going crazy over his fires. He's become sort of a celebrity. He's trending as the Lightning Bug right now."

"Dumb name."

"I know. According to the blogs, it's because in all his fires no one died so he's harmless. Like a bug."

"Harmless?" Thomas growled.

"It's ridiculous! Lancelot almost died because of this guy. This guy's fires—" Abigail stopped. Thomas' hands tightened behind her back causing his nails to dig into her. "Thomas?"

He blinked several times before loosening his hands. "Hearing about his fires is just frustrating."

Abigail ran her hands along his arms. "He's gone now. Maybe work will be less stressful for the both of us now."

"Yeah, maybe," Thomas said absently. "Have you been thinking about our wedding any?"

Abigail grinned, placing her left hand over Thomas' chest. She liked feeling his heartbeat through his T-shirt. "I've thought of *one* thing. I think it's time you meet my family."

He playfully groaned. "I was hoping we'd run away and elope."

"You'd still have to meet them. Eventually."

He sighed, tilting his head to the side in a painfully adorable way. "I guess we'll have a big party then, after all. Let me meet all the aunts, and uncles, and cousins in one go. Have huge centerpieces, tiny bottles of bubbles with our picture on the label, and a slightly bad 90's cover band."

Abigail grinned. "You've thought about this a lot."

"Yeah, since you haven't," he teased.

"I've thought about that kind of stuff too," she defended. "Like the flowers. I want lilies."

Thomas raised an eyebrow. "Like the ones I got you on our first date?"

She swatted his shoulder. "That was not a date."

He grinned, she laughed, and her life was perfect.

"Sanders?"

Abigail and Thomas broke apart to face the host who interrupted them. He held out two plastic menus as a peace offering.

"If you'll follow me, your table is ready."

Thomas snaked his hand into Abigail's and gestured her to follow the host through the tightly-packed restaurant. Peanut shells crunched under their shoes. Neon beer signs flashed on almost every available wall space not taken up with more stuffed animals or black and white pictures depicting the old west. The aisle narrowed as several dining groups decided to add an extra chair on the end of their table. Abigail tugged Thomas in a zig-zag path to keep up with the host.

A man stumbled across the peanut-shell-covered floor from the opposite end of the aisle. The host nearly missed a head on collision, bumping into an occupied seat in the process. Abigail twisted to the side with a practiced move that could have tripped the man if executed properly. With his eyes looking down, Thomas received the full force of the man's shoulder bump.

"Watch it!" Thomas snarled, his fist drawn back and ready to strike.

Abigail smelled smoke. She felt heat burning between their conjoined hands. She saw the spark of blue inside the curl of Thomas' fist. She covered his fist with her free hand and forced him to lower it. Sparks bit into both of her palms.

"Thomas," she called his name, but he didn't budge. He simply glared at the man who continued to apologize with his hands up. "Thomas, it's okay."

He blinked, realizing both his hands were contained by Abigail. When he spoke, the rumble of thunder replaced his snarl. "Sorry man, watch where you're going."

The man didn't stick around and darted down the aisle. The host seated them at the next empty table and set down their menus without any additional pleasantries. Abigail watched Thomas break apart peanuts in the seat across her. He didn't eat any of them, just snapped them open and dropped them to the table. Several of their edges charred in his destruction.

"Talk to me," she said. "What was that?"

He shook his head. "It was a long day at work. I didn't mean to slip like that."

Abigail reached for his hands, but he pulled them away.

"I'm going to the bathroom." Thomas stood from the table. "Will you order me a whiskey?"

Abigail watched him leave. The aisle they fought to get down suddenly opened around him. He vanished inside the shadows looming outside the bathroom alcove. A waitress appeared, took the order, and delivered their drinks before Thomas returned. Abigail drank half of hers before he settled back into his seat with a grin wide enough to sweep away any doubt and discomfort.

"You alright?" Abigail asked cautiously.

"Much better now that I found the emergency exit. I don't think this place is following occupancy code."

Abigail didn't stop the relieved sigh accompanying her chuckle. "That's what had you so on edge?"

He playfully kicked her shoe under the table. "You don't have to be super to have that, what'd you call it? Hero vision. A good firefighter has to put out fires before they happen, too."

"Is that what you were doing in the bathroom for so long?" Abigail raised an eyebrow.

"In one way or another." Thomas pulled a menu to him. "Think this place would cater the wedding? This barbecue burger looks pretty fancy."

"Maybe for everyone not in a white dress."

"Good point. You may be stuck with cheese and crackers all night."

Abigail reached across the table and tangled her fingers with his. Thomas set the menu down and locked his eyes onto hers. The outburst from the aisle was miles away to Abigail. Replacing it inside her mind was Thomas waiting for her at the end of a different kind of aisle adorned on either side with family and rose petals leading her to him. He squeezed her fingers.

"I talked to Kenneth last week." Abigail didn't know why she felt like she was admitting a secret. The way Thomas grimaced at the old hero's name didn't help her case. "He told me what happened the night you came back to San Arbor."

His frown fizzled away. "What do you mean?"

"He told me how you removed his burn." Abigail gestured to the side of her face. "I think it's really noble that you did."

Thomas scratched at his face, but the movement didn't hide his creeping blush. "Well, I gave it to him so I figured I could get rid of it."

"I thought he finally found a skilled enough plastic surgeon," Abigail said. "Why didn't you tell me?"

Thomas tapped his fingers against the menu. Whatever answer brewed behind his lips darkened his face more than his blush. His words came out in a huff. "I didn't want you to think I did it for you. It was part of my atonement, and I didn't want you to think I healed Kenneth to get back on your good side. That required something else."

"Like what?"

The waitress reappeared to collect their menus and their food orders. She hovered closer to Abigail's side of the table and when she asked Thomas for his order, she didn't look up from her note pad. Abigail glanced around their section of the restaurant. The tables nearest to them were kept empty, even if it meant cramming people together elsewhere. Abigail adjusted their dinner budget to include a hefty tip to make up for Thomas' outburst.

"I wanted the new me on your good side," Thomas answered after the waitress left, acting like her interruption never happened. "I didn't want *him* bribing you."

Cinder.

Abigail didn't need any clarification from Thomas about who *he* was. She returned her hands to his and he heated them with his touch. "I love you, Thomas. Cinder is dead."

"I love you, too, Abbs."

Chapter Twenty-Three

Abigail skipped into work the next morning. Her entire mood was as bouncy as her movements. The crowded bus she took to the HRC hadn't bothered her, nor did the perspiring gentleman she sat next to for several blocks, or the gum she stepped in while getting off the bus. She wiped her shoe against the sidewalk curb until most of the pink glob was gone and continued her journey.

She waved at Shannon when she entered the lobby, smiled at Mitch when she caught him leaving the elevator and whistled *Oh What a Beautiful Morning* while she dressed in her Avalon gear. On the way to the Round Table, she realized nothing would ruin her mood, not even if she was assigned another classroom visit. Entering the room, the other Knights looked just as jovial. Merlin and King Arthur laughed with their heads bent together as Lancelot tried to throw tiny chocolate candies through Excalibur's mouth guard. By the number of candies on the floor, it didn't look like Lancelot was having any success.

Abigail took her seat and basked in the communal good mood. A hero saves people; Abigail believed that to her very core. She knew someone would always need saving but, in this moment, she relished the sensation that everyone was safe. Finally, San Arbor was free of the arsonist. The city was safe.

King Arthur's laughter stopped, and Lancelot tossed his remaining candy into his mouth instead of at Excalibur's helmet as President Samuels entered the room. The door slid shut behind him. He did not look as carefree as Abigail and the others felt. As he settled into his seat, a somber air clouded the room.

"What's wrong, Quinn?" King Arthur asked.

President Samuels pointed a remote at one of the monitors hanging on a wall and summoned a brutal image of a man bleeding out in a concrete cell. Despite the poor image and discoloring of the man's head, Abigail saw the tattooed cobra coiling around the arsonist's ear.

"Bryan Riggs was found dead in his cell late last night."

"The arsonist died?" Lancelot stared at the image with his mouth half open.

"Murdered, by the looks of it," Merlin corrected.

"Shanked, if we're being technical." President Samuels turned away from the screen.

"What's our plan?" Abigail asked. "Do we have any reports from the jail yet?"

King Arthur spoke over the president's answer. "This is the police's problem. We won't involve ourselves."

"But this is obviously an inside job. Shouldn't we figure out who targeted Riggs?"

"Your job was to catch the arsonist." King Arthur spoke slowly as if he thought Abigail forgot. "Which was accomplished. He's not a danger to anyone, anymore. We can move on. You did a good job, Avalon."

"You can't be serious." Abigail glanced to everyone at the table. "This is the San Arbor Detention Center, not some state prison with a hundred plus prisoners. Someone arranged this and someone must have seen something."

"You're right." President Samuels raised his hand toward King Arthur to stop him from interrupting. "But so is Arthur. This is a matter for the police and the detention center now. If they require our help, they will ask. The ordinance does not extend to inside the judicial system."

"The killer could be loose in San Arbor right now."

"Or already locked in a cell," challenged King Arthur.

"Enough." President Samuels cut through their brewing argument. "Excalibur, I'm assigning you to patrol the district around the detention center. Keep an ear out for anything suspicious."

"Roger that." Excalibur accepted his duty.

"I'll patrol with him," Abigail volunteered.

The president shook his head. "You're already scheduled with marketing today, Avalon. You're filming a new fire safety campaign. Merlin, you'll accompany Excalibur for a few hours before moving east."

Abigail slumped in her seat and sighed. She'd rather teach another class of gremlins how to brush their teeth.

"Too bad you couldn't have your firefighter friend on the campaign with you," Lancelot said after receiving his assignment to work with King Arthur. He wiggled his eyebrows after the statement and made a terrible-looking and terrible-sounding kissy face at her.

"Shut it, Lance." Abigail kicked his chair, and he rolled a few inches away.

"No, he's got a good idea," Excalibur said. "Bringing on a first responder would help market our camaraderie."

Merlin gasped. "There actually is a brain under that bucket."

Excalibur ignored her and turned to President Samuels. "What do you think?"

"It's not a bad idea at all. With both agencies chasing down the target, it would be good to showcase that teamwork. I'll make some calls, see who we can get on such short notice."

Abigail watched King Arthur. She waited for him to deny their idea. To laugh at the very thought of it. To refuse to associate the names of the Round Table Knights with the first responders, but he didn't. King Arthur sat obedient and quiet for the company president.

"Ladder Company 3 would be a good place to call first." Lancelot snickered as Abigail pushed him further down the table.

Hiding her and Thomas' relationship wasn't difficult. She had enough practice to know that when her mask was on, Thomas Sanders was simply a firefighter she sometimes worked calls with. Abigail could force her hands to stay at her sides, to not respond with an inside joke, to not get hung up in his emerald stare. What was difficult was interacting with his team. She forgot which information Abigail, girl-friend knew compared to Avalon, superhero. She quickly swallowed down her questions about Tawna and her pregnancy as she greeted Thomas and Purvis on the media floor.

Abigail knew Tawna was just over six months, and hoped they were having a girl. Both she and Purvis wanted to be surprised and not find out until the delivery. She knew Tawna already painted the nursery lilac, claiming she knew more things than Purvis as she was the one carrying their baby. She knew Tawna already decided on the outfit they would dress the baby in on the way home from the hospital. Abigail was with her when Tawna bought the onesie designed to look like a fireman's turnout coat, equipped with boot looking socks and a helmet printed beanie.

Avalon didn't even know Purvis' name.

"Hey guys," she smiled walking to them. "Thanks for coming by on such short notice."

"It got us out of cleaning the apparatus floor so I'm glad to be here," said Purvis.

Thomas' eyes locked onto Abigail's, and she wasn't so sure she wouldn't drown in his gaze. "Purvis breaks out into terrible hives whenever he has to work too hard."

"I do not!" Purvis defended.

"Thankfully in our gear you won't have to see the boils if he gets them here," Thomas continued.

"As long as you can read a few lines from a script there shouldn't be any hives," Abigail joined the joke. "And, just in case, we can have someone from medical come watch."

Thomas looped his arm around Purvis' neck, tugging him close to him. "I've had paramedic training, ma'am. I'll take him out if I need to."

"He's had one CPR class." Purvis escaped Thomas' grip and straightened his turnout coat once free.

Abigail stifled her laugh and gestured around the room. Off to the side, a platform stage was being fit with a green screen and three cameras were dollied into position. A handful of HRC staff sporting either a walkie-talkie or headset skittered around the equipment finalizing tiny details that Abigail knew nothing about.

"We'll be getting started soon," she said. "Can I get you anything while we wait?"

"Is there really going to be a script?" Purvis asked.

"A couple of lines," Abigail answered, "but nothing too hard."

"Can we practice them?"

For all his bravado, Abigail had never seen Purvis look this nervous. He tapped his fingers against the sides of his coat and glanced at the cameras like he was waiting for them to combust. When an overhead light flooded the stage, Abigail thought he flinched.

"Let me get the script," Abigail said. "We can go over them a few times together if you want. I think I'm going to get tongue tied over a few parts myself."

Purvis nodded and Abigail left to find anyone with a stack of paper that could be the script. She dodged a boom microphone before it slammed into the side of her face, found a table of tiny sandwiches hidden in a corner, was forced to stand still for a quick powdering of her nose, and finally found a chair marked with director occupied by a woman in her fifties.

"Rosita," Abigail smiled at the director.

"Avalon." Rosita cupped the sides of Abigail's face with wrinkly hands and kissed both of her cheeks. "I hope you're ready to make more magic today. Your last commercial was quite a success on my part."

"Those dolls were one of the hottest selling items last Christmas." Abigail's memory of the commercial was different than how Rosita must have recalled it.

"What can I help you with, dear? Have you been to make up yet?"

"Just got my nose touched up." Abigail tossed her thumb over her shoulder to where the powdering assault took place. "I was hoping you had a copy of the script? I'd like to run it over with the firemen a few times."

"Excellent idea." Rosita shoved several stapled documents into Abigail's arms. "You may workshop the new sections containing our guests. They were drawn up last minute after the call from Samuels."

"I understand, I know this—"

Rosita interrupted Abigail by jumping out of her chair. "No, no, no!" she shouted toward the stage. "I said up lights! Didn't you pay attention in the meeting?"

Abigail took her cue to leave and returned to where she left Thomas and Purvis, but only Purvis was there.

"Here's a copy of the script." Abigail handed Purvis one of the documents. "Where'd your friend go?"

"Thomas said he needed to go to the bathroom," Purvis said distractedly as he began flipping through the script. "Which fireman am I?"

"I don't think it matters." Abigail scanned the room again. "I'll go find Thomas, it's easy to get lost in this place."

Abigail did not find Thomas inside the single room, co-ed bathroom. She didn't find him at the buffet table or mingling with the staff. The woman armed with makeup brushes hadn't seen him, nor did the security personnel at the stairwell door. Abigail scanned the empty rafters and looked behind the stage curtain, but Thomas had vanished.

She almost started to worry until she heard the thunderstorm rumble of his voice snaking out from under the green room door. She gripped the door handle but paused before turning it.

"I won't." Thomas' voice was muffled through the door. "Not here."

Abigail waited to hear a response, but none came. Thomas answered the silence.

"This is not a good place to burn."

Abigail shoved the door open. Thomas stood alone in the room. His reflection glanced toward her from the mirror. His hands were pressing against the glass, the knuckles on his right hand looking red and angry.

"There you are." Abigail kept her voice media-ready until the door closed behind her. "Everything okay?"

Thomas turned away from the mirror and leaned against the counter, hiding both his hands inside his turnout coat's pockets. "Everything's perfect. Do they need me on set already?"

"Not just yet." Abigail crossed the room and linked her arms through his. With a gentle tug she urged his hands free of their confines, but they remained inside Thomas' pockets. "Is there anyone else in here?"

Abigail didn't need him to answer. She could see the entirety of the room from where she stood. They were alone.

"It's just us." A smirk claimed Thomas' mouth as he leaned down to kiss her.

"I thought I heard you talking to someone." Abigail said instead of raising up on her tiptoes to meet him halfway. Thomas pulled back until Abigail's hold stopped him.

"Just going over my lines," he answered, removing his left hand and capturing Abigail's with it. He ran a finger over her naked fingers. The smallest hint of a tan line started to form around her ring finger. "You're not wearing your ring. Did you not like it?"

"You know I can't wear it here." Abigail refused to acknowledge the guilt attempting to twist her gut. "It would cause too many questions."

"So, we're back to secrets?"

Abigail couldn't tell if Thomas' hurt expression was real or a tease, so she pulled out the chain she wore under her costume. Her engagement ring twisted at the end.

"I'm not ashamed of it," she stated. "Or you."

With his right hand, Thomas pinched the ring between his thumb and pointer finger. It looked so fragile in his grip. The sapphire center looked out of place next to his red knuckles. "Promise me something."

"Anything."

"Never take this off."

Abigail kissed him quickly, a peck to seal the promise she thought she already made. "Of course, I won't."

Someone outside the door knocked, and Abigail leapt away from Thomas. He chuckled, his eyes never leaving her.

"Avalon," the knocker said. "They're ready for you."

"Coming right out," she announced.

Chapter Twenty-Four

Abigail stared in disbelief at the photograph taped on the jewelry store's counter. The ring pictured looked like the one hanging from the chain under her costume. The golden band was a perfect circle connecting under a beautiful sapphire stone. The wrapping around the base looked like the detailed work that wrapped around hers. The picture didn't shimmer under the florescent lights, but Abigail knew how the stone would toss around the light. She stopped herself from reaching for her ring. She forced out a shaky exhale and focused on the jeweler across the counter.

"You didn't get anything on the cameras?" Lancelot asked him.

"No sir, they're broken," the jeweler answered. "Wires were cut the night before."

"The night before the robbery?" Abigail asked.

"What else was stolen?" Lancelot added.

"This ring, a few gold chains, and our petty cash," the man answered Lancelot. "The more expensive things were under a better lock, I suppose. I know this is probably below your pay grade, with it being just a piece of jewelry and all, but when I saw you two walking by, I thought I'd ask for your help."

"You can always ask the heroes of the HRC for help." Lancelot smiled, reciting from their PR pamphlet. "Right, Avalon?"

Abigail yanked her gaze from the photo. The image continued to burn into her mind. "Absolutely."

"We'll keep our ears out for anything related," Lancelot said. "Meanwhile, you should call area pawn shops to see if it gets moved."

"And get your cameras fixed," Abigail added. "How did the thief get in?"

"Smashed out one of our back windows." The jeweler shook his head. "I guess I ought to get sensors on the doors and windows too. We just have them in the cases."

"No signs of fire?"

Both the jeweler and Lancelot stared at Abigail. She didn't waver under their perplexed expressions.

"You caught the arsonist, I thought?"

"Yes, we did, sir." Lancelot worked to erase any doubt about the case. "He won't be setting any more fires."

The jeweler turned to Abigail and answered her question, "There was no sign of any fire."

"I just wanted to check all of our bases," she said absently.

The ring still laid guiltily against her chest. Abigail bid farewell to the jeweler and exited the shop before Lancelot could finish wrapping up his final remarks. Her ring was stolen? The thought made her sick. The idea of Thomas stealing *anything* made her sicker. He stole the bike so easily, what would have stopped him from taking a ring? Abigail twisted her heel against the sidewalk, willing the accusation away. The motorcycle was under a different circumstance. Lancelot would have died without Thomas' quick thinking. With her back to Lancelot, she reached for the ring. The gem was cold to the touch.

She couldn't believe Thomas would want to continue their life together by stealing and lying to her. He said he'd been waiting for weeks to ask her. Abigail dropped her hand.

"The robbery was last week?" she asked when Lancelot joined her on the sidewalk.

"Yeah," he answered. "Just like the guy said. Are you feeling alright?"

"I just wanted to get the timeline right." Abigail sighed. There were two rings, that was the only way this made sense. "Things have been a whirlwind the last few weeks. I'm fine, I promise."

Lancelot continued to stare at her for several seconds until he either believed her or accepted her lie and moved on.

"Should we call the police and have them search for it too?"

"Finding the ring will be next to impossible despite the number of eyes we have out for it," Abigail answered. Lancelot frowned under his mask. "It's too small to keep track of. Besides, the jeweler already made a report with them. I'm sure his insurance will help with the loss too."

"I wish we could do more for the guy. Did you see how embarrassed he was to ask us for help?"

"We can talk to Quinn about that." Abigail started down the sidewalk. She didn't like the jewelry store at her back. Like it was watching her, seeing through her costume with its sights on her ring. "We should be more accessible to the public."

Lancelot snapped his fingers beside her. "Let's get lunch! At the park, with a bunch of people."

"Is this a PR stunt or are you hungry?"

Lancelot grinned, patting his stomach. "A hero's gotta' eat, you know?"

After their publicized lunch at a San Arbor park where the heroes were invited to a five-year-old's birthday for hot dogs and cake, Abigail froze on the sidewalk. Her legs locked into place as if she were a doll and not a superpowered individual. Abigail couldn't look away from the electronic store's window display. Lancelot walked forward unaware of her stopping. He continued his story to the open air and squirrels running along the telephone wires. One of the television monitors on display played the afternoon news. The firetruck on the screen taunted Abigail. The painted number 3 on the side was a gut punch. She watched the story recap, saw Purvis and Maddox work the car crash behind the reporter. Abigail's mind swam with unknown questions. She didn't see Thomas on the report, but if his team was there, he had to be too.

Her head flooded with more questions. He was supposed to be helping Maddox paint his porch. Thomas said today was their off day. How could they be painting a porch while fighting fires? Abigail braced a hand against the window as a dizzy spell claimed her. Thomas wouldn't have lied to her. Especially about something as stupid as painting a porch. This had to be an old report. Abigail tried to convince herself, but the time stamp on the news ticker tape kept proving her wrong.

"Checking out your boyfriend?" Lancelot teased behind her.

His voice cleared away part of the fog in her mind. This was real. Abigail continued to watch the report, looking for Thomas. She tried to cover up her obsession with the footage. "We didn't hear this on the scanner."

Lancelot leaned around her to better see the screen. "It's on the north side. Out of our jurisdiction. Looks like it's fine though. The reporter is happy."

The reporter smiled and signed off. As the screen switched to the newsroom, Abigail saw a glimpse of her pale reflection.

"Are you sure you're feeling okay?"

Abigail tried to smile, shoving away Lancelot's concerns. "I think my lunch is fighting me. I'm fine. Promise."

"I'll fly you to the hospital, just say the word."

Abigail hoped he was joking, and quickly changed the subject away from her. She stepped away from the window. "Think you'll change up your costume after you're done sidekicking?"

Lancelot gave himself a dramatic once over. "Is there something wrong with my look?"

"Not unless you like your diaper pants."

Lancelot laughed. "That's harsh, Avalon."

She joined his laugh. He was an easy distraction, and she was grateful for it. Whatever questions she had for Thomas, she couldn't ask them until she was back home, anyway. It was better to settle into Lancelot's distraction than worry about things she couldn't do anything about. They rounded the city corner, waited with a small crowd as the streetlights rotated to red, and crossed the street. It was a typical late summer day in San Arbor. Everything was normal except for the explosion.

Glass shattered ahead of Abigail and sucked the sound from the busy street. The first-story windows of a building on their left were in ruin. Dust, glass, and smoke collapsed from the openings. Abigail yanked Lancelot close to her and shielded him with her cape as a wave of fire followed the glass.

The screams inside the building were louder than the faint sirens across the city.

"Shields up!" she shouted at Lancelot before jumping into the blaze.

The events outside occurred in slow motion. Abigail saw each piece of window glass crash onto the sidewalk. She felt each temperature degree increase from the outpouring heat of the blast. She moved in hyper speed to cover Lancelot before the blaze could scorch him. But, once she was inside, time was not on her side. Fire wrapped around support columns like a greedy python. Dark smoke covered the ceiling tiles. Falling cinders tried to blind her. She searched for the cause of the fire, the central point of heat and destruction, but the building's lobby was a vortex of flame, smoke, and carnage. Desperate cries for help were sucked from the air with each heat wave.

The air suddenly stilled around Abigail. Embers trickled around a protective bubble as if a giant umbrella was above her. Behind her, Lancelot stood with his arms extended into the air.

"Shields up," he greeted.

Abigail nodded, turning her mask's pin light functions on. "I'll bring them to you."

"I'll be right behind you."

Abigail ducked under the psychic umbrella and dashed into the flames. The intense heat of the fire agitated her skin, an alien feeling she was not used to, but she pushed through the flames. Those trapped inside would not be able to withstand the blaze like she could. Agitation to her could mean death to others.

A hand reached toward her in the dark smoke and Abigail pulled the rest of the person close to her. She pushed them under Lancelot's umbrella and kept moving. She didn't have time to assess injuries. She didn't have time to promise things would be okay. She didn't have time to think. Her body reacted to years of training. Person after person, she hauled strangers from the flames and delivered them to Lancelot who kept them protected. The shield covered twenty individuals before Lancelot pulled out of the building.

He returned with a squad of firefighters, their fire hoses pointed and ready.

"Lancelot, take a guy and check the next floor," Abigail commanded. "I'll smother this side of the building and—"

"We'll take the other," one of the helmeted firefighters finished.

"Let's be heroes."

Time became nonexistent as Abigail worked the scene. Cherry-red flames poured from her hands as she snuffed the blaze. It left dirty scorch marks on the floor and up the walls. She burned more pieces of furniture as she moved through the floor, but she beat back the blaze. The smoke thinned around her. Behind her, she was able to hear the water hoses. She felt the cool touch of Lancelot's abilities as he moved past her. She knelt behind an upturned desk on the lobby floor to check for any more victims and instead found a familiar gray box. The outside began to melt but she saw the thermal strip of red tape inside. Another incendiary device.

Her heart stuttered.

"Avalon?"

Abigail covered the switch with her boot and turned to the helmeted firefighter that called her name. She spotted the number 7 stitched into his turnout gear.

"We're ready to clear out of here," he said.

"Good work on killing the blaze." She awkwardly praised him, forcing herself to keep her legs as still as possible as she hid the switch.

"Good work on the rescue." His comment sounded sincere. "I wish we could all have a Lancelot like you."

"He's wonderful, isn't he?"

The firefighter nodded, then said, "We do need you to leave though. Overhaul phase is coming in, and you know…"

"SAFD only," she nodded with a bright smile. "We'll leave it to San Arbor's best."

She waited for him to turn, but the firefighter kept his eyes on her. Abigail felt the blood pulse behind her ears. King Arthur's threat bubbled to the front of her mind.

"Is everything okay?"

"Of course!" Abigail sounded too cheerful. "Just need to tie a shoelace. Give me one second."

Abigail bent down and fumbled with her boots. She shifted her body so the switch was hidden behind her leg. She gritted her teeth. She knew King Arthur would not be happy, but she had no other choice. She fumbled with her laces. By design they could never become untied, but she wouldn't let that become public knowledge. With her left hand she messed with the grieve, and with her right she scratched away the thermal strip inside the device. Once it flaked away under her nail, she pretended to sneeze. She dramatically covered her nose and mouth, and as the firefighter stepped back, she spat a tiny ball of blue flame onto the switch. Without the thermal strip, the metal warped and melted into a heap of unrecognizable trash instead of exploding.

She crushed it to ash with a twist of her heel and followed the firefighter out of the building. Leaving the remains and her secrets to be washed away.

Chapter Twenty-Five

"Your shield worked better than I thought," Abigail admitted to Lancelot while they stood inside the elevator at the Hero Relief Center. She hadn't told him about the device, deciding to wait for King Arthur in case he held any more lies over her sidekick.

"Did you expect any less?" Lancelot asked with a smug grin. His shield kept him untouched from the fire as well as those he saved. Nothing about him, his hair, or his costume was out of place.

Unlike Abigail, who's costume was speckled in ash and soot. She smelled like a fireplace.

"On this first run, a little bit." Abigail playfully punched his arm and regretted it. She busied her hands by flattening her costume's skirt, dusting away a layer of ash clinging to it.

"There's no second chances when you're saving people, right?"

The door slid open with a chime. "You're right."

"Since I'm all cured, want me to handle today's report, boss?"

Abigail rolled her eyes. "I'll take care of it."

"Cool. I've got an interview with Channel 9 anyway."

"Then why did you offer?"

Lancelot shrugged. "Out of habit, I guess?"

"Have I really been dumping the reports on you that often?" Abigail waited for his answer, but Lancelot only shrugged again. Trying to ignore the guilt that bubbled in her gut, she changed the subject. "An interview with 9? Is it with your girlfriend?"

"Monica?" Lancelot tapped his chin with his pointer finger as he thought. "Since my evening has an opening now, I could ask her to dinner."

"Just don't share any company secrets, lover boy." Abigail shoved him down the hallway, then buried her hands inside her pockets so she couldn't accidentally touch him a third time today. "I'll catch up with you when you're done, I need to talk to King."

Lancelot turned around. "About what? I can drop the interview."

"Just about the report, don't worry about it. Go powder your nose or something before your big interview."

Lancelot gave her a final grin and continued down the hallway. Abigail walked past the other offices until she stood outside King Arthur's door. She rarely saw Excalibur's door shut while she worked with him, but King Arthur's office always remained shut off to the rest of the other Knights. She hoped it hadn't been a red flag she'd been ignoring. She knocked and barely heard King Arthur's response on the other side. The office was well lit when she entered. The bay windows on either side of the desk stretched from floor to ceiling. A plush couch in the center of the room looked comfortable enough to nap on. She made a mental note to get something like that in her office. She had the space and spent enough nights trying to sleep in a chair to warrant something better.

"Excellent work downtown." King Arthur smiled at her. "Saw the whole thing on TV."

"Lance is doing an interview with 9 about it," she absently replied, examining the rest of the office. King Arthur's desk was clean enough to perform surgery on. The entire office was pristine and smelled of lemon cleaner. "I didn't mean to interrupt if you're in the middle of something."

King Arthur lowered his gaze to the empty desk before raising an eyebrow at Abigail.

She chuckled nervously. "There was another incendiary device at this fire. I had to destroy it before SAFD found it, though. I'll leave it out of the report, of course, but wanted to inform you."

"I'm glad you did." King Arthur steepled his fingers together and rested his chin atop them. "Did it match the others?"

"Looked like them. Same size, same smell, and same thermal-strip inside. King, does this mean we caught the wrong guy?"

"Riggs was a part of this somehow." King Arthur assigned the dead man's guilty title without a second thought. "He claimed to be working with someone else, or maybe someone got a hold of the switches and wanted to try them out themselves. It looks like your back on the case, Abigail."

"You won't want anyone to know, will you?"

King Arthur smiled. "It's like you're reading my mind. Were the first responders suspicious of you destroying the device?"

Abigail shook her head. "If they were, there was nothing for them to find. Merlin and I discovered the casing melts under the Dragon's Breath. I made sure there was nothing but ash."

King Arthur's smile remained. Abigail hated the way it chilled her bones instead of lifted her spirits. She hoped he was right, that this was the best way to handle the situation. President Samuels would never allow King Arthur to lead if he didn't approve of his actions.

If he even knew of his actions.

"Abby?"

Abigail focused on King Arthur and the question she missed. "I'm sorry?"

"Will you deliver this to Merlin on your way out?" King Arthur held a thumb drive toward her.

"Of course." Abigail accepted it.

"Now, go figure out this arsonist case already." King Arthur's smile tried to deliver the statement with encouragement, but it weighed heavily on Abigail. The mad man needed to be caught and it needed to be before another fire was set.

Abigail dropped off the thumb drive and returned to her office to work up the report of the fire. The middle of the report was as boring as the start, and neither section contained much information. The fire started with a bang, and it ended with a sizzle. When she finally reached the end of the form, she felt little sense of accomplishment. She angrily clicked *save* and the file vanished into the HRC computer system. Even if filling out her reports in a timely manner could save the day, Abigail wasn't sure she could do it. The paperwork was torture.

And, deep down, she knew the bureaucracy did nothing to help her catch the fire starter. Whether this new arsonist was the original all along or some deranged copycat. The files and reports wouldn't show what she was missing in the case. If they could, she would have found it by now. She would have discovered a pattern and figured out what the goal was. Noticed how they were constantly avoiding her, how they were staying a step ahead, how they created an incendiary device that only reacted under a heat few were capable of producing.

If these files and reports could shed any light, Abigail almost hoped they would reveal King Arthur instead of the arsonist, and what he would do if she couldn't catch the bad guy. Fighting fires was easy. If King Arthur turned on her, she wasn't sure she'd be able to win.

Abigail leaned back in her chair and tossed her arms above her with a frustrated sigh. Fighting the bad guys was a lot easier than finding them. Unless she hid inside a random building and hoped the arsonist would target it, all she could do was wait for a lead. She'd start with Riggs' history and investigate those inside his circle.

Before she could open Riggs' record, Lancelot crashed into Abigail's office. She jolted in her chair, her knees banging against the underside of her desk. Lancelot's eyes were wide with either excitement or fear, but Abigail couldn't ask him what was happening before he lifted her with his mental powers.

"Someone saw him!" Lancelot shouted. "The guy who started the fire today! We have a witness that wants to give us a statement!"

"What?" Abigail tried to pump her legs through the air, but Lancelot's psychic touch held firm, and they floated down the hallway.

"DaVodi brought her in. She's at The Round." Lancelot moved as fast as he spoke, entering the stairwell and ascending to the top floor. "King and the others are heading there, too."

"Slow down," Abigail warned, but it was pointless. She buzzed with adrenaline. Her hands sparked in excitement. "We still have to be professional."

Lancelot lowered them to the ground outside the stairwell door marked with a 12. "You're the one who's igniting."

Abigail's cheeks flushed and she defended herself by pointing out Lancelot's own unprofessionalism. "Your mask is off."

Lancelot touched just under his eye and laughed when he felt skin. His mask hung loosely around his neck.

"Did the reporter get you that easily?" Abigail teased.

"She did say yes to dinner," Lancelot answered, tightening his mask into place.

"You'll have to tell me everything later." Abigail ended the subject as they walked into the Round Table and found the rest of the Knights seated at the stone table. She and King Arthur exchanged a heavy look.

Chief DaVodi stood with an elderly woman at the front of the room. The points of her thin elbows stuck out from the holes in her knitted sweater. The woman's graying hair curled tightly around her face, and her choice of perfume reminded Abigail of her grandmother on her dad's side. Too strong and too sweet. King Arthur waited for Abigail and Lancelot to sit before addressing the woman and the police chief.

"DaVodi says you saw the person responsible for today's fire?"

The woman nodded, but DaVodi answered, "She saw something. It isn't a guarantee."

"What did you see?" Abigail asked impatiently. The smallest detail would be more than what they currently had. If a table wasn't between her and the witness, Abigail would have shaken the woman until answers fell from her pockets like loose change.

"I was leaving the Caldwell Building after having lunch with my grandson." The woman's voice was frail. "He's interning there this semester, for school. He's 'learning the ropes' is what he says, but I don't think he's learning any more than he would in the classroom. But what do I know? College wasn't so mandatory back when I was his age."

A polite tap on her arm from DaVodi put the woman's story back on track.

"I needed to sign out at the front desk in the lobby, and from the corner of my eye I saw a flash of blue. I thought it was a car driving by, but when I heard someone shout, I looked over and saw the fire. I know it sounds silly, but I swear on my Daddy's grave it was blue before looking normal."

"Blue fire." Chief DaVodi recapped the woman's statement.

The room spun around Abigail. She couldn't feel her fingers. Each time her heart beat it echoed inside her hollow chest. Her skin lit with goosebumps while the crime fighter in her screamed his name. While the girlfriend she was refused to believe Thomas could do anything criminal.

Excalibur's gloved hand brought her back to the ground. He squeezed her arm and said, "No one suspects you."

A strange relief settled Abigail's breath. They didn't suspect Thomas, just her.

"You were right on the scene." Chief DaVodi did not share Excalibur's belief. "Arrived at the townhouse fire before it was even called in. Have you heard about the hero complex? It's common in cocky first responders. They cause the events that allow them to save the day."

"Avalon isn't one of your cocky responders." King Arthur defended his team, the steel in his voice surprising Abigail. "She doesn't need to cause crime events in San Arbor when your boys can't keep the criminals in line."

Chief DaVodi's upper lip twisted into a snarl.

"Besides, Avalon was with me all day," Lancelot added.

"You're a compromised alibi." DaVodi silenced Lancelot before looking at Abigail. "I need your location and who can corroborate it for each of the fires going back to Jolt Station."

The police chief's eyes bored into hers despite the mask keeping her and her identity safe. Abigail pinched herself under the table and focused on the sharp pain.

"But we caught the guy responsible for all of those fires." Lancelot continued to defend Abigail while she remained silent.

"Bryan Riggs, the person only you suspected who mysteriously died just before he was going to name his accomplice? That will never hold up in a court." DaVodi glared at Abigail, waiting for her to say something.

"I can get you the information if you truly suspect me." Abigail was surprised how level her voice sounded. "I don't have anything to hide. But, if my alibi names someone not in the hero industry? How will you keep them safe?"

"The investigation on you wouldn't go public unless it went to court, but, as you said, you have nothing to connect you."

Nothing except the same blue fire and stolen incendiary devices from the scenes.

"I'll ask you to come to the precinct with me for a proper interrogation."

"Interrogation?" Excalibur asked DaVodi. "Is that really necessary?"

"Yes." There was no room in the police chief's answer for negotiation.

"No." King Arthur rivaled the police chief's decision. "We'll handle this in house."

"Just because you're a *superhero* doesn't mean you're immune to the laws that govern this city!"

King Arthur ignored DaVodi, which infuriated the police chief even more as spit flew from his mouth accompanying his following curses.

"Avalon," King Arthur called across the table.

"Sir?"

As Abigail shifted her gaze off the fuming chief to her leader, her eyes snapped onto his like a magnet. She couldn't look away, she couldn't move, she couldn't think. A purple light filled her vision and her mind. She became suspended in the color. She wasn't sure if she was breathing anymore.

"Avalon, answer my questions truthfully. Did you start the fires in San Arbor?"

The voice vibrated the color, and ripples made of sound lapped against her skin. The gentle caresses knocked the truth from her lips. Her voice sounded inside the purple ocean but didn't disturb the color.

"No."

As soon as she answered, the ocean drained away, and Abigail was back at the Round Table. The same purple shade inside King Arthur's eyes drained away until his normal brown eyes remained. Abigail collapsed into her chair, unable to catch her breath.

"You see, DaVodi, my team is clean," said King Arthur.

Excalibur whispered in Abigail's ear, "Are you okay?"

"I think so," she lied. It felt like a dozen hairy spider legs were crawling over her arms, and her stomach ached like she'd just ran a marathon. Worse of all was how empty her mind currently felt. When the purple ocean drained away it sucked away a piece of her conscience. She could have been submerged for just a moment or an entire lifetime. Abigail suddenly pitied everyone who had been under King Arthur's ability. It was no longer as noble as he made it out to be. Abigail rubbed her hands up her arms and burned away the chill.

At the end of the table, DaVodi glared at her. "I will still need the list of your locations for each of the fires."

"Understood."

"If it was blue fire, could it have been the Flame Villain?"

Abigail whipped her head to Lancelot before he could finish his question. "You know about him?"

He shrugged. "I saw his file when I was cleaning your desk the other day. You have a whole encyclopedia on the guy. It was a little obsessive."

Abigail had to leave. She wanted to dart from the room, but six sets of eyes burned into her. She fumbled for an explanation and what she settled on was as gritty as coffee grounds against her teeth. "After he attacked Volcanic, I needed to keep tabs on him in case he returned."

"You didn't think city wide arson was a tab?" The chief crossed his arms.

"That's not his style. Cinder preferred—"

"First name basis with a villain?" DaVodi interrupted.

From across the room, King Arthur wore the same appalled look as the chief. It morphed into a frown before anyone but Abigail noticed.

Merlin stood and approached the woman who looked terrified standing between the chief of police and the heroes. "Thank you for coming in today, you've helped us a lot. Chief DaVodi, Mitch will escort you and our guest to the front of the building. Ma'am, can we arrange a taxi for you?"

The woman nodded, wrapping herself tightly inside her sweater.

Merlin set her attention back to DaVodi. "Avalon will send you the statements you require, but we have a lot of work to do right now."

After the chief nodded, Merlin escorted DaVodi and the witness to the door and quickly closed it when they were on the other side. She blew a loose strand of her red hair away from her eyes with an annoyed huff.

The target on Abigail's chest felt a hundred times heavier without DaVodi in the room. King Arthur had nowhere else to train his heated gaze.

"The Flame Villain wouldn't need to use an incendiary device." Abigail was surprised at the sound logic that came from her panicked mind.

"Is he in San Arbor?" King Arthur asked sternly.

"Not that I know of." Abigail swallowed the lie, not knowing if she imagined the creeping of purple around King Arthur's eyes. *Cinder is dead.* "I lost him after the Volcanic attack."

"We cannot rule out the possibility," King Arthur decided. "All of us are going out. Split the city and check every room and alley. We will find the real arsonist, or we will find every low life in the city."

"Was Riggs not the real arsonist?" Lancelot asked the room.

Excalibur dropped his head. Merlin looked at King Arthur. Abigail was sick of lying.

"I found an incendiary device at the Caldwell fire," she told Lance-lot. "Riggs wasn't working alone."

"Should we collaborate with SAPD?"

The look King Arthur delivered to Lancelot could have sliced him open. "The Knights will handle this."

"Yes, sir." Lancelot shrank in his chair.

"Report back to me before engaging." King Arthur dismissed them.

Chapter Twenty-Six

Abigail pressed her cell phone against her ear before she made it out of the building. The pure relief when the phone answered flooded her, and she waited to hear Thomas' thunderstorm voice. She knew the low rumble would scare off the darkness currently gripping her chest. Whatever new fire starter was in the city wouldn't frame him. Or her. She needed to warn him. She just needed him. When Thomas did speak, her grip around the receiver tightened.

"Hey, doll."

Her flood of relief crashed into a dam. His voice cracked open the dark clouds in her head like a storm warning. Lightning flashed and something ominous danced on the wind. Goosebumps erupted on Abigail's arms. The fiery sunset around her seemed to be made of actual fire.

"Thomas?" She whispered, pleaded.

"Not anymore," Cinder leered.

"How?" Abigail was ashamed of the tears prickling in her eyes. She wobbled on the Hero Relief Center lawn. "What happened?"

"I've always liked to play with fire." His lack of an answer chilled her bones. "Think you're fireproof enough for me, yet?"

"You were supposed to be dead!"

A passerby nervously glanced at Abigail before they crossed the street. Abigail tucked herself behind the sword and the stone statue. The monument forced her to stand up straight even though her legs turned to jelly. Cinder chuckled and the sound chilled Abigail worse than the stone pressing against her back.

Cinder's dead.

Good job, hero.

"I've missed you, too." Ice clinked against a glass on his end of the phone. "Come have a drink with me. At the place we first met. We've got a lot to discuss."

"Thomas—"

Glass shattered on his end, and Abigail tried again.

"Cinder, I—"

"Come alone, hero. And come quickly. The staff, apparently, is a little frightened of me."

Abigail heard the snap of his finger and a frightened yelp before he ended the call.

Chapter Twenty-Seven

Abigail would never forget when she first met the Flame Villain. She had just graduated from the police academy and worked for a startup hero company in San Arbor. The protective mask she wore then was a sequined strip of fabric that matched the now bankrupt company's T-shirt. The costume was as protective as it was fashionable. So neither. She served drinks at the little bar to advertise for the company. It was the furthest thing from being a hero, but, in the moment, young Abigail didn't care. She would climb every corporate ladder to achieve her dream of becoming a real hero.

She never expected she would return to the bar where Cinder scarred her neck and left her dying on the burning floor as Avalon. The same night the sequined mask burned, so did Abigail's frightened younger self.

Adrenaline and fear pumped her legs as she neared the bar. She wasn't afraid for the people inside. She would save them. She wasn't afraid for the building. It could be rebuilt. She wasn't afraid of the cell-phones capturing her frantic run across town which left melted footprints in the sidewalk. The department of transportation could patch the newly formed potholes. She wasn't afraid of getting separated from the other Knights. Her team would find her with the tracker stitched inside her mask. The fear causing sweat to drip between her shoulders was for Thomas. The man she loved and what had taken him.

Volcanic's voice added to her fear. His words were built like concrete, hard and unwavering. *Whatever came out of that fire wasn't Tommy anymore.*

Memories of the last year flashed painfully in her mind. The life they built together started to fall from under her feet. It couldn't have been a lie. Thomas was real. Cinder was dead. That was the truth. That was Abigail's truth. Any minute she would wake up from this nightmare and find Tommy lying next to her in their tiny apartment that smelled of woodsmoke.

She hadn't woken when she reached the front door of Murphy's Pub. She grabbed the wooden door handle and a splinter ripped into her finger. The blood escaping the cut confirmed she wasn't dreaming. She had no choice but to enter the bar and face her nightmare. Abigail smelled campfire smoke and sulfur the moment she stepped inside. Glass bottles on the back of the bar were shattered, their insides dripping onto the hardwood floor like blood. Scorch marks littered the floor and tables, and chairs were overturned. The look of the room brought more chills down Abigail's arms. She reached for her neck and felt a small relief when she felt soft, unburned flesh beneath her fingers.

"It's like nothing changed."

Abigail turned and found him leaning against the back wall. A neon sign tossed colors across his dark coat. The crooked smile that was handsome on Thomas was deadly when Cinder wore it. His face was damaged with new burns across his cheeks. His eyes scorched her without any flames. He looked so relaxed. He looked so normal. He looked like he belonged here. As a villain.

Abigail swallowed hard, forcing her tears back.

"What did you want to talk about?"

His grin widened, pulling the dark burns across his face, and he crossed the floor. His lanky form allowed him to jump over the bar with ease. He found two mostly intact glasses and poured the remains of a whiskey bottle into each. He passed one to Abigail, the rim chipped and jagged on one side. Cinder knocked his glass against hers and inhaled the drink.

"Go ahead, ask me again."

Abigail's skin squirmed under his daring gaze. She knew what he meant. The year spent with Thomas hadn't removed the connection she built during the months with Cinder. "Did you start the fires?"

"Of course."

The room dropped ten degrees. Cinder poured half a drink more into his glass.

"Why?" Abigail kept her questions short. She knew any more words could break her, and her cracking voice would be a victory to the villain. She snatched the glass from the counter, finding a second of relief of not having to look into the same emerald eyes that either blessed or haunted her dreams.

"You should know this one, doll. To be a hero."

Chief DaVodi's voice echoed in her head.

"A hero complex?"

Cinder rolled his eyes, but his smirk grew. "After I hauled all those people out of Jolt Station, I had to do it again. It felt good."

"Being a hero or a villain?"

He laughed, and it sounded just as it always did. A lightning strike in a storm. "Why does there need to be a difference?"

"Because one will get people killed."

"How's your record?" Cinder took a drink, spitting out a piece of glass that chipped off the rim. The blood dripping off his lip didn't tarnish the amused look on his face. "Don't think your King can keep anything from me. You're quite a killer."

The whiskey in her glass boiled as Abigail tightened her hands around it. She refused to let him bait her. She lashed out with different ammunition, smoke mixing with her words. "So, this past year meant nothing?"

Cinder rolled his glass between his blackened hands. "It was... enjoyable."

"But not enough."

He pinned her with his gaze. "This is who I am, doll. Playing house with you was never going to satisfy me."

"You could have fooled me. Did you ever love me, Thomas?"

Cinder flinched, and the glass shattered in his hand. He wiped his hand slowly on his jacket. He looked just as Abigail remembered when she fought him downtown. She was a fool to believe the crooked smile of Thomas was anything but a hidden smirk from Cinder.

Abigail pulled the silver chain from around her neck and set it and the ring on the bar top. She stepped away from it, the ring, the villain, the promise of her forever with him as her insides shredded beneath her costume.

"Cinder, I am putting you under arrest for the arson attacks on San Arbor," Abigail recited her legal statements with a hollow heart. "You have the right to remain silent, you have the—"

"Even after all our history?"

"What did you think would happen?" Abigail bit the bait this time. "I'd let you run wild in my city then invite you back into my bed?"

"It worked pretty well before." Cinder smiled darkly. "You never had a problem with me in our bed before this. Did becoming a hero change you so much?"

Abigail swallowed hard. Red fire sparked around her wrists until flaming gauntlets covered her fists. "It never should have happened to begin with."

Cinder *tsked*. "I get it now. I was only welcomed when I offered you something. But now that I can tarnish your hero name, it's over. Such a shame, Abbs. I thought you were better than them."

Abigail gritted her teeth. She wouldn't argue with him. She wouldn't play his game. This needed to end.

She wished she was strong enough to do so.

"Tommy please. Whatever this is we can figure out and fix."

Cinder glared at her. His look was ten times more intense than any of his indigo flames. "How are you going to fix this? This is who I am."

Abigail shook her head, two tears tipped over her eyes. "What happened to the kid who wanted to be a hero, too? Wildfire. A firefighter. That is who you are."

Cinder laughed. "You're still so naive."

"Snow carrots on the mountain." Abigail wildly tossed everything she had at him. "That's what you wanted, not whatever this is. I know you, Thomas. I know being a villain isn't you. You've fought too hard to give in like this."

Cinder exhaled and ran a hand through his hair. He looked tired. Abigail thought she was making ground. She could reach Thomas; she knew she could. Cinder slid over the bar top and snatched the ring. He twisted it between two fingers.

"I stole this."

"I don't think you did."

"I stole my badge."

"You earned it."

"All I've ever done is lie."

"Not to me."

"You're a terrible hero."

"You're a shitty villain."

Cinder looked up from the ring. The force of his stare surprised Abigail. The return of the emerald wastelands of his eyes surprised her more. He slipped her ring inside his coat pocket. "One choice, doll. Come with me, or take me in."

Abigail hesitated. Her immediate answer stuck in her throat like a bad cough. She'd follow Thomas anywhere. His voice called her home with every word he spoke. But it wasn't his warm smile beckoning her. Cinder's crooked smirk waited for her answer.

And he did not appreciate her hesitation.

Dark blue spheres formed inside his hands. Sparks fell to the floor. The spilled liquor shimmered like gasoline in the dangerous light.

"Better find the hostage, hero." Cinder taunted and shot one of the spheres into the back of the bar. "Before this place burns to the ground."

He blasted the area around him with dark fire. More bottles burst under the heat, and the wooden bar stools snapped apart. Abigail charged forward with her hands outstretched to grab him, but she only caught smoke.

"Cinder! Thomas!" she shouted, but only the fire's roar answered.

And the muffled sounds of someone in the back.

Tapping on the lights built into her mask, Abigail rounded the small corner into the bar's kitchen. Vats of grease boiled and popped into the hot air. Abigail searched the kitchen until she found Cinder's hostage. An older woman was tied to the steel counter leg and gagged with a dirty kitchen rag. Abigail only recognized her as the bar's owner by her photos on the wall. Blood dripped from her nose and streaked the gag. A nasty bruise was blossoming under her eye. Abigail eased the rag out of her mouth and worked on the restraints. The old bike chain was welded together and had burned the bar owner's wrist in the process.

"Just hang on," Abigail melted the chain links between her fingers. "I'll have you out in a second. Is there anyone else here?"

The owner winced as Abigail freed her wrist. "Just me."

Abigail hauled the woman to her feet. "Keep your head low. Stay by my side. We're running to the front door."

One of the bubbling grease vats popped and flicked boiling grease onto them. The bar owner flinched and swatted away the liquid. Abigail yanked her cape off her shoulders and covered the woman. Abigail grabbed her hand, and the woman squeezed the hero's fingers. Abigail hauled them to the front, wishing she had access to Lancelot's shield. Blue sparks rained down on them as the fire climbed up the walls and devoured the Irish themed décor hanging from the rafters. Abigail exhaled a Dragon's Breath at the main door and pushed the owner through the opening.

The air outside was rancid and didn't ease the burning Abigail knew the bar owner was feeling in her throat. Flames burst through the roof of the bar, and Abigail watched the woman's face turn to horror. Interior walls collapsed. The bar crumbled. The coming sirens sounded miles away as the fire raged. The bar's history vanished as the smoke did into the sky.

Abigail grabbed the woman's shoulder and forced her to look away from the bar. "It can be rebuilt. You're alive and safe."

A single tear trailed down the owner's face. "Get that bastard, Avalon."

"I will."

Abigail guided the woman across the street and offered her a silent condolence as the bar continued to burn. The water cannons would kill the remaining flames, but it was too late. Cinder had claimed his victory.

Abigail connected her comms and contacted her team's shared frequency. "It is the Flame Villain. I lost his trail, but he's here."

Excalibur's voice came in a huff. "We have reports of blue flames at the Aroma Community Center."

Abigail could see the edge of the nature preserve down the hill from where she stood. She was close to the community center, but not close enough. She found a parked car under a streetlight and smashed in the window with her elbow. "I'm five minutes out."

"Avalon," King Arthur said while she hotwired the car, "use lethal force. This rat has been around for too long."

Abigail left her shattered heart on the sidewalk and sped toward Cinder.

Chapter Twenty-Eight

Embers drifted aimlessly through the air and bounced off tree branches like a swarm of enchanting fireflies. The path Abigail ran up looked like a fairytale dream, except for the structure fire waiting for her at the end. The bright orange flames beckoned her with a dangerous beauty while the heat warned her to stay away. She wasn't entranced nor threatened by either. She sprinted faster and ignited her hands when she pushed through the decaying door. The ash claimed her bare skin, and the further she went the thicker the coat on her became.

She wasn't sure how she would do it, but she knew what she had to do. Find Cinder and stop him. Kill the blaze and find the man she knew was still inside. The good man who just wanted to fight fires. The man she loved. Not the villain who continued to toy with her.

The Aroma Community Center was empty this late at night. Abigail chose to believe Cinder picked the building for that reason. His fires wouldn't be able to hurt anyone here. The burned wrists and bloodied nose of the owner of Murphy's Pub flashed in her mind and forced Abigail to rethink her belief. She shoved it all aside and continued through the molten first floor and up the smoldering stairs. She found Cinder on the third floor observation deck. His back was turned to her, overlooking the park and the city lights of San Arbor.

Orange flames reflected off the windows and caused the view to also burn. Everything she loved twisted inside the flames. Cinder's reflection smiled at her. Everything burned.

"Beautiful, isn't it?"

"It's time to end this."

"Not yet." Cinder turned to face her. "Not before the big finale."

"You're not leaving." Abigail's words sounded concrete while her insides squirmed under his stare. "Your plan is over."

Cinder shook his head, his dark hair whipping around his face. "It's already set in motion. You've got the best seat to watch it with me."

Abigail looked past him through the window. All of the downtown skyline was visible. "Another bomb?"

"Bingo." Cinder tapped his head, awarding her correct answer. "Hidden in the park. It's only a matter of time before the fire ignites it."

"Why don't you do it yourself?"

"And show you where it's hidden?" Cinder laughed. "I don't think so."

Abigail shoved a strand of hair off her shoulder, secretly turning on her communicator in the process. She said, "A bomb hidden in the nature preserve isn't anything we can't handle."

Cinder arched an eyebrow and closed the distance between them. "You think I left my ending to one tiny explosion? This one will burn the whole city down."

"How will you save anyone?" Abigail challenged. "If all this is to feed your ego, how will you save anyone in a blast that big?"

He laughed again. The cruelty shocked her but not as much as the familiar undertone that brought to life a hundred memories of the same laugh from the year prior. "This is much bigger than that, Abigail."

"Any location where?" Lancelot buzzed in her ear. "Are you okay?"

"Fine." Abigail answered quickly. "But, under the Ponte Vecchio Bridge, you made me stronger. I won't fail."

Indigo flames snaked around Cinder's arms, burning away the sleeves of his coat and curling around his neck and chest. "I doubt you could lay a finger on me."

Abigail inhaled sharply, and her cherry-red flames became boxing gloves on her hands.

"I'm coming, Avalon." Lancelot said in her ear.

Abigail leapt on Cinder, crashing a fist into the side of his jaw.

They crashed onto the floor and Abigail pinned Cinder's arms under her knees and walloped several blows across his cheeks. His fireproofing was as strong as before, her flames rolling off his face like water, but blood smeared his teeth from her relentless impact. He spit a mixture of saliva and blood toward Abigail. She recoiled in disgust.

With her knees still pinning him to the heating floor, Abigail reached for the handcuffs in her pocket. She knew it wouldn't hold him for long, but she needed to try something. The Knights would be here soon, and the firetrucks would be close behind. If she had any hope of saving the man she loved, she needed to snap the villain out of him before any of them arrived.

"You have learned some new tricks." Cinder commented, his eyes never left hers. "Can I show you one I learned from you?"

Abigail felt the heat before she saw his flames. It was wild, hectic, and chaotic. Blue fire oozed from Cinder's skin like sweat. She couldn't get away from all of it. One second there was nothing, and then she lost him under the rapid expansion of heat, fire, and light. She exhaled her own blue flame, creating a barrier between them, and rolled off Cinder, protecting her face with her forearms.

The two flames twisted together until they collapsed inside one another. Only hazy smoke remained. Abigail ducked down and tried to inhale a clean breath, but the fire downstairs was creeping closer. She was trapped between two walls of smoke. She allowed a glance down her arms. They were bright red. Nasty blisters bit through her skin. She hadn't become as strong as she thought.

As she needed to be.

She returned to her feet and called out, "That was a cheap shot!"

"You'll love this one then."

Cinder's voice was right behind her. His fist collided with her side. The impact snapped against her ribs. Abigail staggered to the side. Cinder vanished inside the smoke and returned with a similar blow to her other side. As he disappeared again, Abigail was ready for the third strike. She caught his fist and pulled him into her using his momentum and bashed his forehead against her shoulder.

Cinder pulled free of her and stumbled backward. The smoke was quick to envelop him again.

Abigail leapt forward, grabbing what remained of his shirt and slammed her head into his nose. She held him hostage against her.

"This isn't you!" Abigail yelled at his bloody face. "You never wanted to be bad. Whatever this is, we can fix it."

Cinder laughed but he wasn't happy. "You can't cover this up, doll. There's only one way to stop this."

His statement hit harder than any punch.

"I'm not giving up on you, Thomas."

Blue flames coiled out from Cinder's neck. Abigail tightened her hold around him and prepared for the searing heat, but the flames stroked her cheek without any heat as if they were a comforting hand. His eyes burned her instead of the fire. She lessened her grip, and it was the only opportunity Cinder needed to break free of her. He grabbed onto her forearm and flipped her over his shoulder.

Her back slammed against the floor, and the air evacuated from Abigail's lungs. Whatever ribs he cracked earlier were definitely broken now. Gritting her teeth, she forced oxygen in through her nose, wincing as her lungs pressed against the internal injuries. She returned to her feet.

"Better than I expected," Cinder taunted, running the back of his hand under his bleeding nose.

Abigail ran at him, but her boot crashed through the floor. She sank into the lower story with it. The fire below had weakened the structure while they fought. With her added weight, the floor caved in completely, and Abigail could only grip an exposed floorboard to keep from falling into the vortex below. The fire trying to chew through her fireproof costume and body didn't scare her.

The fall did.

Desperately, Abigail kicked up but the movement only resulted in her slipping further. The floorboard creaked and dipped down from her hold. The wooden fibers started to crack. Abigail scrambled to reach for something else to pull herself up, but her fingers only scraped through smooth ash.

The floorboard groaned before snapping completely and dropping Abigail into the inferno.

The next thing Abigail saw was unexpected. Her vision filled with the endless green of emeralds. Two strong hands latched onto her forearm, and Cinder hauled her up. She collapsed beside him. Soot stained both their faces. Cinder yanked his hands away from her, but she reached back for him. Once captured in hers a second time, he didn't pull away. Behind the soot, behind the scars, Abigail couldn't deny the man beneath.

"I love you," she said desperately.

"You loved a villain once, too." Cinder reminded coldly.

She squeezed his hand and when he didn't pull away, she pulled them to their feet.

"Help me put out these flames and we'll figure things out."

"You keep saying that."

"Because I won't give up on you."

Cinder stared at her for a long moment and Abigail stared back. She watched the flames sneak closer from the reflection in his eyes. Fire creeped out from the hole in the floor beside them. A section of the ceiling collapsed behind them. Smoke filled every pocket of air. He finally looked away and slipped a hand free of Abigail's. Relief rippled inside her chest as Cinder raised his free hand and coaxed one of the escaping flames into his palm. Abigail's heart soared. He freed his other hand and absorbed a red flare coming up the stairs. Abigail stepped aside to watch him work his ability. An ability so wonderful she was lost in it. Within minutes the observation deck was clear of smoke and flame. They descended to the second level, and each took a side of the room.

Abigail snuffed the fire that climbed the walls, leaving a dark trail of alligator char behind. The faster she cleared the blaze, the sooner she'd bring Thomas home. They'd run to the cabin in the mountains and stay there forever if that's what it took. She just had one more fire to put out.

"Hey Abbs?"

Abigail turned from the last of the flames. Cinder stood in the middle of the clear room. His hands glowed indigo blue. Every bit of fire he absorbed burned just below his skin. His face became distorted in the dancing shadows produced from the light. Abigail searched for his eyes, his crooked smile, anything, but she only saw darkness.

A monster hidden in the flames.

"It's been fun."

He snapped his fingers and the blue orbs exploded around him.

The blast sent Abigail through a window where she crashed outside. She rolled across the ground until a tree stopped her momentum. Despite the pain pulsing through her entire body, she clawed against the grass to stand. She shot flames through her feet to propel her back to the second story, but she couldn't scale the building in time. It collapsed. Blue sparks clashed against the night sky. A wave of heat and smoke erupted out and incinerated the closest tree branches. Abigail ran to the front door, her falling tears singeing her face. She met the flashing lights of Fire Company 3 as they worked the flames from the outside. The hissing of the water was deafening.

A force snagged around Abigail and prevented her from reaching the building. She screamed and fought against it, banging her arms against the air, but was pulled away and dropped next to Lancelot between the firetruck and Chief Warren's vehicle. Lancelot grabbed her and pulled her into his chest as she slammed her fists against him to escape.

Lancelot didn't let go.

"You're hurt," he said. "You're *burned*."

"Let me go." Abigail growled through the memory of Cinder igniting. "I have to save him."

She felt Lancelot flinch. "The building is gone. No one could survive that."

"He could."

Lancelot tightened his hold around her. Abigail stopped fighting. Held captive in his arms, she saw the last of the community center collapse. A plume of blue smoke and sparks lit the sky before disappearing.

"Excalibur and Merlin found the bomb. It was under the bridge, like you said." Lancelot's statement was a consolation prize.

"And your villain will be destroyed by his own fire." King Arthur's voice was not comforting as it came behind Lancelot. "Good work, Avalon."

Abigail twisted out of Lancelot's arms and the sidekick reluctantly let her go. She glared at King Arthur but was unable to say anything.

His smug grin was another blow to her breaking heart. Her fists shook at her sides. She wanted to burn his mouth off.

"Can we get a medic over here?" Lancelot called to no one in particular.

"I'm fine." Abigail lied.

"We'll need you to look fine before media arrives." King Arthur's statement sounded absurd.

Abigail dissected the remains of the community center. Smoke and water obscured most of her vision, but she prayed to find a body moving inside. Thomas had the best fireproofing of all of them. He could survive this. He had to survive this.

Lancelot and King Arthur muttered behind her, and she took the opportunity to dash forward. Lancelot shouted after her, but his psychic touch never came. She was back inside the center and ripping through the fallen debris.

She peeled away a fallen floor joist and damaged drywall until her fingers bled. She punched through charred doors. She kicked away smoldering tables. Ash fell around her as did her hope as she only found destruction. She didn't smell the rancid but familiar scent of burnt flesh, but the air was so thick with other chemicals it could have covered it. Something glinted in the center of the floor. Abigail's eyes snapped to it.

Even half hidden in the rubble and ash she recognized it.

The bronze badge of Thomas' fire company.

Abigail collapsed to her knees and clutched the badge to her chest. Sobs shook her body while remaining embers sizzled against her skin. This was all there was left.

Chapter Twenty-Nine

Abigail left the community center's remains sometime later. Ash and soot covered her skin and costume. Dying embers clung to her hair, and she smelled painfully of a fireplace. The filth on her face did little to hide her feelings. Her puffy cheeks and red eyes didn't look very heroic. Each step threatened to shatter apart her heart that barely beat inside her chest.

She hadn't found Thomas. His body was still somewhere inside the remains of the community center. The fire had claimed everything.

The surprise of finding Ladder Company 3 waiting for her didn't shock her like it should have. The fire that laced her arms with burns also stripped her of nerve endings. Numbness clung to her as much as the ash. It should have been her team outside the scene, but it was Thomas' who waited for her. Her legs attempted to give out as she walked closer. She tightened her grip around the badge for support. It did little to help as she locked eyes with Maddox. He wrung his hands together unsure of what to do or say.

Purvis spoke into the night; his voice carried a weight she never heard before. "Tommy didn't pull out."

"Chief ordered it, but he didn't listen," Maddox added.

"He does it a lot, but nothing bad ever happens."

Abigail didn't understand. She looked between the two men and their fire chief but couldn't understand. Thomas hadn't been with them. They were called to stop the fire that Cinder started. A glow of purple shined behind their backs. Abigail focused on the glow and saw King Arthur looking at her. His ability rewriting the memories of Ladder Company 3.

Relief and disgust twisted in her stomach. Ladder Company 3 didn't know the truth. Abigail didn't know what their new truth was either.

Abigail ran her thumb across the half-melted fire badge. Her tears dropped onto it and washed away some of the ash. She reluctantly handed it to Chief Warren. Her hand felt cold without the scorched metal. Her legs were weak without its support.

"I couldn't save him." Her throat burned as she said it.

Chief Warren accepted his badge. "Neither could we."

Abigail's chest shook, and she forced herself to breathe. She didn't remember how difficult it was to inflate her lungs. Each inhale was painful, but she welcomed it. Her lungs pressing against her aching ribs meant they were working. She nodded to Ladder Company 3 before retiring to her team. They looked like strangers in the shadow of the firetruck. The red lights bathed them in blood. They looked like monsters. Abigail waited for King Arthur's repercussion, but he only watched her in silence. It was just as torturous. Lancelot was the only one to speak.

"You need to get checked out."

Abigail looked down and saw the burns and cuts on her arms. A side of her face pulsed angrily. She didn't feel the injuries. She didn't taste the blood in her mouth. Despite the embers in her hair, she was cold.

"I'm fine." Her voice sounded as far away as she felt.

"Take her to San Arbor Medical," King Arthur decided. "Merlin and I will run point here. Excalibur will collect you later."

"Yes sir," Lancelot responded and picked himself and Abigail up with his mind.

The flight to the hospital was cold. The night air that slapped against Abigail didn't bother her injuries even though the cuts and scrapes started to bleed again. She was either too tired or too uncaring to fight Lancelot's arm around her as he led her to the check in desk. She didn't care about the not-so-subtle camera flashes from cell phones or muttered whispers around her. She barely noticed being cut from her costume or dressing in a green gown. The sting of antiseptic didn't faze her, and Lancelot answered most of the questions asked by the nurses.

The entire ordeal could have lasted 12 hours or 12 minutes. It was over before Abigail realized she was bandaged and laying in a bed. An IV machine beeped next to her, and the coming sunrise bathed the room in orange light. Abigail shut her eyes and prayed the next time she opened them she would be in her apartment. Thomas in the kitchen. The past 24 hours nothing but a bad dream.

She hadn't fallen asleep before the door opened. She glared at her intruder.

"Hey." Lancelot's smile lost its charming effect. He shook a juice bottle before setting it on the table next to her bed. "Doctor said you need to hydrate. They had apple juice downstairs. I remember the water tasting funny when I was here."

Abigail tried to turn away, but the IV tubes protested her motion. "When can I leave?"

"I think after 48 hours of observation."

Abigail didn't reply. Lancelot pushed the only chair from the corner to her bedside. He sat down and waited eight minutes before saying, "I heard everything on the comms."

"I wanted you to find the bomb," she answered curtly.

"And we did, thanks to you." His smile was lost to her again, so he dropped it. He wrung his hands together. Several of his knuckles popped in the process. "I also heard the stuff you said to him. Was it true?"

Abigail remained silent, and Lancelot figured it was his cue to keep talking. Abigail considered strangling herself with her IV tube.

"I'm sure the others heard it too, but we can work a story together. Blackmail, coerced, something. I don't want you to get in trouble. King is pretty upset as it is. Did you know the fireman was the Flame Villain? It's crazy that—"

"Lance?" Abigail cut him off. "Shut up. Please."

"What do you need?" he asked anyway.

"To be alone."

Lancelot hesitated in the chair. The sun broke through the clouds before he stood. "Please drink the juice. I'll come see you later."

When the door shut, Abigail tossed the juice bottle in the wastebasket.

Abigail never felt more alone despite a nurse coming to check on her each hour and asking if she would like to see her visitor outside. Yesterday she would have thought Lancelot's persistence was a good hero trait, but now she found it extremely annoying. Abigail desperately wanted to leave. She was useless in the hospital room; she was vulnerable under the white ceiling. All she wanted to do was bury herself in a hole and break. She wanted to break down just as her heart was doing in her chest. The wrappings around her ribs might as well be holding her heart together, too.

Cinder is dead.

But now Thomas was too.

Her hand felt empty without holding onto his badge. Without holding onto him. She regretted handing it over to Warren.

Abigail twisted in her bed and tried to stand but pulled her IV too hard and a nurse was quickly at her side.

"Please stay still," the nurse urged, tucking the scratchy blanket around her like she was a child and not a hero. "Your wounds will open up again."

"I don't need any of this." Abigail grumbled.

"You don't have to be so super in here." The nurse didn't meet her mask-covered eyes. "Heal up and then you can go back to saving the city."

Abigail didn't think she could save anyone after last night.

She couldn't save one person, what luck did the city of thousands have?

Nice job, hero.

His voice haunted her and threatened to shake her apart. If there were any pieces left.

The day dragged on without any hope of peace. Abigail watched the sun pointlessly rise and set through the window.

She gave into a dreamless sleep at some point over the night because she woke the next morning to another blazing sunrise and unwanted visitors. Lancelot placed another juice bottle on the table and sat on the edge of the chair. He twisted his hands together waiting for an order. His fidgeting fed into Abigail, and she wished she could tell him to stop, but King Arthur's gaze weighed ten pounds on her chest. He stood at the foot of the bed. His smile could start the next ice age.

"Doctor says you're improving," he announced. "You'll have to stay on bedrest, but they'll let you go home soon."

Abigail didn't have the patience to wade through a minefield of a conversation with her leader. "When do you need my desk cleared out?"

His grin didn't falter, although Lancelot flinched at her question.

"Why would I want that?"

Abigail shot him an annoyed glance but listed off her offenses. "Disobeying orders, reckless endangerment, harboring a villain."

"I told you to stop the arsonist, and you did." King Arthur's smile finally warmed. "Wouldn't look too good if the HRC fired the city's savior, would it? It is a shame about that firefighter though, running bravely after you to help. Lancelot, make a note to send something to that firehouse."

Lancelot meekly said, "Yes sir."

"Why did you change their memories?" Abigail asked. "Wouldn't San Arbor's first responders working with villains be good PR for you?"

King Arthur glared, and the thin ice Abigail stood on cracked. "Between a first responder helping my heroes or my hero working with a villain, my story looks better for us. Kind of you to be thinking about your real team for once."

"Tell me what you want from me." Abigail would do anything to end the conversation.

He was quick on his checklist. "Get cleaned up, give HRC your statement and take a few days off. I'll need my Dragon Slayer back in tip-top shape."

Abigail sunk deeper into the hospital bed. "Sure thing, boss."

King Arthur smiled and excused himself from the room. Abigail glared at Lancelot, hoping he understood her message. Either her sidekick did not, or he refused to listen. He rustled through the pockets of his track jacket. A sports team logo was stitched into the breast pocket, and the lime green color palate made him look like a Sprite can.

"This was found during the overhaul." Lancelot held out a small chunk of metal.

The object may have been golden at one time, but now the circular shape twisted in on itself several times with unknown debris disfiguring it even more. Running down the length of the garish pendant was a cracked blue shard that still tried to sparkle under the fluorescent lights. Abigail grabbed the pendant and rubbed her thumb over it. A tear slipped down her cheek. This was her ring.

Abigail choked on an incoherent word.

At least she could keep one promise; she'd never take it off.

"If you want to talk about things," Lancelot never looked more nervous than he did now, "I'm always here for you, Avy."

The remains of her ring bit into her barely healed fingertips and chipped away at some of the shield she'd been hiding behind. It wasn't fair to not reward Lancelot for his kindness. He could have easily tossed the ring away, stored it away in an evidence locker, destroyed it.

"Not right now, Lance." Abigail attempted to smile at him, but her mouth hardly moved past its straight line. "But thank you."

Chapter Thirty

Abigail stared at the firehouse. The painted 3 on the front of the building reflected upside down on the car's windshield. The sight stole her breath. Abigail clutched her chest, her hand knotted into the clasp of her cape. Her external injuries had mostly healed, but the rest of her still ached in his absence. The dark gray turnout jackets moving inside the apparatus floor made her think of Thomas; how well he had worn his, how bright his smile was compared to the dark material, how he stepped out of every smoldering building with it protecting him.

Thomas was no longer inside the firehouse.

Tears welled inside Abigail's mask before streaking down her face. Attempting to keep a level breath inside this car was a thousand times harder than keeping one in any fire she'd been in. She knew the feeling would only worsen once she was inside the firehouse. When she would confirm that he really wasn't there.

"Do you want me to go with you?" Lancelot's voice sounded much farther than just the driver's seat.

"I have to do this alone." It's what she told King Arthur after he gave her the *assignment*. It's what she told Lancelot before he decided he'd drive her anyway. It's what she told herself every time she looked in the mirror.

It shouldn't be Avalon, Dragon Slayer, paying her respects on behalf of the HRC. It should have been Abigail, mourning girlfriend, trying to find comfort with Thomas' second family. But that didn't fit into King Arthur's narrative. If Abigail was to protect Thomas' name, she would need to play up the fabricated story. San Arbor firefighter, Thomas Sanders, running into the burning community center to help Avalon and her fight against the arsonist. It didn't matter how good he looked in the turnout jacket, it couldn't protect him from the fire like a real hero's fireproofing.

"You don't have to wait for me," Abigail said, her hands balling atop her legs. "I'll walk back."

Lancelot reached past her and opened the car door. "I'll be right here. Take all the time you need."

Abigail refused to acknowledge him, or his kindness, and exited the car. With the firehouse looming above, her knees buckled as another intense wave of sadness crashed into her. Each step forward felt like she was walking under water. An unseen pressure keeping her back. Abigail was shocked she didn't collapse after each step. She arrived at the garage door without any more preparation than she had earlier that morning.

What she wanted to do, she couldn't, and what she could do would never be enough.

A few heads shifted in her direction, but no one stopped their current duties. Abigail kept herself from crossing the floor, entering the house, and arriving right at Chief Warren's office. Avalon didn't know how to get there. Only Abigail had been able to join Thomas for lunch a few times while on shift. Only Abigail knew who Thomas was.

"Excuse me," she interrupted the next person she saw. "Can I speak to Chief Warren?"

The cadet, the title of probie taped to his shirt giving his position away, blinked twice before finding his words. "Uh, sure. Right this way."

Abigail followed the cadet through the apparatus floor, around the firetrucks and ambulance, and into the rest of the house. The inside smelled vaguely of burnt chili. Just like it had the last time she visited. *The last time.* She froze after they passed the kitchen. Hanging on the wall was something that hadn't been here last time. A collage of printed photos taped around a framed photo of Thomas in his uniform. Abigail couldn't look away from the displayed memories of Thomas and his firehouse. Selfies between him, Purvis, and Maddox. Pictures from training sessions on the lawn. Newspaper clippings. A picture of all of them from the mayor's banquet. The selfie Thomas took of himself and Avalon. Her fingers trailed over it.

The two of them together, grinning, and alive. Abigail's knees buckled and she pressed a hand against the wall to keep steady.

"He was quite fond of you." Chief Warren said behind her.

"I loved him so much."

"Pardon?"

Abigail cleared her throat of the tears that burned it and turned to the chief. "I loved working with him. He was an incredible man."

"Best damn firefighter we've had in a long while."

The cadet shifted on the other side of Abigail, and after a look from the chief he left the two women.

"SAFD is filling his spot pretty quickly." If Abigail's growl upset the chief, she didn't show it.

Chief Warren's voice remained calm and steady. "It's company policy. San Arbor requires a set number of firefighters and paramedics. Is there something I can help you with?"

Abigail rubbed her forehead, coaxing the scripted lines to her mouth. The HRC media team wasted no time in writing the condolence Avalon was meant to say. "The Hero Relief Center wanted to offer their condolences to you and your company for—"

Abigail's voice cracked on each word and Chief Warren finally took pity on her by raising her hand and stopping Abigail. "Nothing you say will lift the fog over this house. Nothing will for awhile."

"I know." A sob rushed out with her statement. "If I could've done anything different I would. I would give up everything to make this better. To go back and…"

Abigail didn't know what she would change. She didn't know which moment led to Cinder's return. What moment led to Thomas' death.

"Let me show you something." The chief didn't allow Abigail to decline. She started down the hall and Abigail followed before she could be left alone with Thomas' ghosts. The specter haunted her enough at their apartment. "No one's had the heart to take any of it down."

The chief led Abigail to the sleeping quarters of the firehouse. Abigail's heart sank like a cannonball. She knew exactly which bed was Thomas'. A collection of Avalon memorabilia sat atop it. Chief Warren picked up a deck of Round Tables Knights playing cards. All but four were removed from the box. The four aces that contained Avalon's image tumbled into her hand. She set them down and picked up an action figure and handed it to Abigail.

"Deep down, I knew Sanders would die in a fire. That was the kind of person he was: stubborn. He never pulled out when I told him to, always going too far into buildings and putting himself in danger just so his friends wouldn't have to. The only thing I saw him love more than running into fires, was you. If he had to die in one, I'm glad it was fighting one with you. Gave his life a bit of purpose."

Abigail collapsed onto the bed behind her. Tears fell rapidly from her face. Her shoulders shook and she sobbed. She cried until the toy Avalon in her hands drowned in her tears.

"He never thought there should be a divide between us," Chief Warren said, sitting next to Abigail. "Between us first responders and you heroes. I think that's why he pushed himself so hard. To stack himself next to you."

"Thomas would have been an amazing hero." Abigail wondered if he had worn a mask instead of a turnout jacket that night things may have been different. She wondered if he never donned a mask in the first place if he would still be here.

"Thomas *was* an amazing hero."

Abigail nodded, wiping her face clean of the liquid debris with her gloves. "Thank you for showing me this."

Chief Warren squeezed Abigail's shoulder and the comforting touch reminded her of Excalibur, minus the armored glove.

Chapter Thirty-One

It was difficult to believe it was still summer. Filled with shapeless gray clouds, the sky crouched inward. The cold air matched the somber mood in the small town's cemetery. The visitors were ghostly silent as they followed a priest through the headstones, most of their tears already shed inside the church where the service was held. Now, they were as numb as the cold ground.

Abigail slid one of her arms through Kenneth's. The gruff man didn't protest her touch. They both wore black. It had been years since they matched outfits. But no matter how hard Abigail tried, she couldn't pretend they were on assignment together. They wore black for the same reason everyone else did. Everyone approaching the newly minted headstone belonged to the same team. The team of mourners. Abigail was grateful Kenneth came with her. At times, it seemed his arm was the only thing keeping her upright.

The group formed a half moon around the headstone. It was bright gray compared to the dull and faded ones around it. The newest tenant to the graveyard, except there was nothing buried under this stone. Thomas' body was never recovered from the community center. His remains were mixed too terribly with what remained of the building to be separated.

Across from Abigail, Tawna offered a meek smile. She held Purvis the same way Kenneth held her. It was strange not to hear him shouting, but she guessed without Thomas to shout at, Purvis' taunts didn't have a target. Abigail couldn't stop seeing his absence. Maddox and his husband Harvey stood beside them with their hands knotted together. Harvey rubbed his thumb in small circles over Maddox's hand. The motion was small, easily missed if you weren't staring. It was all Abigail could look at. She'd lose count if she tried to remember all of the little touches she and Thomas had shared. At the time, each touch seemed insignificant. But now that he was gone, Abigail regretted not cherishing every second of them. They promised each other forever, but she never thought forever would be so short.

"Are you ready?" Kenneth asked, nodding to the headstone filling up with white carnations.

Abigail held a flower in her free hand. She didn't remember taking one. Kenneth held one too, maybe he grabbed one for her from the priest.

"Yeah." Abigail lied.

They joined the line waiting to add their flowers and final goodbyes to the stone. The points of Abigail's heels sunk into the damp ground. Each step closer she wished for the ground to swallow her whole, but she arrived at the stone before the ground could answer her plea. Kenneth dropped his flower without a word and stepped back so Abigail could have a private moment. Nothing felt private with a crowd of mostly strangers watching her. Even without her mask, Abigail couldn't escape her fate filled with onlookers. Whether she pulled someone from a burning house or wept above a headstone, someone was always watching. She knelt and moved some of the flowers to read the stone's inscription.

It was simply his name. Marked on the side with an image of a fireman's hat. Below it listed his credentials: son, brother, and friend. Abigail's chest heaved. He meant galaxies more than just those three words. Words should have spilled off the stone and filled the yard to commemorate his life. Only good words. Only words that belonged to Thomas. Glancing to the left, she read the stone beside his. *Ethan Sanders*. This was the family plot, she realized. If there was an afterlife,

Abigail desperately hoped they were together. It would be the only good thing to come of this.

Abigail set her carnation on the stone and ran her fingers over his name. The raised edges snagged against her fingertips. When she stood, Abigail snatched Kenneth's arm before she could lose any remaining strength. Surprisingly, Kenneth placed his free hand over Abigail's and squeezed. He was using her for support just as she was. If the San Arbor hero world could see them now, they would laugh. The city's once most powerful duo struggling to keep composure in a graveyard. They were both so very fragile.

Kenneth led them to the final hurdle of the funeral. The one Abigail didn't think she'd ever be prepared for. She tried using the train ride to Thomas' hometown to think of something to say, but her sobs left her weak and her mind beaten to a pulp each time she did. She listened to Thomas' team ahead of her as they gave their condolences to his mother. A wave of jealousy crashed over Abigail and surprised her. She was jealous of how easily they spoke; how easy it was for them to recount their time together with her son. Abigail was jealous of how real their interactions sounded.

They didn't know the dual sides of Thomas. They would never have to question which version of him was truthful. Abigail craved their blissful ignorance.

Thomas. Cinder. Firefighter. Villain. Abigail loved some form of him, perhaps even all of them, but she could never say that out loud. She only had what she believed to be the truth, and a terrible part of her demanded to know if it was true to him too.

She was no more prepared to speak to Thomas' mother when it was finally her and Kenneth at the front of the line.

Kenneth's massive hands consumed her frail ones. "Ma'am, I'm so sorry."

He choked on the words but stood stoic as he always did.

Evelyn Sanders nodded. "Thank you."

Her voice sounded as hollow as she probably felt. Her eyes were dry and tinged red. Her tear ducts as spent as Abigail's.

"Did you work with my son, too?"

"I did a long time ago," Kenneth answered. "He was a good kid."

She nodded again, and then looked at Abigail.

Abigail knew only one truth, and she admitted it. "I loved your son. I loved Thomas so much. I wish I met him sooner." *I wish I loved him longer. I wish I could have saved him.*

Evelyn didn't look surprised at Abigail's statement. Very slowly, the hint of a smile pulled at the thin lines around her mouth. "You must be Abigail."

Abigail gasped. "You know who I am?"

"More or less." Evelyn removed her hands from Kenneth and slipped them around Abigail's. "Tommy told me," she paused, her throat moving as she swallowed. "He used to tell me about this woman he met in San Arbor. How he planned on marrying her."

"He said that?"

"He came by and asked me for my old necklace a couple months ago." Evelyn dove into a memory. "The first piece of jewelry his father gave me. Tommy said he wanted to make something special for her… for you, I mean. He wanted the sapphire from it."

Abigail ripped the melted pendant from under her collar. Hints of blue still shined between the carnage the fire made of the ring. "I said *yes.*"

Evelyn reached for her, and Abigail thought she was going for the pendant. The only thing she had left of Thomas. Abigail felt heat rush to her hands, ready to defend the ring, but Evelyn only wrapped her arms around her. The fight in Abigail dissipated, and she hugged the woman back.

Both bodies shook together as more tears squeezed from their eyes.

"Thank you for loving him," Evelyn whispered as she pulled away from their embrace. Her eyes contained the same emerald wastelands that were Thomas. "I know at times it may not have been easy."

A dozen questions, statements, and promises rushed onto Abigail's tongue, but she couldn't say any of them. Abigail squeezed Evelyn's hands, hoping she received the message Abigail wasn't even sure she tried to convey. They were two strangers locked together by a dead son and his secrets. Evelyn squeezed back, sending her own silent message that somehow comforted Abigail.

Abigail followed Kenneth away so the next person in line could advance. Kenneth offered her his arm, but she refused it. She felt stronger now. Ahead of them, Tawna waved them closer to their group. Abigail heard snippets of their conversation about getting lunch before the train back to San Arbor departed.

"What will you do now?" Kenneth asked.

Abigail knew two truths now and vowed to continue the one she was able to. "Go back to work. A hero saves people."

Acknowledgments

Thank you to both my agent Nancy, and Kurt and Erica at Speaking Volumes for your support.

A huge thank you to Mark, Crystal, Bill, Mike, Nick, Sam, Anna, Tobias, and Jodi at my writing group for reading (and rereading) random chapters of this novel and helping make them better. I'm excited for you guys to see it all together. I wouldn't be the writer I am today without you all. Love you, mean it.

Thank you to my friends at Rockin Rooster Comic and Games for supplying me with enough heroic inspiration to last a life time. Thank you to my Mom for showing me enough firefighting shows to create the scenes throughout this book. Thank you to my husband for putting up with my writing playlist on repeat for a full 12 months. Thank you to Allison for loving these characters as much as I do.

And finally, thank you for continuing this journey with Abigail and Cinder.

About the Author

Jordan S. Keller is a Cincinnati based writer whose love for stories started at a young age when she preferred to write in a spiral-bound notebook rather than play outside at recess.

The thirst for stories grew in college where she majored in print and radio journalism, sharing the lives of the incredible people who live in Eastern Kentucky through the city radio station and multiple area newspapers. She possesses a bachelor's degree from Morehead State University for Convergent Media.

She sharpens her writing skills while recounting the heroics of her Dungeons and Dragons characters over dinner and co-running The Central Cincinnati Fiction Writers Group.

Jordan S. Keller lives with her husband, their bearded dragon, a goblin disguised as a cat, a puppy with airplane ears, and fourteen koi fish inherited when they bought the house.

Upcoming New Release!

JORDAN S. KELLER'S

Ashes Over Avalon Trilogy
Book Three
COMBUSTION
"The Fall of a Kingdom"

Villains are killing heroes…
Abigail Turner is sent undercover to investigate…

For Abigail, working alongside villains is bad enough, when she starts to understand their reasonings she questions everything she believes. When their target is aimed at King Arthur, Abigail must choose to keep the status quo of heroes with all its flaws the same, or help usher in a new world where having abilities doesn't make one good or evil depending on the media's camera lens.

Changing the world has a price Abigail isn't willing to pay…

For more information
visit: www.SpeakingVolumes.us

Now Available!

TONI GLICKMAN'S

BITCHES OF FIFTH AVENUE SERIES
BOOK ONE – BOOK TWO

**For more information
visit:** www.SpeakingVolumes.us

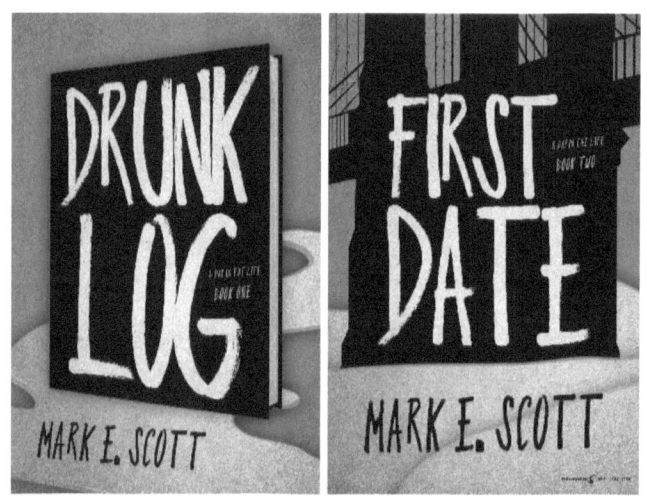